May the Best Man Win

Mira Lyn Kelly

sourcebooks
casablanca

Published by Sourcebooks Casablanca, an imprint of Sourcebooks, Inc.
P.O. Box 4410, Naperville, Illinois 60567-4410
(630) 961-3900
Fax: (630) 961-2168
www.sourcebooks.com

Printed and bound in Canada.
MBP 10 9 8 7 6 5 4 3 2 1

To my beautiful family. I love you!

Chapter 1

ON THE UPSIDE, THE PRELUDE HAD ALREADY BEGUN, and chances were good that Mozart's Sonata in E-flat Major pumping through all those organ pipes would cover any sounds of distress emanating from St. A's sacristy.

Jase Foster crouched in front of Dean Skolnic, groom du jour, and cursed. This had to stop happening.

"You think she's gonna notice?" Dean asked, wincing as Jase pulled one strip of duct tape after another off the garbage bag of ice currently secured to Dean's shoulder.

"The arm?" Jase clarified, because while he wasn't an every-Sunday kind of guy, they were in a church so he couldn't flat-out lie. "No, man. I really don't."

Lena would take one look at her husband-to-be's swollen black eye, and she wouldn't see anything else.

Strike that.

She might notice the greenish-gray pallor of Dean's normally ruddy complexion, because coupled with the way he was gulping air like a goldfish, it didn't bode well for his stomach or anyone within splatter distance.

The door opened behind them, and Father John plowed in, five foot six inches of bristling irritation and grizzled holiness. Scowling at the scene in front of him, he snapped his fingers and pointed at the guilty-looking crew of lesser attendants—mostly Dean's cousins who'd driven in that morning—plastered to the back wall. "Crack the fucking window."

Jase steeled himself against the laugh clawing to get free. Because, yeah, Father John had a mouth on him. Something Jase had discovered when he, Max, Brody, and Sean were muscling Dean out of the limo, barely clearing the door before the driver peeled off. The priest had stopped dead in the mostly empty back parking lot, taken one look at Dean, and let loose with enough four-letter words that even the guys—seasoned professionals in the expletive arena—had been coughing into their fists, studying the thick canopy of trees above and the new asphalt beneath their feet, basically looking any-where but at the pint-size priest with a bear's temper.

"How we doing, Father?" Jase asked, pulling the bag of ice free and stepping out of blast radius. "Need any help?"

More grumbling as the priest elbowed one of the groomsmen out of his way and opened the window himself. "Seems you've done enough already."

Probably. But Jase was chalking this morning up as a learning moment. No matter how bad the groom's nerves, a quick game of hoops on the way to the church was not the answer, especially when evening out the teams required bringing the limo driver into the mix.

Cutting a look over at Max, Jase pushed to his feet. "Let's get his jacket on."

Max Brandt was working his cop stance with his legs apart, his arms crossed over his chest, and a don't-fuck-with-me scowl firmly in place. He nodded down at Dean. "Get serious. He's gonna blow. We don't put it on him until he does."

Hell. Jase glanced around the tight confines of the sacristy to the cabinets stocked with candles, chalices, napkins, and the rest of the holy hardware, and he mentally amended *Fuck* with the requisite apologies applied.

Jase wanted to think Dean could pull it together, but when it came to hurling, Max could call it from a hundred yards away. Even before the Chicago police force honed his powers of observation to a sharpened critical edge, the guy had had a hinky instinct about when to clear a path. That, and about women too. Both handy skill sets to have.

Grabbing a plastic trash bin from next to the hanging rack of choir robes, Jase shoved it into Dean's good arm.

"You heard him, Dean. Make it happen, and we'll get you out there."

That was a promise, because unless one of his grooms had a definitive change of heart about marrying the woman waiting down the aisle, no-shows didn't happen on Jase's watch.

The door opened again, and Brody O'Donnel stepped inside. He wasn't as tall as Jase or as menacing as Max, but the guy had presence. He was solidly built with a broad chest and a wild head of russet waves that fell well past his ears, which he'd only half bothered to tame for the morning's nuptials.

Whistling out a long breath, he eyeballed Dean, who was doing his best to manage the task assigned to him. Then nodding around the room, Brody grinned. "Father. Guys."

Father John looked up and broke into a beaming smile.

"Brody," he boomed like the guy was his prodigal son returned, even though the two had only met the night before. Then shaking his head with a warm laugh, he declined when Brody pulled a flask from the inner pocket of his single-button tux jacket and, shameless grin going straight up, held it out in offering.

"Aw, come on, Father John. It's the good stuff," he ribbed before passing it to one of the braver cousins.

Brody could always be counted on for two things: his uncanny ability to make friends with just about anyone and his propensity for always having a flask of "the good stuff" on hand for emergencies. Which made sense, considering he owned Belfast, one of Lakeview's most popular bars. Booze was, in fact, his thing.

"Brod, so what're we looking at?" Jase asked, knowing they had to be running out of time.

"The girls are about ready to go. Sean's smooth-talking the Skolnics, and I've got the safety pins, but...uh..."

Jase knew that drawn-out qualifier. Whatever Brody had to say, Jase was sure he wasn't going to like it. "What?"

"Maid of honor had the pins and wouldn't give 'em up if I didn't tell her what was going on."

Emily Klein. Fucking fantastic. Because after managing to avoid her throughout the entire engagement, now, with everything else that morning, Jase was going to have to deal with her getting up in his grill?

"She's coming?"

"Nah, I talked her down pretty good, so—"

And that was as far as Brody got before the sacristy door swung open again and that old familiar tension knuckled down Jase's spine. He took her in with one sweeping glance and then—just to piss her off—went back for a second, slower pass. She should have looked like Natasha Fatale from those old Rocky and Bullwinkle cartoons. She had the height, all right, but instead of the severe black hair, wickedly arched brows, bombshell body, and calculating scowl, Emily was every kind of soft. Soft strawberry-blond hair spiraling in loose curls over her shoulders. Big, soft-brown eyes. And a soft, shy smile that hid her poison-dart tongue. Even her body, tall and athletically lean, had a softness to its modest curves—curves that had distracted the hell out of Jase in high school but that he'd become immune to in the passing years.

Since he'd finally seen through her *soft* snow job to the cold, hard ice queen beneath.

"Jackass," she greeted, with a soft smile just for him.

"Emily. What can I do for you?"

"Brody mentioned Dean had—"

Dean coughed into his trash can, and Emily's superior scowl shifted to the man of the hour.

She looked from Dean back to Jase, her mouth gaping open in soundless horror. "*Is that dislocated?*"

The shoulder looked bad, Jase knew. And with anyone but Emily, he would have been all about the explanations, apologies, and assurances. Dean was going to be waiting at the end of that aisle, ready for Lena, even if Jase had to hold him up there himself. But since it was Emily... "No."

He waited.

Emily's toe started to tap, a nervous habit she'd had forever. One he took unhealthy pleasure in exploiting.

But Brody, a perpetual fixer fortunate enough not to have any history with Femily Fatale, stepped in with a reassuring shrug and his signature lopsided smile. "A little roughed up is all. Don't worry about a thing. He's fine."

Which was when Dean retched up the contents of his stomach and a round of applause sounded from the attendants stationed around the room.

Go time.

"Nice job, man," Jase offered, taking the trash-bag liner out of the bin and shoving it in Emily's direction. To his utter delight, she was so startled that her hands came up before she'd had the chance to think. And then she was stuck quite literally holding the bag.

Hauling Dean up by his good arm, Jase and Max worked the guy into the jacket and started pinning his sleeve to his coat. It wasn't perfect, but if ever there was a pinch, this was it.

"Oh… Oh no… Oh… What am I supposed to do with this?" Emily asked shakily behind him.

Jase didn't look back. "See if one of the groomsmen can help you with it."

He'd love to leave her hanging, but this was Dean's wedding, and he wouldn't be doing his friend any favors by screwing over his bride with a missing attendant. Even Emily.

"Uh-uh, no way," Brody said, laughing. "That has 'best man' written all over it. You know the drill, dude. With great power comes great responsibility, or some shit like that."

Not a chance. "Power to *delegate* responsibility. Hey, you with the braces, take this to the Dumpster out back and meet us up front."

The skinny kid let out a groan but hopped to, taking the trash bag from Emily and scurrying out the door just as Sean Wyse strode in. Smoothing back his immaculate hair, he flashed a picture-perfect smile at Emily. "Looking breathtaking today, but I think you're mixing with the wrong crowd here. Can I walk you back to the girls?"

Emily was chugging Sean's BS like it was a Starbucks mocha latte, cocking her head appreciatively but declining all the same. Then she was out the door, and the too-small space around Jase opened up enough that he could breathe.

About time.

Sean reached into Brody's pocket and helped himself to a swig of what was probably Jameson. "You ladies ready yet?"

Brody started lining the guys up in order for their trip to the other end of the church, while Jase took care of the sweat beaded on Dean's forehead with a handkerchief he knew better than to attend a wedding without. Then grabbing Dean by the side of his face, he looked him straight in the eyes.

"You good, man?" he asked, hoping like hell Lena was in it for the duration. Dean was too good of a guy to get screwed over. "Ready to do this?"

Dean swallowed and nodded. "Yeah. I am."

The same thought that tore through Jase's mind every time he got one of his grooms ready echoed then—the thought Emily Klein had played no small part in reinforcing:

Better him than me.

Jase smiled his most confidence-inspiring smile, the one that closed deals, and jutted his chin toward the door. "Then let's get you married."

Chapter 2

STICKING TO THE FAR SIDE OF THE LEFT AISLE, A pinch of floor-length blush chiffon in hand and her smile straining at cheek-cramping proportions, Emily Klein skimmed past an usher seating the last of the late arrivals as she hustled toward the bridal room where Lena was waiting with the girls.

Best man her butt.

Seriously, how did Jase Foster keep getting this gig?

Obviously, the guys loved him. Couldn't get enough of the whole bromance business Jase had perfected back before it was even a thing. But the women? Come on, like they hadn't heard about the time Jase got Neil Wallace to the altar a mere two hours late—because the boat they took out that morning on a whim ran out of gas. Or when Jim Huang wore an eye patch to the altar because of some "epic" game of finger football gone wrong. Or when Trey Wazowski needed to start a suspicious course of antibiotics before leaving for the honeymoon.

Cripes, Emily had heard them all, and she hadn't even been at those weddings.

And now, because Lena had turned the same blind eye to Jase's questionable record as all those other brides, here *she* was, saddled with the task of preparing her friend for the fact that her husband-to-be looked like he'd been jumped in a dark alley on the way to the church.

Stopping in front of the paneled door not solid enough to muffle the twittering chatter within, Emily took a bracing breath.

A chuckle sounded from a few paces away, and she turned to find Paul Gonzalez shaking his salt-and-pepper head at her. "I thought the bride was supposed to be the nervous one."

Emily gave Lena's dad—who'd been her boss before his retirement—an affectionate smile. Like his daughter, the man was small in stature but big in heart, and Emily had always had a soft spot for him. "I don't know, Paul. Seems like someone ought to have a case of the nerves, and Lena's as cool as a cucumber."

Stepping over to her, Paul laid a reassuring hand on her shoulder. "Relax, Emily. Everything is going to be fine. Even if nothing goes according to plan—though something tells me since you had a hand in all this, it will—the day will still be perfect. Lena's marrying the man she loves. Nothing else matters."

He was such a sweet old guy. And so misguided.

But that's what she was for.

"You're right. Okay, I'll relax." And then flashing a wink as she slid into the bridal room, she quietly added, "Just as soon as the cake is cut and the bouquet is thrown."

"Yay! You're back," Lena sang out, delightedly rushing to Emily's side.

Dressed in formfitting raw silk with a mermaid flare that emphasized her curvy physique, the bride-to-be looked gorgeous, every lustrous mahogany coil pinned in place, her warm complexion flawless, lips glossed, and each lash curved in exacting detail.

Lena was ready to go.

"Is Dean nervous?" she asked in a hushed voice, leaning close like she was protecting the other bridesmaids from the truth. "Remember how he was before he got his car? With the pacing and all those lists—and that was just *leasing* a Bimmer. This is *forever*. He's got to be nervous. He is, isn't he?"

Emily stared into her friend's deep mocha eyes and shook her head. "Nervous? No way." Not anymore, she didn't think.

Lena bounced in her beaded pumps. "So tell! Is he completely devastating in his tux?"

Yes, completely. Only Lena probably wasn't talking about Jase, so no need to clarify the whole ugly-on-the-inside business.

And this was where it got dicey. Because while Emily knew Lena needed to be prepared for what Dean was going to look like—*before* she hiked up her skirt and started sprinting down the aisle barking out orders to call 911—she didn't want her friend freaking out before she'd even set foot down the aisle. So time to employ some of those well-honed public relations skills and put a little spin on the situation.

Emily took Lena's hands and pulled her friend over to sit on the floral love seat beneath the window.

"It's a gorgeous tux, Lena. We totally nailed it with the cut. The guys are all ready to go. But just so you're prepared, Dean took a little spill on the way to the church." When the limo driver got overeager for a rebound, started throwing elbows, and knocked him down. Yeah, she'd caught up with Braces, and he was a talker. "He has a bit of a black eye"—*a bit* because it was really way more red and blue and disgustingly swollen than actually black so far—"but he can't wait to marry you."

Lena looked past Emily to the door, like she was already considering that sprint. "He's okay?"

Okay would be stretching it. "He's waiting for you up front, hon. I guess his shoulder is banged up a smidge"—and his arm is safety-pinned to his jacket to hold it in place—"but it's nothing that would keep him from marrying you today." True story.

Satisfied, Lena smiled at Rachel, Marlene, Lorna, and the rest of the attendants hovering around the mirror, helping one another straighten straps and smooth hair. "Time to line up, ladies. I need one minute with Emily, and we'll be good to go."

The girls filed out the door, and then it was just the two of them.

"Today is because of you, Em," Lena said, squeezing Emily's hands. "If you hadn't been there three years ago...I don't think I would have been able to leave. I wouldn't have found Dean. None of this would be happening today."

Emily's heart gave a soft thud as she looked into her friend's sweet face. She was so happy, so confident: so different from those first months Emily had known her, when there'd barely been any light in her eyes at all. Emily had recognized in Lena the kind of quiet despair that had shaped her own life so significantly.

"No, Lena. You'd have gotten through it on your own." She had.

Lena shook her head. "You were with me through the worst days of my life. And nothing makes me happier than to have you here at my side through the very best one."

Blinking past her tears, Emily pulled Lena in for a tight hug. "You deserve this."

Lena pulled back and, with an arched brow, replied, "You deserve this too."

"Someday, maybe," Emily said with the smile she wanted Lena to believe. "But today's all yours. Are you ready?"

Her friend blinked back her own tears and nodded quickly.

"Then let's go."

Paul was standing at the door, his arm out, waiting to walk his only daughter down the aisle.

Emily adjusted Lena's skirt and handed her the bouquet before taking her spot in line ahead of them. The groomsmen who'd been waiting to the side paired up with bridesmaids.

A text alert vibrated the phone she'd managed to camouflage within her bouquet, in case of any wedding emergencies. Heart pounding, she checked and, seeing the message was from Jase, stifled a groan.

> You got your end done?

Jackass.
She texted back what was bound to be the truth.

> Better than you.

Then, with a tilt of her head, she flashed a winsome smile toward the front of the church, where Jase was waiting to walk up with Dean. He saw. The scowl said it all.

The music changed, and a hush fell over the church as the processional began.

Lena's words echoed through Emily's mind. *You deserve this too.*

She might, but that would mean inviting someone to get closer than she ever let people get. It would mean opening herself up to something she wasn't so sure she could handle again…whether she deserved it or not.

———

"I said it was an *accident*," Emily hissed beneath the celebratory din of laughter, big-band sound, and clinking crystal.

Cold blue eyes fixed on hers, hard and flat. Readable only in their blatant accusation.

Not surprising, considering first, she'd just skewered the butter-soft leather of Jase's tuxedo shoe with her stiletto, and second, when it came to Jase, who was groaning like she'd just run him over with a tractor, accusation was about the only thing he had to spare for her.

And after ten years of it, Emily had about reached her limit.

"I heard what you said," Jase growled through clenched teeth.

The implication being that he hadn't missed her omission either. He invariably considered an *apology* his due, but it absolutely, unequivocally, would *not* be forthcoming. Because if Jase hadn't been practically tripping over himself trying to avoid physical contact during this stupid, mandatory wedding-party dance, she wouldn't have nailed him. And while her misstep had, in fact, been accidental, after Jase's little stunt with the trash bag that morning, she didn't feel bad about it in the least.

The guy ought to learn to lead.

Or, better yet, take off. Get out of her hair, get out of her life—just get lost.

"Christ, lady!" Jase jerked back, his face blanching as he sucked a breath through his nose.

Oops. Now she'd nailed both feet.

She really wasn't a very good dancer—at least, not when it required coordinating shared floor space with another person.

"Oh, man up and stop being such a crybaby."

Jase seemed on the verge of apoplexy, so she flashed her widest smile and leaned in close—reluctantly conceding that it was nice to go onto her toes rather than lean down to whisper in a man's ear—to murmur softly, "Or do I need to get you a tissue, princess?"

He tensed, the air between them beginning to crackle.

The hand that had been barely hovering above her waist through the first half of the song firmed against the small of her back as he jerked her into hard contact with the solid planes of his body, the unexpected impact pushing her breath out in a whoosh. She barely had time to tell herself to breathe when the world spun. Suddenly, Jase had tipped her back into a dip so deep that she had no choice but to cling tightly to his shoulders and meet his unyielding stare.

His breath rushed over her jaw and neck, leaving a wash of unwelcome chills in its wake.

"Emily, you're going to apologize for stepping on not one of my feet, but both. *Nicely.*"

Like he'd apologized for the vomit?

"You're delusional."

"Oh, you'll apologize, all right, and you'd better make me believe it. Because if you don't, in about five seconds, I'm going to dump your sweet ass on this floor."

The breath froze in her lungs. "You wouldn't."

"*Test me.*"

Her fists tightened in the fabric of his jacket as her mind latched on to one thought: in the history of truly horrible bridesmaid gifts, Jase Foster was hands-down the worst.

Because, yeah, that's how Lena had sold him at her New Year's Eve engagement party eight months before. She'd been going on about how he was one of Dean's best friends and how much she loved him and how great he and Emily would be together. And since Emily's last interlude had been a while ago, the idea of a little masculine attention held a certain appeal. For about fifteen seconds, she'd entertained the idea of *maybe*. Maybe just for a few dates.

But then Lena had said it. "Dean was agonizing over who to pick as best man—you know how close he is to all the guys—but then I thought about the pictures, and this guy is tall, Emily. Like, way taller than you, even."

And right there, her spidey-senses started to tingle. Because coming in at five foot eleven and a half, she knew the list of guys who were taller than her by enough to earn a "way" qualifier was quite short. Sadly, Jase was among them.

Sure enough, when Lena had grabbed her arm and pointed to the six-foot-five stretch of broad-shouldered, lean, all taper-cut and tuxedo-fine male striding through a sea of formal wear… Ugh. Of course, it was him.

"His name's Jase Foster. And seriously, all tuxed up tonight"—Lena's voice had dropped to a conspiratorial whisper—"tell me he doesn't look *gift wrapped*!"

He might have, except that the bow tie dangling open at his neck, coupled with the roughed-up mess of dark-brown hair topping his ruggedly handsome face, suggested that at some point during the elegant engagement party the man had already been unwrapped and played with…*extensively*.

Typical.

"Any chance he comes with a gift receipt?" Emily had asked, keeping her voice light and teasing for her friend's sake.

And that's when he'd spotted her. She could tell by the way his steady progress through the crowd came to an abrupt halt and his mouth formed a four-letter word familiar enough to her own tongue that she recognized it on sight.

Real classy, Jase.

What a dickhead.

But then Jase had rubbed a hand over his mouth and jaw, wiping it clean of the flash of hostility he'd let slip. They were at an engagement party for friends close enough to slot them as the honor attendants in their wedding—and there was no place for a decade-old grudge in this celebration. Besides, she could rest assured that the depth of her loathing for Jase Foster was as clear to him as his was to her. And if not, she had the next eight months to reinforce it.

Now, staring up into the hard lines of Jase's face as he held her suspended precariously over certain humiliation, she couldn't believe she'd once thought this man could be her whole world. She'd thought he was her *friend*. She'd thought…

Well, lesson learned. Through bitter experience, she'd come to realize that Jase could only be counted on to let her down at the moment she needed him most.

Which meant she *really* needed to apologize—and fast.

Chapter 3

"Sorry."

One word. Grudgingly issued. But still, Jase was taking it for the victory it was. Not that he'd have actually followed through on his threat. Not a chance. And that she believed he would… Well, he wasn't quite sure how he felt about that.

"Very big of you, Em," he offered, prepared to pull her back up when her soft eyes narrowed on him.

"And typically *small* of you."

He sighed, looking down at the woman still caught in his arms, wondering when he'd finally be able to put her behind him.

Those damn legs of hers were the problem. Miles long and distracting as hell, they'd been strutting through Jase's life since he was sixteen, walking over whatever bit of peace he'd found and then strutting right back out, leaving nothing but a path of destruction in their wake.

Still, he was the lucky one. Thirty seconds had decided it. Thirty seconds difference, and maybe he'd be the one whose life never recovered.

His molars ground down, because that wasn't something he ought to be thinking about at Dean's wedding, but every time he saw Emily working that honey-and-sunshine routine of hers, he wanted to puke. Why did she even bother? It had to be exhausting to pretend you were someone you weren't 24-7. But maybe she liked the collection of friends that hiding the truth had garnered her.

Or maybe she actually believed her own bullshit, which was even worse, because how the hell was the population at large supposed to defend itself against that?

Jase pulled Emily up to standing, restoring the distance between them that he never should have breached.

"Thank you," she said, and then winced as if annoyed to have given him even that much.

"You bet," he answered, keeping the civil smile.

The song was almost over, and this dance was the last of the forced interaction with her—at least, until the next time their circles of friends happened to overlap in holy matrimony, and genetics once again threw them together as the tallest pairing in the wedding party. Maybe they'd luck out and it wouldn't happen for another year or so... or, better yet, ever again.

The song ended, and sure enough, Emily wasn't about to linger. No niceties being offered tonight. Without even looking back at him, she turned out of his hold. Fine by him.

Or it would have been, except that in her typical obliviousness to anyone beyond herself, Emily seemed unaware of how her body was lining up with his. Before he could pull out of the way, the bare skin of her arm met the back of his hand in a mesh of contact that could only be classified as a caress. Emily's sharp intake of breath had Jase's attention snapping to the widening of her eyes, then back to where his knuckles skated down the remaining length of her arm.

A second passed, and neither of them moved, both seemingly caught in the aftermath of a train wreck that never should have happened, in that jolt of electricity at first contact and the lingering low charge that seemed to sizzle through the duration.

Jesus, some things never changed.

———

"You lying little hooker!" Lena gasped, her eyes bright with excitement. "You told me there was nothing between you and Jase, but then right there in the middle of everyone—"

Emily waved her off, walking past the new Mrs. Skolnic to the east bar, where the hunky bartender was as generous with his dimpled smile as he was with his pours. "That dip was just Jase being showy. Hey, Jimmy, could I get another glass of the pinot, please?"

Fresh drink in hand, Emily turned back to Lena, who was still staring at her with an all-too-smug look on her delighted face.

"I'm not talking about the dip, which was spectacular, by the way. I'm talking about after. When you guys had that"—Lena bit her lip and stepped closer, lowering her voice—"*moment*. It was like fifty shades of hot."

Taking a cool sip of the crisp white, and then a slightly heartier swallow, Emily shook her head. "That was no Jamie Dornan moment, please."

Lena's neatly sculpted brow pushed up, and then, pulling Emily by one hand, she led her back to the table where six of the bridesmaids were sitting, all of them with their eyes locked on her.

Trying not to slosh the wine, Emily went for another sip, because the second she sat down—

"Oh my God! You and Jase—"

"That touch. *Hawt*—"

"And the linger? Like a slow burn, only—"

"And when she was looking back all slow and stunned—"

Okay, so maybe she could have waited for the wine until she sat down, because apparently no response was required here. The girls were completely absorbed in this fantasy they'd concocted about some fictional *moment* that didn't exist.

"And he had that broody, WTF look—"

"Like he was *struck* by her—"

"I'm *super sorry* I half hit on him last night—"

"She is. Rachel had *no idea* you guys were—"

"But he totally wasn't interested, so don't worry about—"

"And if you get with Jase, you've gotta hook me up with Max—"

"Oh my God, you guys, let's agree: Emily gets the bouquet—"

The bouquet? Oh, no way. If that thing came hurtling in her direction, Emily was spiking it straight into the ground.

"Enough!" she pleaded, looking from one expectant face to the next. "It was *not* a moment. There is nothing, I repeat, *nothing* between Jase and me."

Lena crossed her arms on the tabletop, leaning forward and staring Emily down like a vendor trying to up their price. "So when did you guys meet? *Exactly.*"

As a rule, Emily wasn't a huge fan of talking about that part of her life—or her past in general, really. She'd much rather listen and focus on the now. But with all eyes on her, she could feel the heat creeping up her neck.

These girls were relentless. There was no way she was getting out of there without spilling something.

"High school. We were friends for a while, but it didn't stick."

Rachel leaned in then, same posture as Lena. "Friends, like friends who have something hot and unexplored between them?"

More heat crept up Emily's neck. Because for a few months, there *had* been something between them. Something that made her heart beat twice as fast when their eyes met in the hall, holding just that extra second. Something that left her a little breathless when he smiled at her. Something that felt like it was growing, getting bigger every time they talked. But whatever it was, one day it was there, keeping her up nights with her belly twisting and churning, wondering if he'd finally ask her—and the next day it was just gone. Jase was as *friendly* as ever, but apparently the guy's attention span toward females was the same then as it was now—not exactly the stuff of legend.

She'd been confused at first, but then she'd accepted it and moved on.

"Friends, like I dated his best friend for about a year."

This time, Marlene was closing the circle around her, her eyes gleaming. "So you were his best friend's girlfriend, but you're not anymore. Maybe he's thinking about a second chance?"

"No." In this, she was confident. Jase would never see her as anything *but* Eddie's girlfriend. The traitor who ruined Eddie's life. The scapegoat Jase blamed for everything, because if he didn't, he'd be forced to take some of the responsibility himself.

But she couldn't say any of that, so instead, she kept it simple. "Honestly, Jase and I don't get along very well. You'll just have to believe me. Neither of us would *ever* consider something more."

One by one, the girls sat back, and Emily relaxed.

"Sure, I believe you." Marlene nodded, casually smoothing a few strands of her jet hair back into place. "But just out of curiosity, why hasn't Jase taken his eyes off you the entire time we've been sitting here?"

———

It was after midnight when the party finally shut down. Dean and Lena had said their good-byes a half hour before, and the band had already cleared out. The Skolnics had taken the gifts, and Emily was doing one final sweep to make sure nothing had been left behind when she came to the black tuxedo jacket hanging from a chair at the wedding party's table.

Someone would definitely be missing this.

Draping it over one arm, she caught the barest scent of cologne—good cologne—and raised the jacket to her nose. It was familiar, but she couldn't remember which one of the guys—

"Not going to lie, Em." The gruff voice from the doorway brought her head up in a rush. "The jacket huffing is kind of creepy."

Jase, he of the persistent, pointless glare. Of course.

Bow tie hanging loose from his open collar, sleeves cuffed to just below his elbows, he started across the ballroom with an easy, long-legged gait. "But I'm betting they've got some twelve-step program to help with it."

Not bothering with a response, she pinched the jacket between finger and thumb and held it out for him as they met in what had been the middle of the dance floor. "You leaving a mess for someone else to clean up. Why am I not surprised?"

Taking the jacket, he paused. "Sure you're okay? One more whiff for the road? Something to hold on to?"

"Pass," she answered, her heels clicking against the floor as she walked out. "I can't forget about you fast enough."

"Hey, Emily?"

She stopped and let out a weary sigh, because really, with this wedding over, all she wanted was to put Jase Foster behind her. She glanced over her shoulder to where he was frowning after her, a disconcerted look in his eyes. "What?"

"You're not friends with Sally Willson, are you?"

Her brow furrowed as something heavy settled in the pit of her stomach. "Sally was my roommate in college. We're like sisters."

She didn't want to ask; she didn't want to know. But by the way Jase was cursing into the palm of his hand and staring at her with those accusing eyes, she was fairly certain she already did.

Sally had been dating her boyfriend, Romeo Santos, for two years, and just this weekend, he'd taken her up to some cabin in Wisconsin.

"Oh no."

Jase shook his head and walked past her. "See you *soon*, Em."

Chapter 4

September

ONE MORE GOOD TOSS AND JASE HAD THIS. HE COULD feel Max at his back, standing closer than strictly necessary, even with the press of Belfast's perpetually healthy weeknight crowd.

Trying to intimidate him into screwing up.

Not gonna happen. Jase had his head in the game and—

"So what's it like having your *work wife* knocked up?"

Too late to stop the throw already in progress, Jase knew as soon as the dart went sailing that he wasn't looking at the bull's-eye. Or even the board, apparently.

Jase muttered under his breath as Max and Sean bumped fists.

From the high top that had been their regular Wednesday night table since before Brody opened the doors to business four years ago, Molly Brandt groaned. "Seriously, dude, you did *not* just let my brother psych you out! What are we, amateurs here?"

Yeah, he was better than that, but come on. *Work wife?* Even in the platonic context of a work relationship that rocked—which was how it was with his assistant, Janice— the word *wife* made his balls retract.

Still kicked back in his seat, Brody stretched out his burly arms. "See what you get for teaming up with Jase, Moll? Shoulda picked me. We'd be taking a victory lap right now."

"Yeah, yeah." She laughed, but the big guy wasn't done yet.

Brushing off his broad shoulder, Brody grinned. "Pop you right up here. Queen of Darts."

Well, the copper-plate ceiling was tall enough for it, and while Brody definitely had the muscle to do it, Molly wasn't really the girl-on-your-shoulders type. Jase glanced down at the black motorcycle boots she loved to wear. More like the steal-your-bike-for-a-joy-ride type.

"Sorry, Moll." Jase shook his head and cut a look at Max. "Dare you to say that to Janice's face."

Max adjusted his pants. "Hell no, the jewels are just fine where they are, thank you."

Smart. Janice had been Jase's assistant since he started at the bank right out of grad school. A few years older than Jase, she had a disapproving mother's tough-love way about her that Jase had come to adore, and even a badass cop like Max usually had enough sense to respect.

Truth? He was already freaking out about losing her for maternity leave. *She was good.*

Jase slid into his seat and ruffled the shock of chartreuse in Molly's otherwise white-blond hair.

Swatting at his hand with a laugh, she turned to her brother. "How about *your* work wife?" she asked, talking about his partner on the force. "I hear CJ's been looking at rings. Getting jealous?"

Max opened his mouth, but Sean leaned in, flashing the half-cocked smile they'd all come to recognize as a precursor to trouble, and made a crack about Max being the *wife*, at which point the conversation degenerated into the trash talk they'd been slinging since college. The kind Jase wasn't in any hurry to outgrow.

These guys were his best friends. The guys he'd lay down his life for and knew without question would do the same for him.

Eventually, the conversation wound back to the coming weekend. The engagement party none of them were looking forward to.

The one Jase had already confirmed Emily would be attending.

"How the hell is it that Sean's the one who gets out of this thing when just hearing the words *black tie* is enough to get him hard?"

Sean shrugged. "I'm hard right now."

Molly snorted beer out of her nose, and Sean shot her a wink from across the table.

"Pretty sure it has something to do with him nailing the girl Romeo was following around first semester sophomore year," Max suggested helpfully, then seemed to be thinking back. "Was she the girl from behind the Dumpster?"

A thoughtful furrow appeared between Sean's brows. "Nah, that was Nadia, the TA from econ. Gina was…"

"Gina was on the fire escape outside Teddy Burgdorf's party," Molly offered helpfully. "And Sean's not the only one who isn't going to be there Friday."

Brody shook his head. "That asshole boss of yours making you work again?"

"Yeah, but he's paying me double time for picking up the shift—so I only loogied in his beer once."

The big guy made a sick face and looked into the black depths of his half-consumed Guinness. "Starting to wonder if maybe I need to consider a separation from my work wife."

Molly leaned back, laughing like the imp she was. "Good luck. You'd never find another manager as good as me."

"Don't I know it." Brody tipped the glass back and downed the remaining half in a single swallow that had the rest of them staring at the empty glass uneasily.

No way she'd done it.

No way.

Molly grinned. "Have fun without me on Friday."

Engagement parties could be a hell of a lot of fun. And as a rule, Jase looked forward to them. These were his friends after all, inviting him to celebrate one of the most monumental decisions of their lives, so he'd be a dick not to. But this party—Jase shot a glance through the trees to the Willsons' three-story, multiwinged stone mammoth, currently lit up like a Caribbean cruise liner washed ashore in the depths of the western suburbs—had been racking up strikes since before the question even got popped.

Strike One: Emily. How was he supposed to look forward to this thing when every time he thought about it, he thought about *her*? About those damn legs tangling up his whole night.

And was she hair-braiding besties with every marriageable female in the Chicago area between the ages of twenty-three and thirty-five? He couldn't believe he was getting screwed with her again. He would too, thanks to their ninety-ninth percentile status on the national height charts. Fucking genetics.

Strike Two: The Willsons. Jase could live with the black-tie attire and what Romeo had guaranteed would be the stuffiest, most unpleasant sit-down dinner any of them had ever had the misfortune of attending. After five years in private banking, Jase could knock out a night like that without batting an eye. But Sally's parents? Man. He'd only met them once the previous summer at one of the Santos's backyard barbecues, where Romeo's parents had invited fifty friends and two hundred family members.

Watching Mrs. Willson treat the Santos's relatives like they were the staff, while Mr. Willson had stood in front of the house barking into his phone the entire afternoon—yeah, once had been plenty. Especially knowing how they'd picked Romeo over when he'd asked them for Sally's hand. Add to that, he'd bet they were looking at a seating chart, which again meant *Emily*. Possibly hours of her.

Strike Three: The heart attack he'd had pulling up the winding drive just minutes before. It had been an hour-plus drive out from the city. Brody had been riding shotgun—while from the back Max bitched about his bow tie strangling him—when Romeo had sprung out from behind one of the trees lining the drive, looking like a ghost. He'd banged on the hood of the car before jumping in the backseat.

"Jesus, man," Max growled, glaring at the guy like he was ready to put a bullet in him. "You scared the ever-livin' shit out of me."

"Hey, Romeo," Jase offered, cranking around in his seat to give the guy a once-over.

Definitely not looking good. "What's going on?"

"Thank God you guys are here."

Running a hand over his neatly gelled black hair, Romeo directed Jase to veer right at the fork and park over by the stables. Then he stumbled out of the car and, leaning back against the east wall of the structure, rubbed his hands up and down over his face.

"She's pregnant."

Oh man. By all rights, Jase should have already been out of there. But since this was a good friend and not baseball, the three-strikes rule didn't apply—which meant escape wasn't an option.

Brody was quick with his congratulations, slapping Romeo on the back a few times and laughing about how he'd been worried it was something bad. Max stood off to the side, his cop look fully engaged as he sternly told the guy it was a good thing *they were already getting married* then. Typical Max.

"Max, give the guy a break. When did you find out?" Jase asked.

Romeo looked back with shell-shocked eyes. "About twenty minutes ago."

Jase whistled between his teeth.

"Yeah, timing. I know. But I guess Sally was getting ready with her sister and got sick. Again. Peg was teasing her about a baby being on the way, not thinking anything of it. But then Sally started putting a few things together, and I don't know—next thing, there's an emergency run to the pharmacy, and she's peeing on a stick, and—"

Romeo swallowed, and swallowed again, like his stomach was about to revolt.

Jase took a step back but caught the subtle shake of Max's head and relaxed.

"We're going to be parents. I'm going to be *a dad*. And I'm not even married yet."

Jesus. No wonder the guy had looked like he was running from a horde of zombies! Even when they were planned, babies could be scary. But the fact that the news was less than twenty minutes off the press and Romeo was out here instead of inside with Sally was setting off some alarms.

"So she told you…and you left?" Jase asked as gently as a guy like him could.

"Hell no," Max cut in, turning that lethal stare on Jase as he shouldered closer to Romeo. "It's a lot to swallow with a house filled with a few hundred guests. Our boy here just needed some time to let the news digest. He's solid, and he's going to do the right thing. *Aren't you, Romeo?*"

The poor guy shrank back against the wooden siding. "I only left because she was afraid her mom would figure something was up and go crazy before the party. I swear, it wasn't my idea. I'm solid, Max."

"Yeah, but if you *weren't solid*…" Jase said, giving the guy a meaningful look. Because the engagement had come up pretty fast. "Like, if you had any doubt at all… Now that you're bringing a kid into the mix, more than ever, you need to be honest with yourself about how you feel. Doing the right thing isn't always doing what everybody's *telling you* the right thing is. Understand?"

Probably not. Romeo came from the kind of family they based Thursday night sitcoms around. But speaking as the product of a marriage that never should have been—a marriage that nearly destroyed his father and that Jase had only survived thanks to Eddie's parents all but adopting him for the month after his mom took off—Jase had no problem explaining it to him.

Okay, no problem, other than Max escalating into that wide-legged, "don't even think about screwing with me" stance. It had to scare the crap out of the punks unfortunate enough to be on the wrong side of the law when their paths crossed, but Jase had seen this guy choking up over a Budweiser Super Bowl commercial. Which meant he couldn't totally give the glare the credit that maybe he should. Besides, Max's arms were still crossed rather than tensed with his fingers twitching restlessly around his hips. Like he was ready to swing or fire. So Jase figured he was okay.

"Guys, I'm solid," Romeo said wearily. "Mostly. I mean, my knees feel like Jell-O and my guts like I put them through the spin cycle. But as far as Sally and this baby— *our baby*—go, no doubt in my mind. I want them both."

"Then that's all that matters," Brody said, throwing an arm around Romeo and giving him a rough shake. "So the timeline gets pulled in some. Who cares?"

Romeo let out a short laugh and started walking back toward the house. "You've met Sally, right?"

—⁓—

"Don't try to talk, Sal," Emily begged. She was kneeling in front of her friend, who was perched anxiously on the edge of a silk vanity stool and turning a shade of blue almost as disturbing as the surrounding decor of her frilly childhood bedroom.

"But the hall…is booked…a year…in advance," Sally managed, each punctuating gasp and following string of words weaker than the ones before.

Emily nodded her understanding and tried again to pry the satin binder from Sally's fingers. But either the loss of oxygen had constricted her fingers, or the mere thirty minutes her friend had had to come to terms with the fact that she was pregnant wasn't quite long enough for Sally to give up her hold on the wedding plans she'd been making from about the time she'd started collecting those creepy dolls encased in the mirror-backed glass by the corner.

The binder wasn't going anywhere.

"Yeah, but there are so many beautiful spots for a reception in the city," Emily tried again, giving it her optimistic best. Because this was bad—or not bad, because what a terrible thing to think about a baby— but the timing was going to take some getting used to. "The wedding can still be out here at your family church, just like you wanted. And the reception… Well, we'll find the perfect spot, sweetie. We can start looking tomorrow."

Sally's words came back to her, urgent and alarmingly thin. "I *had*…the…perfect—"

"No tears!" Peg Willson squeaked, casting a panicked look behind her as she rushed in and hurriedly swung the door closed. The reverberating *bam* of wood meeting frame had her eyes bugging and the blood draining from her face. Cracking the door, she peeked out before turning back.

"This is the only paper bag I could find," Peg whispered, shoving at Emily the contraband she'd gone all *Mission: Impossible* to retrieve as though she were afraid being caught with it would cost her an arm.

Emily stared, wondering how Peg thought her sister

breathing into the stiff, glossy, handled work of art with little leaping frog cutouts would be any help.

Peg was a sweet girl. Mostly. And smart as a whip when it came to school. But when it came to basic common sense…

"Mom can always tell when you've been crying from that ugly red business you get under your eyes." Peg made a face as she leaned in closer. "I can see it starting already."

…not so much.

"What? *No!*" Emily countered quickly, thinking of the dangerous cocktail of nerves, tension, and hormones currently raging through Sally's system. "You look fine. A little powder and you'll be good to go. But first—"

Fingers flying over her phone, she searched for tips on hyperventilation.

"Hey, how about you try covering one nostril and breathing through your—"

The room suddenly shrank as one broad-shouldered, tuxedo-clad groomsman after another started wedging his way in, Romeo in the lead.

Thank God.

He knelt in front of his fiancée. "Sally, baby, you look terrible." He looked back over his shoulder, a frantic look in his eyes, and then, totally missing the warning look in Emily's, went on. "Jesus, maybe somebody should call an ambulance."

Emily was about to open her mouth to reassure him that no ambulance was necessary, that she had it under control if they would just give her another minute, when a deep voice cut in from too close behind her. Jase.

"Now, Romeo, that's just all those overprotective instincts kicking in. Your girl here is fine. Aren't you, Sally?"

And then he was crouching next to Emily and cutting her a quick look of disdain before concentrating on the bride/mother-to-be.

"Are you serious with that bag, Emily?" He let out a patient sigh and then smirked at Sally. "No wonder you haven't caught your breath, sweetheart. But I'll have you back to rights in no time at all."

Emily could feel the heat rushing into her face. She hadn't been the one to get that ridiculous bag. And the fact that Jase thought she had? Well, of course he would. The guy was notorious for selling her short.

"In fact, how about you guys give me some space here with Sally?"

Emily blinked. Had he just…?

A cold glance from those obnoxiously long-lashed eyes confirmed it.

He had. That ass had just dismissed her.

Unbelievable.

Typical.

Emily gave Sally's hand a squeeze. "Not necessary. We've got this."

"Yeah, but I've been waiting to get Sally alone for years." Jase made a ridiculous face and edged closer, shooting a mischievous look back at Romeo, who appeared to be about to have a heart attack himself. "And now the clock is ticking before she's a married woman. How about you guys all excuse me so I can make my move?"

Cripes, all that oozing charm was enough to make

Emily gag. And worse yet, it seemed to be working. Sally had stopped those desperate little sucking breaths, and she was getting the color back in her face.

"That's quite a canopy you've got there, Sal," he said, his voice going midnight-low and naughty. "*I like the ribbons.*"

Perfect. And there it was, Sally's smile breaking through that panicked frown. Because of Jase.

Within five minutes, Sally's makeup had been touched up, and Jase was standing by the door, ushering everyone through as they headed downstairs to join the party. Emily left the binder by the window seat and then followed suit, noting Jase's smile lost its warmth and his eyes went hard as she passed.

"Emily." Dry. Annoying.

He closed the door behind them.

"Jase," she replied in kind, hating that irritating tension winding through her with the knowledge that he was a step behind. That she could practically *feel* him there.

At the bottom of the stairs, Brody stopped short as a round of applause filled the room upon Sally and Romeo's arrival. Emily curbed her steps, but Jase must have been looking past her or not paying attention—because one minute she was smiling, searching for a tray of champagne, and the next, she had the full six feet five of Jase Foster bumping into her backside.

Her breath caught as she pitched toward Brody, but then she had the press of Jase's palm, wide and secure, across her abdomen, pulling her back into all that muscled heat.

"Sorry" came the quiet growl at her ear as he held her close.

Her heart was racing, her fingertips tingling. It was definitely because of that abrupt jolt forward. Nothing to do with the strength and ease with which she'd been drawn back.

Or Jase's breath rolling across the bare skin of her neck. Warm and wet and—

"Emily?" he asked, the way he said her name curling around her ear with a deep rumble.

She turned slowly, meeting his waiting stare. Not knowing what to make of how her senses were going haywire.

Jase's face was filled with a smug sort of satisfaction. "You can let go of my arm now."

Her eyes bugged. She looked down, and there they were. Her hands wrapped tightly around the arm he'd caught her back with.

God, she hated him.

Chapter 5

WHAT AN IDIOT.

It was bad enough that he'd been so caught up in the swing and curve of Emily's hips in that shimmery, low-backed dress that he'd actually walked into her when she'd stopped. But then he'd had to try to even the score by taunting Emily with a look that said he knew she wasn't unaffected by the feel of his arm around her.

Really, what did he think that was going to do for him? The only scoreboard was the one in his head, and unless she was keeping score too, where was the satisfaction? He should have caught her after that karmic misstep, made sure she was steady on her feet, and stepped away.

But once his hand spread over the flat expanse of her middle and he felt the breath leave her lungs, the guy in him had recognized that short expulsion of air as something entirely different from being jarred by the initial contact. Yeah, he had enough experience with women and the myriad types of breathless gasps to know one from another. And that it was Emily giving up that little gasp when he knew full well she would hate that he heard it, well, he couldn't resist making sure she knew he had—and that he'd recognized it for what it was.

Attraction, reluctant as it might be.

Priceless. But then he caught the subtle shift in Emily's eyes. It was more than just a narrowing or all that softness turning hard. There was something else in her eyes. Something he recognized all too well.

Challenge.

Enough to wipe the smirk from his face.

Because if payback was a bitch, her name was Emily Klein. And as much as he detested her, the woman was not without her wiles.

"Whoops," she murmured, one slender brow rising in his direction as she rested her hand on his arm and leaned forward to adjust a black stiletto heel he'd bet didn't need any kind of adjusting. But knowing what she was up to wasn't any defense against that sexy stance right out of a magazine shoot. The near-criminal fold of her body emphasized the gentle arch of her back as she peered up at him from beneath a fall of strawberry waves.

The air punched out of his lungs, and just like that, one unbidden leggy, lithe, flexible, toned, and sexy thought after another started crashing his mind the way his hockey team used to crash the net.

She swept her hair around to one side, giving him an unobstructed view of her smooth neck and shoulder, and that standout freckle he'd first seen at the beach the summer before senior year. The one he hadn't wanted to notice.

Blinking thick lashes at him, she smiled. "You okay, Jase?"

"Yep, Emily, I'm good," he managed with only the slightest croak.

Fine, she'd gotten to him. And okay, so he deserved it. Now they were even, which should have been reassuring. But he'd known Emily for a long time. He'd watched her volleyball games and competed with her for the highest grade in their AP classes. And he knew that competitive streak ran as deep and strong in her as it did in him.

No way was she letting him off with a tie. Not if she saw victory within her reach.

She'd go for the win. It was just a matter of time.

Dinner, as he'd suspected, was a seating-chart affair, but some angel of mercy had placed Emily across from him at their table for ten, leaving the chairs to his right and left filled by a cousin and sorority sister of Sally's. Both women were drop-dead in the looks category but he couldn't say on personality, thanks to Emily sucking up his attention from beyond the candle-and-sugared-fruit centerpiece.

More specifically, Emily and Mitchel Beekman, the poor schmuck saddled with the seat next to her. Mitchel was a decent enough guy. Jase knew him through Romeo, and while he wasn't about to invite Mitchel on a weeklong fishing trip, just the two of them, he liked him enough that the idea of Femily giving him her soft snow job didn't sit right.

So he'd kept an eye on them.

Watched as they chatted through the carpaccio and she laughed at his jokes through the bisque.

Yeah, Mitchel liked the sound of it too. He could tell by the way the guy's focus seemed to lock on her to the point of completely ignoring the hottie parked to his left. How his mouth sort of hung open in that dopey, awed way, while Emily rambled on about *whatever* through the poached salmon and filet.

Jase started playing with one of the grapes on his

cheese plate, his ears straining to hear what they were talking about. Probably one of her name-dropping war stories about working PR for some celeb.

"…needless to say, I found a new Laundromat…"

Or maybe not. Whatever.

Mitchel's mouth was still half open in that increasingly irritating grin.

Jase rolled the grape between his fingers. He could totally make the shot. Especially with that gaping, vacuous target.

Mitchel burst into laughter, covering his eyes as he rocked back in his chair. And then, almost as if it were happening in slow motion, the guy leaned in again, this time closer, and that peekaboo hand landed on the back of Emily's chair.

Jase's molars connected, and his jaw clenched.

He waited for Emily—who had most definitely noticed the arm breaching her space—to brush Mitchel off. Pull back and put the requisite polite distance between them. Flash a few of those no-go signals females mastered sometime around the tenth grade.

Only she wasn't doing any of that.

Her eyes just flicked to the arm at the back of her chair, and then she went back to talking, her smile as sweet and soft and steady as ever.

By the time dinner was over, Jase couldn't wait to get out of there. Mitchel's street credit had taken a serious hit.

And Emily? Well, if that was the kind of guy she was into, then have at him.

"Jase, about fucking time."

Max clapped him on the back and started pushing

firmly toward the door where a small crowd was waiting in a reverse receiving line to thank their hosts and make their escape.

Jase looked back, recognizing the strained look on his buddy's face.

"Officer Friendly, got girl trouble again?"

"Bite me," came Max's tight reply.

And then Brody was falling in, catching them each by one shoulder and pulling them in together for his quintessential bear hug. "She's cute, Max. A nurse."

The low growl coming from Max had Jase scanning the crowd for incoming cute nurses—but the woman in question must have exchanged her Florence Nightingale getup for one of the sparkling, jewel-toned dresses and high heels. He had no idea.

Even narrowing it down to the women eyeing their little cluster didn't do him any good, because the three of them tended to earn a fair amount of female attention.

"So what's the problem? You kissed her beneath the willow tree out back, and now her dad wants you to make an honest woman of her?"

"Worse," Max ground out. "She's Romeo's little sister."

Max looked about as uncomfortable as he could get, and considering he wasn't a guy who ever really relaxed, that was saying something. Jase whooped and scanned the crowd for Maya. Max could do a hell of a lot worse if he was interested in settling down. Only he wasn't anywhere near the one-woman-for-the-rest-of-his-life stage—and even if Maya was of the same mind, Max had a hard-and-fast rule about his friends' sisters. Probably scared shitless about turnabout being fair play.

"Relax, I don't see her."

He did, however, see Emily, who was deep in conversation with Romeo's aunt Ginger. But not so deep that she didn't bust him staring at her from across the room.

Great.

He flashed her a wink chock-full of empty promise and confidence he didn't feel. Then let his mouth fall into the smile that got him into all the places he shouldn't go.

There it was—the falter in her step and crack in her cool. Score one for Jase.

"Yeah, guys, we ought to get out of here," he said, suddenly feeling the need for a quick escape. Not that he was running. Whatever Emily could dish out, he could take. But still. "Maybe we could bypass the Willsons and just give them a wave good-bye. Skirt around the side or head out the back door."

Just then, he caught the soft, sexy scent and light touch of a hand too familiar for his taste.

"Oh, excuse me," Emily murmured, choosing that minute to sort of shimmy between him and the guy in front of him, letting hints and bits of her hair, arms, hips, and ass barely graze him as she leaned through the line to reach for a glass resting on the table to his left.

Then flashing him the softest, sweetest smile, she winked before brushing those killer legs across him in the other direction.

Catching the pained look on his face, Brody gave him a sly grin. "What, did she get you with her heel again?"

Jase positioned his coat in front of himself and cleared his throat. "Yeah. She got me."

Joe Foster was out front when Jase pulled up to the small bungalow in Oak Park that had been his childhood home. Hopping out, he squinted up at the roof, checking the gutter they'd fixed the week before.

"Any problems when it rained Wednesday?" he asked, meeting his old man at the side gate and following him around back to the garage.

"Nah, think we got it." Then waving a hand at the rake Jase was reaching for, Joe added, "Put that away. Pregame's going on. Let's get inside."

Jase shrugged and returned the rake, half disappointed he wouldn't have a chance to burn off a little of the tension he'd been banking since the night before. But he was here to hang out with his dad, not exorcize Emily through landscaping. "Sure thing."

"Christ, kid, sounds like some party," Joe said some twenty minutes later, settling into his recliner with his hands folded over what was still a moderately lean stomach. "Romeo handling the pressure?"

"I think so," Jase answered from the kitchen. Then popping the last bite of banana bread—his dad's specialty—into his mouth, he scanned the contents of the fridge to take inventory for when they hit the grocery store. "I had some concerns when he was getting ready to pop the question."

"They had that blow-up fight not too far back, right?"

Jase grinned at the sparsely stocked shelves, eternally amused at how Big Joe Foster was such a sucker for gossip. Seriously, put his dad and Janice in a room together, and they'd be in hog heaven. "Yeah, but I think it was just your typical guy pre-ring panic attack. We talked a lot, and he loves her. Like, forever loves her."

Yep, and that would be his mushy-hearted old man letting out a wistful sigh. "That's the way it ought to be."

"I guess." Then moving on to the cabinets, Jase called back, "You want chicken tonight?"

He could throw a pack of thighs in with one of the bottled marinades and give it a couple of hours to soak before grilling.

"Sounds good to me."

Jase walked around to the main living area and pulled one of the chairs from the dining table to face the TV. In the twenty years since his mom left, the only change his dad had allowed in the decor was the position of the living room furniture. And Jase was about ninety percent sure that was because, at sixteen, he hadn't asked before moving the couch that had acted as a divider between the table and chairs and the cluster of living room furniture to the opposite side of the room, allowing for easier viewing of whatever was on while they ate.

Change wasn't something his dad typically embraced, particularly when it pertained to the house his wife had decorated, so Jase wouldn't have even tried if undoing the move hadn't been an option. As it turned out, the old man had walked in that first night, stared a moment at the spot where the couch had always been and then, seeing the game on, nodded once and dropped into his chair at the end of the table to dig into the spaghetti Jase had heated up for dinner.

From his beige recliner across the room, Joe let out a warm chuckle. "Kid, you look wiped. Getting your vitamins?"

Jase rubbed a hand over his grin, both touched and amused at the way his father still looked after him. "Yeah, Pops. Every day."

"So what's with the walking around like you've got lead in your boots?"

Jase could try to dodge, to change the subject, but his dad had asked him a direct question, and, well—his dad didn't ask him for much.

"It's nothing. A woman."

Joe sat forward, a glint in his eyes. "Special?"

"Especially annoying." Irritating. Pecking her way into his thoughts even after he'd dropped the guys at home the night before. Hell, she'd still been there when he'd collapsed into bed. Flashing that smile. Laughing. The sound of it doing shit to him he wasn't a fan of. Particularly when he was on the brink of sleep and that sexy laugh and the memory of how she'd brushed so very close to him started to mingle in his mind, forcing him to get up and put in a few hours of work before he was willing to brave sleep again.

"You remember Eddie's girl, from before the accident?"

"Emily? Sure I remember, and from before she was Eddie's girl too. Always liked that one. How's she doing these days?"

Grudgingly, Jase told the truth. "Good. Real good, from what I can tell. She's a senior account supervisor for one of the bigger PR agencies downtown. I heard she's kind of a hotshot—lands all the big accounts. Lots of friends—friends who keep marrying mine."

"Well, good for her," his dad stated enthusiastically before leaning forward to ask, "She still such a looker?"

Jase couldn't deny it. "She is."

"You know, I always thought you two would have made a better couple than her with that Eddie. She was too smart for him. And, yeah, yeah, I know he's had it rough, but—" His dad shook his head, cutting that thought off, and then grinned at Jase. "So Emily's back. That's fantastic. You taking her out? Somewhere nice, I hope. Not one of those showy places where you can't even have a conversation. But *nice* nice. So you can talk. Get to know each other again."

"Dad, it's not like that with us." Not even close.

But it was too late, because his dad had that gleam in his eyes. The one that said he was getting way too far ahead of himself.

"What matters is how she gets to you right here." He thumped a fist over his heart and grinned.

Jase had way too much respect for his old man to suggest he wasn't sure the guy ought to be giving dating advice to anyone, considering the way his marriage had turned out. But he was thinking it.

"Sorry to disappoint, but you're off base, Dad. The only way Emily gets to me is like nails down a blackboard."

Joe looked anything but disappointed.

"I'm serious, Dad. One look from her is all it takes, and I'm torqued off for the next two days. Not a big deal when I only see her once or twice a year, but suddenly, it's like…" Jase rubbed his hands over the top of his head and then fisted them at the back of his skull. "It's like I can't get away from her. She's everywhere."

"She bothers you that much?"

"She shouldn't. I don't know why, at close to thirty, I'm still letting this girl get under my skin."

"You think it's because maybe she never totally got out?"

Jase's head snapped up.

"Come on, Jase. I remember how you used to be about her. Never saw you look at another girl that way."

"Dad, that was before—"

"Yeah. She was Eddie's girl. I know. But she's not anymore, now, is she?" Then before Jase could jump in with more protests, his dad held up a hand. "I know. She's under your skin. But I could list more than a few marriages that started just that way."

Choking out a cough, Jase shook his head. "If that's the case, then I really oughta stay away from her."

There would be no winning this one. He could tell his dad how Emily disliked him even more than he disliked her. He could spell out all the reasons why. But he wasn't up for the disappointment he'd see in his dad's eyes if he got into too many details.

When Jase looked up, the eyes that met his were frayed around the edges, faded from the years but still so eerily similar to his own that it was like looking in the mirror. "You know they don't all turn out like your mom and me," his dad said.

"I know," Jase answered evenly.

Honestly. Because sure, he'd seen a lot of marriages where one member hadn't climbed into a rusted-out Dodge pickup and taken off for California with the latest guy she'd been banging on the side.

But the marriage he knew best was the one he'd felt the repercussions of through most of his life. The one that ended with his father, the biggest, strongest man he knew, broken down so bad that it had taken years and the support of half a dozen guys who loved him like brothers for him to recover. And the truth was that even two decades later, Big Joe Foster still wasn't the man he'd been before that blow.

Jase cleared his throat, heading back to safer ground. "So adding the baby to the mix… Sure, it moves things up for Romeo and Sally, but aside from the wedding plans themselves, it doesn't really change anything."

His dad nodded, settling deeper into his chair and turning his attention to the game. "Good to hear."

Chapter 6

October

SALLY AND ROMEO DECIDED ON AN INTIMATE POST-Christmas, pre–New Year's wedding, and the now-truncated wedding party had assembled for a planning dinner at Wood, a Boystown neighborhood staple. The place was one of Jase's favorites, guaranteed for a great meal with a slew of awards backing up the hype. It had warm, low lighting, keeping your meal an intimate affair, and a dining-room-length bar that ran opposite the wall of booths where they'd been seated.

Romeo's little brother Martin had scored the best man slot, and thanks to an overabundance of cousins and Romeo's refusal to pick favorites, Jase, Brody, and Max had made the groomsman cut. Martin was a cool kid—twenty-one, a senior at Loyola with plans to start law school the next year, and a decent sense of humor—which meant nights like this one ought to be a whole hell of a lot easier to get through.

Or that's what Jase had thought until Emily breezed through the door, unwinding a burnt-caramel scarf from around her neck and then sliding one button after another free from her narrow-waisted wool overcoat. She looked polished, neat, and somehow sunny coming in from the late-autumn night.

So she'd made the cut too.

Jase took a deep swallow of his beer and set the glass down slightly harder than he should have. He'd had a feeling but, hell, a guy could hope.

She spotted him first. And he had to give her credit. The flash of hostility in her eyes was nearly gone before he'd seen it, replaced with warm smiles for everyone else. She was good, even offering a chipper "Perfect" when Sally suggested she sit next to Jase to leave room for Peg.

Those long legs slid in next to his, all but ensuring she'd end up in his space under the table. Great.

"You again," she murmured, then tuning up a smile even he wouldn't spot as a fraud, she asked, "Shitty day, I hope?"

"Worse every minute," he assured her, meeting her grin and raising her a friendly shoulder bump that should have had steam shooting from her ears.

But they were on good behavior so she capped it, offering him a smarting pinch on the cheek and a sing-song, "That's what I like to hear."

Yeah, that was his girl.

By the time his pork chop arrived, the booth was straining to accommodate a wedding party of ten, the now-defunct wedding binder, the post-baby-bombshell replacement binder, and Peg's newly fractured fibula—which was expected to be healed in time for the maid of honor to wear matching heels at the wedding—kicked out at an angle so no one would bump it.

He might have been more relieved if he wasn't so aware of Emily beside him, her thigh touching his every time someone at the table jostled or needed to reach across for a bite of whatever plate everyone else was moaning over.

To her credit, Emily didn't seem fazed. If anything, she appeared to be enjoying her opportunity to exchange a few barbs beneath the din of Sally's chatter about the seasonal merits of one flower over another.

And, okay, maybe some sick part of him was getting off on it too. Hell, they'd spent the better part of a decade without an outlet for their mutual hostilities.

A decade. Could that be right?

He turned, propping his arm on the booth back behind her so he was angled in a way where his words would be for her and her alone.

"What?" she asked, giving him her profile.

"Out of curiosity, when did you actually start to hate me?"

The question caught her by surprise, earning him a startled look from those big, brown eyes. But then he could see the wheels turning as she debated a response.

Would she be thorny because it had become almost a sport between them, or would she give him a straight answer?

A put-upon breath was the compromise, and then she leaned in closer to his ear to answer. "Eight years ago. After the accident."

Right. But Eddie flooring the gas and driving into that concrete train support hadn't been any kind of accident at all.

He turned, brushing a bit of her hair from her face. "Just then? I would have thought longer."

Her posture became somehow more relaxed, and her

brow furrowed slightly in consideration. She licked at the soft, pink bed of her lower lip.

"No. Before that, it was more disappointment. Frustration. Maybe even a little confusion. I don't know. But after the accident, it matured."

He pulled back and nodded. "Into this white-hot loathing we have today."

"Just," she said with a smile he couldn't help but return, and maybe even got a little caught up in.

And then Sally was leaning in his direction. Okay, his and Emily's.

"You know how much I want this to work. And you guys probably have more weddings between you than the lot of us combined. So let's talk reception ideas. The church is secured, but the reception… We need venues. A list of what's available, capacities, whether they will let us cater or bring in our own cake. You guys know what works and what doesn't, so I'm hoping you can scout a few locations."

Scouting. She didn't want him to just do a quick Internet search.

"Honestly, if you two go together, we'll have the best feedback and"—Sally smiled, but there was an alarming glossiness in her eyes—"I just want it to be special, you know?"

Damn.

Jase turned to Emily just as she faced him. Their eyes met in dismay. Because there was no cool way to turn down a pregnant woman on the brink of tears.

"I can't wait," Jase said, almost choking on the words.

"We've got you covered." Emily reached past him to give Sally's hand a squeeze. "Me more than Jase, but he'll be a help too."

Outside the restaurant, Emily was on her phone, her gaze trained on the sidewalk in front of her toes. She'd gotten a call after they'd settled the check and excused herself to take it. Something about the spokesperson for one of her accounts falling through.

Half the group had already taken off, and the rest were inside deciding where to go next. But Jase had an early morning ahead of him helping Molly pick up a couch she was buying off some guy down in Hyde Park. He'd been saying his good-byes when he checked the front window and saw Emily still on her call, her shoulders hunched against the cold.

So he'd grabbed her coat and, after tapping her shoulder, held it open as she mouthed "thank you" to him, slipping one arm and then the other into the sleeves.

After reassuring someone named Calista on the other end of the line about the product spot, she wrapped up her call and walked over to the corner where he was waiting to flag a cab.

"Are we actually going to do this?" Emily asked without looking his way.

"Do what? Help our friends the way we promised we would? Sacrifice a few hours of our time to help provide them with a memory they'll keep for the rest of their lives?" he asked, his voice dripping with the kind of superiority that was sure to get a rise out of her.

And, oh yeah, there it was.

That soft head of hair coming up to reveal sharp, narrowed eyes and a wicked smile.

Just the way he wanted her.

Her lips parted, and he could see the pink tip of her tongue sliding across the even row of her bottom teeth. Like she was contemplating the best way to eviscerate him.

His pulse jacked, and even though he knew with every ounce of his being that he should step back, he moved closer instead. Brushed her hands away from the lapels of her overcoat and started buttoning it like he had any right to touch her at all. Like he was doing it to torque her off, and not because some messed-up part of his brain just couldn't help himself.

She was slim, the long coat wrapping easily around her. Even with it cut to her proportions, he still had enough fabric to bunch in his hands as he buttoned her up.

What would happen if he reversed his actions, working his way back down that line of onyx disks and sliding his hands beneath the wool to skate over the narrow cut of her waist and the subtle flare of her hips?

His fingers flexed as he realized the wayward path his thoughts had taken.

What was he doing thinking about his hands on Emily's hips? The heat of her body? Or anything about her body at all?

Yeah, and Emily seemed to have snapped out of whatever temporary trace she'd succumbed to as well, because suddenly she was smacking at his hands like he was a gnat. Insignificant and annoying. Unwelcome that close to her.

Good.

That was better.

"You ass. Of course I'm going to follow through on

my commitment to my friend. You're the one with the track record of letting friends down, which is why I was clarifying that you were actually planning to hold up your end. Though even if you didn't, I could handle this venue thing with my eyes closed."

Yeah, yeah. Emily had skills when it came to making nuptial miracles happen. No doubt. But—"*I'm* the one who lets my friends down? Not ever, Em."

She met his eyes, and something that looked like hurt flashed within them for the barest instant. But then it was gone and she was back to doling out the cutting glare he'd become accustomed to the handful of times they'd seen each other over the past few years.

"Right. So how do you want to do this, then?"

They talked briefly about the reason they'd been called to action. Each agreed to put together a list of venues with potential, and then they'd coordinate visits to those with availability the weekend after Christmas.

They'd narrow it down to a short list so Sally and Romeo could make the final decision. A Yellow Cab pulled up, and Emily crossed her arms while taking a step back from the curb to give him the ride.

His mouth was running before he'd had the chance to check it. "We're only going a few blocks apart. Hop in and we'll share."

The words had barely left his mouth before he was ready to drag himself around the corner for a solid ass kicking. Because seriously, what was that?

Share a cab with Emily?

So he could sit in close quarters with her even longer. Soak up even more of that subtle scent she was wearing, the one he couldn't quite identify but made him curious

enough to want to burrow his nose into her neck and see
if he could figure out what it was.

Maybe their legs would touch again.

Maybe if they did, she'd look at him. Their eyes
would meet and hold.

Maybe he'd get to hear that little catch in her breath,
see the heat slip beneath her skin and—

"Pass," she replied succinctly, her eyes dropping
back to her phone.

Christ.

What was he thinking?

Suddenly the more familiar, definitely more comforting sensations wrapped around him snug and warm.

Annoyance. Frustration.

Hostility.

He didn't like Emily. So what did it matter if she
didn't want to ride with him?

"Fine. Get in the cab," he said flatly, his hand already
circling her arm and firmly pulling her toward the waiting car. "I'll take the next one."

What. The. Fuck.

Chapter 7

STANDING ON THE TERRACE OF THE WESTIN CHICAGO River North hotel overlooking the water, Emily tried to tell herself that the anticipatory high she had going was solely the result of excitement over helping a friend. It had nothing do with the fact that, after a week, she would be seeing Jase again. That they'd be alone.

No one there to keep them civilized.

Too bad that jump in her pulse when he strolled through the lobby doors with his overcoat open, the wind catching the short waves of his hair as he squinted into the morning sun—yeah, *that jump*—was calling her a liar.

"Morning, Em," he said, meeting her at the garden's edge to hand her a steaming cup of coffee. "Eye of newt and toe of frog, just the way you like it."

The laugh was out before she could stop it, but then she took a piping-hot sip of what could only be described as an incredible cup of coffee, indeed dressed just the way she liked it. So maybe she'd let Jase slide for making her crack a smile before she got her first jab in.

"Morning."

He looked like he was waiting for her to hit him with a zinger. She smiled. Let him wait. "Thanks for meeting me early. I'm hoping we can hit most of these venues today."

Jase leaned closer, checking the list she'd pulled up on her phone.

"Nice picks. Yeah, but there's a major renovation starting next month on this second one, so we'll have to see. Number three, though…"

Her gaze cut to where he was leaning over her shoulder, to the day-old stubble roughing up his solid jaw and the way the muscles along his neck moved as he spoke.

"…Anyway, there's room to dance, so it's got that." He glanced up then and nodded at the river in front of them. "Too bad it's going to be the middle of winter. The view right here is pretty spectacular."

She'd been thinking the same thing before he arrived. While Indian summer temps were already behind them, the sun was shining, casting a golden glow over the bridges, skyline, and Riverwalk. The terrace wouldn't accommodate the number of guests Sally and Romeo were planning, but the view really was something else. "The ballroom downstairs is still gorgeous, though. Ready to get started and have a look?"

Clearing his throat, he stepped back. "Sooner we start, sooner we're done."

Right.

Six hours and eight hotels later, they were standing outside Subway where Jase had just inhaled a twelve-inch turkey on seven grain and Emily was still nibbling the last of her crack-addictive white chocolate chip and macadamia nut cookies.

He'd done it again. Found a new way to get under her skin and make her writhe with frustrated discomfort.

Those little unnerving touches throughout the day. The supposedly inadvertent contact.

The way his lips turned up at the corners when she railed at him, all but *baiting* her to do it again. Making her think that, on some level, maybe he *liked* their charged interactions.

Making her wonder if *she* was the one enjoying their confrontations just a little too much.

"Emily, now you're just being difficult."

She snickered, taking another bite. "Like you refusing to even set foot inside my favorite pick?"

And what had she been thinking, telling him about the boutique hotel she'd fallen head over heels for the day she'd taken a client to brunch, and in front of the entire dining room, a guy had gotten down on one knee and proposed. It had been beautiful. Elegant. So romantic, that even standing on the sidewalk outside America's biggest build-your-own sandwich chain *beside Jase*, she couldn't contain a wistful sigh.

If she'd been on her game, she would have told him it made her skin crawl. Thrown in a traumatized shiver for effect and then sat back gloating when he sold it to Sally and Romeo like no other spot would do.

Stupid.

"Damn it, Em—"

"Damn it, *Jay*," she cut in, exaggerating the nickname just for kicks.

Pointing her half-eaten cookie at him, she laid it out. "You want to go talk to the manager at your restaurant, but I want to go to my hotel."

Jase looked ready to blow a gasket. She thought about taunting him some more, but then the wind picked up, catching her hair and whipping it around her face in a way she couldn't ignore. She tried to sweep it aside with a hand, but the gusts were unrelenting. Finally, she popped the three-quarters of her remaining cookie in her mouth and used both hands to tame the beast. Of course then she had a mouth overfilled with cookie and Jase staring down at her, his shoulders quaking with repressed laughter.

Chewing desperately, she fought her own rising laughter.

"Oh Christ, please don't choke," Jase urged, shoving his soda at her, the amusement in his eyes making them bright.

After a swallow of that disgusting concoction he'd made at the fountain using all the flavors, her laughter spilled free as she peered up at him. *What is that?*"

"My own special recipe. I'll never tell."

He really did have quite a smile.

Her hair was back in her face, but this time, Jase was the one to gather it up. And then they were standing there on the sidewalk, Jase's hand in her hair, his eyes locked with hers.

And that's when everything inside her went a little haywire. When her throat got tight, and her fingers started to tingle. Her belly slid into a slow churn she wished was disgust but definitely wasn't.

His gaze dropped to her mouth, his own curving into a smug little smirk. She was even more dismayed to admit she knew that, because her eyes had dropped to his mouth as well.

Mutual mouth staring.

So wrong.

Especially because instead of being able to muster the same smug smirk that stupid Jase had working, she was just…completely undone. Reacting like the sixteen-year-old girl she'd been when he'd first caught her eye. Before she knew what a world-class jerk he was. Before she'd had it confirmed in the most unpleasant ways, over and over again, that Jase Foster wasn't and hadn't actually ever really been her friend.

Unbelievable.

Shoving a hand through her hair, she brushed his aside and returned his soda. "Thanks."

He nodded and stepped back to toss the drink into the can in front of the store.

When he turned back, he'd lost that too-confident look. Shoving his hands into his jeans pockets, he grumbled, "I used to date the event coordinator at your hotel."

Emily raised a brow. "I'm listening."

Intently.

"Look, it didn't end well. She misread the relationship and thought there was more going on than there was. I tried, really tried, to let her down easy, but—"

"Now you won't even set foot in her hotel?"

"Now I wouldn't let her get within a thousand feet of a single thing she knew I might care about."

Her heart softened. "Like a friend's wedding."

"Yeah."

Damn it, why did he have to show her he wasn't always the total bastard he liked to be around her? Why did he have to remind her of what a good guy he could be to everyone else?

Why did she care?

She shouldn't.

She wouldn't.

"Fine. We can check out your restaurant." She would have anyway. It had a great reputation, and the fact that they'd had a cancelation was a minor miracle. Besides, raking Jase over the coals had lost its luster.

Jase stood at the bar, his beer tight in the death grip he'd had going since he'd heard it. That laugh. Light and bubbly, melodic and soft, floating over the ever-present Café Ba-Ba-Reeba crowd. No way this was happening again. It had only been five damn days since they'd been sampling mini crab cakes and caprese skewers with Romeo and Sally. What was it going to take to get a break from Emily?

Jase told himself to calm down.

Ba-Ba-Reeba was a popular restaurant, a Chicago favorite.

And it wasn't like this was the first time they'd ended up in the same space.

They frequented several of the same restaurants and a handful of the same bars, though thankfully she stayed clear of Belfast. So her being at the same establishment tonight—not a big deal.

They wouldn't be seated together. Hell, chances were they wouldn't even be in the same room, because in addition to being packed, Ba-Ba-Reeba was also pretty huge.

She probably wouldn't even notice he was there.

Only then he felt it. Fuck. *He knew*. She'd seen him. He shouldn't look. Shouldn't care. Shouldn't…

His eyes were moving over the crowd toward where he'd heard that laugh, the one he wasn't hearing now. And sure enough, there she was.

Several inches taller than most of the women around her. She was probably taller than most of the men too. And she was looking right at him.

Damn.

Eye contact.

The kind where too much passed between them before he had the good sense to pull back and break the lock. A deep breath and a long pull on his beer later, Jase braved another look. She was still standing there, but her focus had shifted to the hostess, who was scowling down at her seating chart with grim determination.

Which gave him the opportunity to catch what he'd missed on that first pass. The soft coils of hair tumbling around her shoulders, the wide-necked sweater too thin to do anything but draw his eyes to everything it didn't hide, and the trousers cut to keep his attention torn between the perfect curve of her ass and the teasingly short stretch of softly toned bare legs ending in—

He gulped.

The heels.

If ever a pair of shoes had earned the moniker, this red-spiked business she had going most definitely did.

Fuck-me heels.

He couldn't look away. Couldn't stop thinking about those red leather spikes sliding up the backs of his thighs, or the miles-long legs that came attached wrapped tight around him.

Holy hell.

Look away, man. Look away.

He tried to, but she looked too good.

Finally he gave in to the pull, accepting there was no escaping the vortex of *hot* he'd just fallen into. It didn't matter anyway—he was a guy. And he'd been admiring Emily Klein's good looks for years already.

He'd never done a thing about it.

So what was the problem? There wasn't one.

Only then she reached up to brush the hair that had fallen forward behind her ear, slowly, tentatively. Her gaze slipped back to him, and his beer hit the bar with less finesse than he usually mustered. He hadn't been braced for the punch that caught him square in the gut.

Emily. Looking less than tough.

Looking vulnerable.

Because of him.

There was no satisfaction in it. None at all.

No, they didn't get along. And yes, they got off on trying to one-up each other in the insult arena. But Christ, even he was feeling the strain of how much time they'd been spending together lately. The dinners out with Sally and Romeo to make sure all the plans were coming together. Working the peace in public and then laying into each other in private. All the while with that *thing* in the air between them—the one he wasn't having quite so much fun with anymore—screwing with his thought process.

Yeah, Emily had probably needed a break as much as he had. But now here they were. Together. Again.

Only not really. Because then the hostess was leading her toward the back of the restaurant, and suddenly Jase couldn't see her. Couldn't see who she was meeting. If it was some guy she'd gone to all that trouble for. If she had a date who was going to be able to rest his fingers over the flare of her hips and brush his thumbs against the rise of her ribs.

Feel the way her pulse accelerated. Know it was for him.

Forcing himself to stop staring at the empty doorway

she'd disappeared past, Jase downed the second half of his beer.

Picking at the label, he wondered who he knew that might be able to tell him if Emily was dating someone—without it getting back to her. Because that would be even worse than flat-out asking her himself.

"There he is!" proclaimed Marcos Nicks like he'd been on an epic quest searching for Jase, instead of just walking into the place where they'd agreed to meet. Two hands gripped his shoulders and shook until Jase's brain rattled in his head.

Turning around, Jase pulled the guy into a one-armed hug and then gave him a clap on the back. "Hey, man, how's it going?"

They caught up on the day, which included Marcos's account of his girlfriend waking him up with a hummer that morning and how he'd been late all day because of it. Jase was happy for the guy—because, come on, who wouldn't be—but didn't encourage elaboration because locker room talk hadn't really interested him even in high school.

Involuntarily, his thoughts drifted back to Emily. To her sliding out of the booth where they'd been devouring doughnuts at 2:00 a.m., leaving Eddie watching her go with that hot look in his eyes.

"She's going to give it up. Finally. You know how I told you what she kisses like. With that hot, wet tongue sliding all over my mouth. I nearly lose it half the time I'm kissing her good night. Think about what that's going to feel like on my dick, man. I think she's ready to do it."

Jase sat there with that placid smile ready to crack

on his face. Yeah, he knew how most guys talked. That there were milestones they were all working toward, and when one of them finally scored it, the rest were supposed to be there on the sideline, cheering them along.

But Jase just wasn't built that way.

His head cranked around to see whether Emily was within hearing distance, hating the idea of her being embarrassed by the guy she was dating dishing up what she undoubtedly thought would be private between them. Hating how much he hated the idea of her giving up any of the things he knew—thanks to Eddie running at the mouth—she'd been holding on to.

"I got her to touch it last night, man. Over the jeans. We were making out, and I kind of caught her hand and, real slow, put it on my package. She got up to go right after that, but for a second she totally left her hand there. Soon, man. Soon."

From the start, Jase had been trying to compartmentalize everything with Emily and Eddie in his head, but in that moment, the walls were down and Jase was sitting with his fists balled. Willing his best friend—the guy who'd been like a brother to him—to shut the hell up before he did something totally against his code and knocked Eddie's teeth in. Because the idea of Emily—

Fuck.

She was walking back to the booth and sliding in next to Eddie, who took her hand in his and held it, turning to flash Jase a quick wink.

Jase pushed out of the booth, set on distracting himself by…shoot, maybe going over to the table of girls at the other end of the place to say hi.

A glance over his shoulder told him Eddie didn't

mind the opportunity to work a little magic with Em,
who was laughing quietly at something the guy had said,
that smile in her eyes probably making him feel like the
king of the whole damned world.

Good.

He wanted that for him. Really. He did.

"—so it's going to be a few more people tonight. Figured
you wouldn't mind, or at least you'd get over having to
share me for the night."

Jase slid back into the present and what Marcos
was saying with a jolt. The memories of Emily from
high school were still too fresh in his mind to really
pay attention to what his buddy was saying.

Which was bull, he knew. Emily was no one to
him now.

Almost. Except that somehow he'd managed to work
his way another five feet down the bar looking for a
different view into the other room. Nothing.

So he still didn't know whether she was there with a
date or not.

"Hey, Marcos, thought I saw someone I knew in the
other room. Give me a minute, will you?"

Marcos was making deep eye contact with the bartender, willing the guy to come over and take his drink
order. "Yeah, but hurry up. I saw O'Donnel pulling up
to the valet when I came in."

Jase headed over to the doorway, feeling like a
world-class puss for needing to look in the first place.
But he wanted to know if Emily was there on a date.
If there was another guy—correction—*a guy* she was
involved with.

He almost hoped there was. Because that would be enough to deep-six the kind of thoughts he'd been having about her lately.

But the slow cruise past the doorway just left him feeling like more of an ass. Especially when he couldn't see jack.

Rubbing at the tightening muscles along his neck, he turned back to the bar to find Marcos headed his way, beer in hand and Brody and two other guys in tow.

"Table's ready, girls. Let's go."

Jase smiled, exchanging a few fist bumps and shoulder checks with the new arrivals as he fell in beside Brody.

"Something's up," Brody said conspiratorially, nodding at Marcos.

Jase frowned, looking ahead at Marcos.

"Why do you say that?"

Brody gave him a sympathetic look. "The guy is practically bouncing off the ceiling. He can't stop fidgeting. And haven't you noticed the peak in trash talk?"

Jaw shifting to the left, Jase gave Marcos a closer look. The guy was definitely jumpy. Boisterous, as he followed the hostess through the maze of the restaurant, cracking one joke after another with barely a breath in between. His hands going a mile a minute to match his mouth.

"He on something?" Jase asked, concern creeping up beside the guilt he was feeling, because he hadn't even noticed how Marcos was acting when he first got there. Because he'd been distracted. By Emily.

Who he shouldn't be thinking about at all.

"I'm going to go out on a limb here," Brody said with

a grin, nodding at the table ahead of them, "and say this isn't about drugs."

Jase followed his buddy's stare to the table where the hostess had stopped. Where Delphine Allen was beaming up at Marcos with pure adoration in her eyes and what looked like the Heart of the Ocean flashing from her finger.

Engaged.

They'd gotten engaged, and this dinner was their way of sharing the news with—oh hell—their friends. Their best friends. Four of them each. And sure enough, there was Emily, seated two chairs down from the bride-to-be.

———

This was not happening. Not again.

Emily had kept her smile in place for nearly twenty minutes following the news Delphine had just sprung on them—the wonderful news, really. But beneath that smile she definitely meant on some level, a few other emotions were at play.

Emotions that required the employment of letters like *W*, *T*, and *F* to convey them accurately, as well as other emotions that tended toward an uglier, self-pitying bent. Because this was supposed to be the Jase-free, sanity-restoring girls' night she so desperately needed. But there he was. Seated just across the table to the right—and not even a pitcher of white sangria with a crazy straw in it or hoarding a whole plate of those little beef skewers with the horseradish cream for herself could make it better.

On the bright side, their one moment of eye contact had been without any gloating or one-upmanship. He seemed as genuinely dismayed as she was.

Only somehow that didn't feel like any consolation at all.

After an acceptable period of time had passed, her smile was on the brink of collapse and Emily excused herself from the table. Cutting toward the narrow stairwell that led down to the ladies' room, she let the facade go and started gulping air.

Oh God, she was going to cry.

She could feel it bubbling up her throat too fast to swallow back and pushing at her eyes.

Jase. Again.

She was barely managing the time they were forced to spend together as it was. And now, just when she thought she was closing in on that light at the end of the tunnel, here he was again. Waving her through to that next expanse of winding, crowded darkness where she was a person she didn't entirely love being. A petty, biting, bitchy woman with a lacerating tongue and, worst of all, a past she couldn't let go of, forcing itself into a present where it didn't belong.

The door was at the bottom of the stairs, only feet away, when she heard someone on the steps behind her.

She didn't have to look; she already knew. Something about the way her heart skipped a beat and then started to race. About the way that spot deep in her belly tensed and her skin started to tingle.

"Emily, wait," Jase said, his deep voice rumbling around the claustrophobic hall surrounding her.

No way.

"Sorry, just give me a minute, and I'll meet you back at the table," she said, barely turning her head so he wouldn't be able to see her face.

She pushed into the ladies' room, but there wasn't even time for the door to swing shut before Jase came in after her, shocking her into stumbling back a step.

His hand shot out, catching her elbow.

"Are you okay?" he asked, maintaining that hot grasp on her arm even after she had steadied on her feet. The fact that she was thinking of the way that touch felt, that it was good, suggested that, no, she most definitely wasn't okay.

"I'm fine," she whispered, but the tremor in her voice gave her away. "You just startled me coming in here."

Jase's eyes were locked with hers, the look in them telling her that wasn't what he'd meant when he asked. "I didn't know about the engagement until tonight. Honestly, I didn't even know you were Delphine's friend."

Emily nodded, more embarrassing tears pushing at her eyes.

"I knew you were friends with Marcos." Of course she knew. Women loved talking about Jase. Handsome, funny, such-a-great-catch Jase. Even when they were fully committed to someone else, they rambled on about him. Maybe especially then. "But I didn't think… I didn't know how close they were to getting engaged."

Not the way Delphine had been talking. But apparently that was behind them. And now Emily was going to be standing up in her friend's wedding, and Jase was too.

Emily felt her lip start to tremble and she blinked, but the tears were coming as quickly as the words tumbling past her lips. "I'm at least five inches taller than the other girls."

Jase nodded, his brows furrowed as he stroked a comforting thumb over the sensitive inner skin of her elbow.

"Brody's the only guy even close, and I've got an easy three on him."

Emily blinked again, peering up into Jase's face as she gave in to the tears completely.

"But I hate you."

"I know, honey." He pulled her to his chest, closing those powerful arms around her back so all she could do was crumble into him. "I feel the same way."

God, how could he make her feel so much better? How could burrowing her face against his shoulder feel so right?

She drew a shaky breath, catching the scent of his cologne as he brushed his fingers through her hair. And then something wholly different from the overwhelming frustration that had sent her running from the table moved through her body. Something warm and quiet. An awareness that shouldn't be there.

Jase turned his head, speaking quietly into her ear. "We'll be through this in no time. It's not going to be like with Sally and Romeo where we've had to be in each other's laps for months at a stretch."

He paused and Emily tried not to think about what it might be like to venture into his lap. This man who was so much bigger than she was. She never sat in guys' laps because she was self-conscious about looking like her legs would fold up from the floor. But when Jase said it, she imagined a totally different visual.

Completely inappropriate.

"They'll have an engagement party. A shower. The rehearsal dinner and then the next day, done. It'll be stretched out over six months. Easy."

She knew what he was saying. That she wouldn't

have him in front of her every other day. That when she
saw him, it wouldn't be like reopening this raw wound.
They'd smile politely and then, if they were lucky, have
five, maybe ten minutes to spit nasty somethings into
each other's ears.

It would be fine.

But suddenly Emily couldn't take comfort in that future.

It didn't feel like a relief to think she wouldn't be
seeing him.

Slowly, Emily shifted within Jase's comforting hold.
She turned her head so she could see his face. Because
something was different, something she didn't understand. And maybe for once, it felt like Jase might have
the answer for her. The answer she needed.

His eyes met hers, the deep blue of them seeming to
darken even as she watched. The look in them leaving
her feeling vulnerable. Exposed. Uncertain.

Aware.

"Jase?"

He took a step back, stuffing his hands into his pockets.

"We're good?" he asked, looking again like the Jase
she'd known forever. The Jase who didn't make her feel
things she shouldn't.

"Yeah, I'm good."

Chapter 8

December

EMILY WOKE UP WITH A HANGOVER.

Not exactly her MO when it came to bridesmaid duties, but the night before had been a trial, to say the least. Half the wedding party hadn't made it to the rehearsal, thanks to Mother Nature sticking it to Sally with the near-blizzard conditions that had blocked roads and brought down power lines in the western suburbs.

Emily had only made it out of the city herself because she'd taken the afternoon off to spend with Sally at the Willsons' house and then stayed overnight.

From the groom's side, only Brody and two of Romeo's cousins had been able to make it through. Which had given her another day's reprieve from seeing Jase again. One she'd gladly taken, and today, well, he wasn't a priority.

Today was Sally's day. And despite all the rough patches leading up to this point, Emily knew—*knew*— all the blood, sweat, and tears would be worth it when the wedding went off without a hitch.

Things had already started shaping up. The snow had stopped falling sometime around eleven, and the plows had been going all night. Now at six thirteen in the morning, Emily was up, showered, and dressed in a pair of gray yoga pants and a mint-green hoodie for their trip to the salon where Sally would have her hair and makeup done. A quick glance at the Victorian-era porcelain clock on the nightstand next to her bed, confirmed by her phone that she trusted about a thousand times more, said she had about twenty minutes before they needed to leave. Plenty of time to grab a banana or some yogurt to go with the Advil she'd toss back as soon as she could find it.

Downstairs, the kitchen was empty, but the coffee had been put out in one of those oversize silver dispensers caterers used, along with a spread of pastries and fresh fruit.

Checking her phone again, Emily started getting nervous, wondering if she was going to have to go room to room looking for all the necessary parties. But then voices sounded from the stairwell.

"It's nerves, Sally. That's all."

Emily smiled at Mrs. Willson's wedding-day advice.

"It's morning sickness, Mom. It still hasn't gone away."

At least Sally's mother was trying. For as stiff and generally unpleasant as the woman could be, she had to have a softer side to have raised a girl as sweet as Sally.

"Well, you don't have to walk around with your hand on your stomach and that look on your face. Couldn't you, for one day, try not to look quite so pregnant?"

Emily blanched, staring down at her coffee, and contemplated dumping it down the drain and sprinting into the frozen tundra to avoid participation in the coming conversation, but she'd only made it halfway to the sink before Mrs. Willson was in the room with her.

"Don't you agree, Emily? *One day.*"

Emily turned, her most polite smile in place. "Wow, good morning, ladies! Sally, you look radiant."

She looked a lot like she'd been exposed to gamma rays, her greenish pallor daring anyone to get too close. But that wasn't what a bride-to-be needed to hear.

"How close are we to getting over to the salon?"

Sally poured herself a glass of milk, and her mother filled a coffee cup about halfway before walking into the pantry to top it off with something not on the buffet. Neither answered.

Emily tried again.

"So it looks like your Aunt Louise and Romeo's cousins' flights are going to make it. Great news."

Sally nodded tightly and took a deep breath through her nose.

Mrs. Willson shook her head in dismay.

"Why don't you sit down and have a few crackers," Emily suggested, retrieving the open sleeve from the cabinet where she'd seen Sally store it the night before. "Or would it be better to just let everything out"—she made a rolling motion with her hands—"and be done with it?"

Sally bolted for the bathroom tucked around the corner from the kitchen. And with the sounds of retching in the background, Emily and Mrs. Willson sat silently, smiling politely at each other.

So after *this*, the rest of the day was going to be perfect.

The bathroom door cracked open, and Sally stepped out and leaned against the doorway.

Her mother took a long sip of her coffee, then pointing with her index finger and a gentle smile, offered, "Dear, you have vomit in your hair."

She was right. Which meant rock bottom had most definitely been achieved. There was nowhere to go but up.

—⁓—

Emily handled high-stress situations without batting an eye. They were par for the course in her line of work, where TV spots fell through at the last minute, high-profile spokespeople suffered changes of heart, and anything that could go wrong on a campaign for a client it had taken years to land would. No matter what happened, she was the woman who saw everyone else through to a solution even better than their original plan. She was the one who turned the worst case into the best possible outcome. She got things done. And this wedding wasn't going to be the only exception.

Not even if one attendant or critical family member after another had started stumbling through the Willsons' front door wearing a thicker blanket of snow on their heads than the last, and there was no more denying that the storm they'd been hoping would head around them had solidified its commitment to rage right on through. They were still getting this wedding done.

The mimosas were flowing, the chatter on the rise. Emily had been hustling for hours, but it was all coming together. Jase was the only outstanding groomsman, and he'd been in communication with Romeo about heading straight to the church with an on-time ETA. Sally had rewashed her hair, promptly thrown up a second time, then pronounced herself good to go. They'd hit the salon, transporting Sally with an arsenal of umbrellas and plastic wrap to prevent the piled curls and generously applied makeup from going limp or runny.

It was showtime.

Sally was in the first car with her parents, poor thing. The handful of honored relatives at the house had taken a second car. And the bridesmaids were loading into the third where all their coats and boots had been stored in the trunk until after-the-wedding photos when they could afford to have their gowns slightly crumpled. Emily hopped in last, grinning at the girls as the driver closed the door behind her.

Slumping back in her seat—but not so much that her hair would take a hit—she let out a relieved sigh. And then her phone rang.

Sally's panicked voice spilled through the line. "The ring, Emily! I forgot to pick up Romeo's ring. The jeweler is on his way to the house to drop it off. Someone needs to stay and bring it to the church."

Emily looked down the drive into the falling snow. She couldn't even see the main road. No telling how long it would be before the jeweler showed up. The car couldn't wait.

"I've got it. The girls will leave now, and I'll drive myself once I have the ring. Be there before the wedding starts. We've got this. Everything is going to be fine."

Chapter 9

JASE THREW THE CAR INTO PARK AND LEANED BOTH arms over the wheel as he stared out the windshield in disbelief.

It was Emily, all right. Sprinting across the icy church parking lot with her strapless gown hiked up around her knees, a pair of heels hugged close to her chest and—what the hell?—bare freaking feet.

A quick glance at his car's temp display showed it was a whopping thirteen degrees outside—then add, or subtract, from that the windchill factor. She was beyond asinine.

And she was still only halfway across the sprawling lot to the church.

With a curse, he slapped at the temp control, cranking the heat, and then flung open the driver's door, exchanging one curse for a fresher, more potent variety. The wind sliced at him as he started to jog across the lane of cars, undoing the buttons on his coat as he went.

Each step was like a thousand tiny needles stabbing into the soles of her feet, between her toes, and around her ankles.

She'd been so careful, navigating the roads with skill and attention—determined to get to the church and deliver Romeo's ring. All the way from the Willsons'

she'd been fine, right up until she'd crept into the far
entrance to the church lot and her car had started its
horizontal slide across the ice and landed her in a ditch.
There was no way her little Fiat was going to pull out
without the assistance of a tow. A tow Emily couldn't
call for, thanks to the jeweler's son knocking her phone
from her hand when he slipped on the ice in front of
the Willsons' house. Fortunately, he'd been fine, but her
phone…not so much.

So no phone meant she'd been stuck several hundred
yards from where she needed to be, no help in sight, in
fresh snow up to her ankles and only one solution she
could see working. Run for it.

Her only consolation in this disaster was the hope
that if she was picking up every bit of bad luck within
a six-thousand-mile radius, there wouldn't be any left
for the bride and groom, and their special day would go
off without a hitch. That and at least there were no wit-
nesses to her total idiocy. Specifically, no Jase Foster.
Who would have called her names and laughed in her
face, letting her abject misery warm that vacant chamber
in his chest.

The ground was as slick as she'd ever encountered it,
and within a few feet of the car, not only was each step
terrifying and riddled with face-planting possibilities, but
it was clear she'd never be able to navigate it in her heels.

This just got worse and worse. She stripped off her
shoes and started again. The ceremony was set to begin,
and with so many people missing from this important
day, she didn't want to be another. She'd make it. She
pushed forward with that resolve past the next lane of
parked cars, right onto the raised shard of ice that sent

her tumbling forward into an awkward split and skid, facing a wipeout of epic proportions. She was going down, and it was going to hurt bad.

At the last second, her fall was arrested when strong arms and a black…blanket—no overcoat…engulfed her. And then her descent wasn't just arrested; her trajectory was completely reversed. Instead of going down, Emily was being pulled back. Her breath left her in a rush as she slammed into a solid wall of muscled chest. She wanted to put a hand out to brace against it, but the coat she'd been engulfed in wrapped her arms close to her body and nearly covered her face completely, leaving only a sliver of tuxedo shirt visible. It was a groomsman. Thank God.

And his coat was so very warm around her. Nothing had ever felt as good as this. She wanted to pull her legs in, because the burn of her feet was bad enough that she was starting to wonder if her toes were going to break off before she got inside.

Wiggling her arm between them, she tried to work her fingers past the lapel to get a better view of her savior. It had to be Max. The guy was built like a linebacker and so solicitous to all the girls. A real protector. She wanted to thank him, but as she fiddled with the fabric, his grip tightened and a voice that most definitely didn't belong to Officer Friendly filtered in through the wool.

"Don't move."

Not exactly a gentle suggestion.

Jase.

Instinctively her muscles went still. Frozen in a way that had nothing to do with the bitter elements she'd stupidly found herself caught in.

Jase was carrying her princess-style across the lot. Her number one least-favorite person in the world— the guy who made her angrier than she'd ever been in her life without doing anything more than locking that damned accusing stare on her—was now doing her a solid, the likes of which she'd never known.

God.

She was going to have to be nice to him after this.

And not fake nice. Real. Honest-to-goodness, would-you-like-something-while-I'm-up, how's-your-dad, thank-you nice.

Suspended in Jase's arms, she shivered as he adjusted his hold, swinging her around so his arm banded beneath her rear as he held her upright facing back over his shoulder, allowing the coat to slip open revealing…the wrong view.

Her breath sucked in as she swiveled around, confirming that Jase hadn't been carrying her toward the church at all.

"Hang on to my shoulder, Emily."

"W-w-what are y-y-you d-d-doing?" she stuttered as her body dropped a few inches, sliding down Jase's front before he secured his grip. "The ch-church. The cerem-m-mony. We have t-to—"

Emily's heart dropped as she was swung forward and pushed into the front seat of an SUV. The door slammed quickly beside her, and she looked out the window to where Jase was already rounding the car, his eyes locked on hers through the glass, a dark scowl etched across his features as he pointed a single finger at her and mouthed the command "Stay."

Then he was jerking his door open and sliding in fast,

bringing another gust of biting cold into the car that was amazingly, incredibly warm.

"I wrapped the damn coat around you for a reason, Emily. Turn around in the seat and give me your feet."

Okay, maybe the cold and the adrenaline and the worry and the hangover were getting to her. Because she had no idea what Jase wanted with her feet. Which had become a general pain that seemed to exist outside of anything as specific as shape. She tried to move her toes, but they were stiff and the shaking was making it hard to do anything.

"A-a-are you g-going to d-d-drive up t-to th-the f-f-front d-doors?"

The eyes that met hers were hostile and as dark as the curse he gritted out before turning to lean into the backseat for what ended up being a blanket.

It seemed she didn't need to wonder whether he'd be painfully polite with her after all.

"Give me your legs."

Normally, she'd have come back at him with an offer to give him something else altogether, but right now, she was shaking so hard she couldn't bring herself to make the effort. Jase wasn't worth it. Even if he had rescued her from the arctic church parking lot, and even more than that, from falling on her face in the middle of it.

"Can you even move them?"

This time, his voice wasn't quite so harsh, and she realized there was an undercurrent of concern she never would have associated with this man—at least not in the context of her well-being.

Looking down at her legs, she started to pull at them,

but it seemed as though her entire body had lost mobility. She just needed another minute…

A minute Jase apparently wasn't going to wait for. Shoving the blanket into her hands, he reached down and gripped both her knees, pulling them up and, in a series of swift moves, laying them across the console so they rested in his lap.

"J-Jase! Wh-what are you d-d-doing?"

He looked down at her feet, which had taken on a mottled, angry appearance, and growled, "What the hell were *you* doing?"

Opening her mouth to speak, she snapped it closed again when those big hands started rubbing over her abused flesh.

"Barefoot. No jacket. Running across the—" His eyes went to the roof of the car, and Emily had the distinct impression that Jase was within a hellfire's throw of blaspheming the sacred parking lot. "What? Didn't want to ruin your shoes? Couldn't be bothered with the hassle of a jacket? Is your vanity skyrocketing so high that the oxygen's too thin to feed your brain?"

Her chattering teeth ground together as heat born of too many years listening to Jase Foster sell her short started to burn inside her. Her arm snapped out, one finger pointing in accusation. "I appreciate the r-rescue, but I-I've about had it w-with the rest of your b-bull. I d-don't need you l-looking to tear me d-down every opportunity you can f-find. Not that you d-deserve it, but here's the d-deal."

Through chattering teeth, she detailed the chain of events leading up to her rescue, starting with the missing ring, the limo driver taking off before she could get her things out of the back, her car, and the fact that no one seemed to even notice she'd gone into a ditch. With each clarification she warmed a little more, her teeth chattering a little less. "With all the ice under the s-snow, I thought I'd probably kill myself t-trying to cross the l-lot in those heels and figured my only option was to r-run. It wasn't about vanity, you arrogant, accusing j-jackass. It was about necessity. So screw off!"

She finished on a rush of breath and then snapped her hand back under the blanket, quickly looking across the lot at the church. This guy didn't deserve an explanation. She wasn't supposed to care enough about what he thought to feel the need to give him one. But after everything else that had gone wrong today…

Whatever.

The heater blowing was the only sound. Then, "Are you okay?"

"I'm frustrated, Jase. Not about to b-break down and s-sob all over you or anything. Can you just drive up to the entrance and drop me? I c-can get in on my own from there."

"Physically okay is what I'm asking. Your car is in a ditch. Did you bump your head or strain your neck?"

"Oh. Um, no. I was taking the turn into the lot pretty carefully, so when the wheels lost traction and started to slide, it was kind of a slow-motion event." At his skeptical look, she let out a laugh. "I can't believe you care, but really, it's the truth. My heart was going faster than the car, I think."

He gave a stiff nod. "That's good, then."

Okay, so they were back to being civil. "Do you think you can drop me at the front?" she asked again.

Jase looked out the windshield. "I'll carry you in, but yeah, I'll get by the door first and then run back out. Can you wiggle your toes?"

Her feet were in his lap, her legs stretched across the console between them. Her heels rested between his thighs, and he was rubbing the life back into her abused soles.

She wiggled her toes, and while they were a little stiff… "I don't see an amputation in my future."

Jase laughed, then seemed to catch himself and look out his driver-side window. But she could see through the reflection that he was still looking at her.

His hands moved over her feet, rubbing and squeezing the blood through them. Circling with his thumbs at the center of her arch. Stroking the muscle that ran along the bottom. It felt good. Really good. Like maybe even a little too good because that slow, steady, warming touch was starting to relax her in a way she wasn't accustomed to when it came to Jase.

He palmed her heel and rotated her ankle, his fingers extending just the slightest bit up her calf. Enough that for one second Emily thought about how it would feel to have those big hands coasting up past her knee.

She gave her head a solid shake and tried to pull her foot back. But Jase just told her to relax—because he wasn't taking her anywhere until he'd gotten her warmed up—and then moved back to her other foot. His long fingers spread over her chilled flesh. Pressing exactly the right spot. Rubbing so it took everything she had not to moan.

The silence was starting to feel strained, but maybe that was just because for a second there she'd thought about Jase in a way she'd been working very hard not to. And that wasn't cool. They had mutual loathing down to an art form. They were good with it.

Anything else would just be…weird.

He rotated her ankle and then knuckled up the sole of her foot—and this time, the moan of pleasure slipped past her lips before she was able to yank it back.

"Wow, Em. You need a minute alone?"

Heat rushed into her cheeks, but she wasn't going to let Jase have the last word or the upper hand. Even if he had just pulled off what could only be described as a rescue of Prince Charming proportions.

"Yes, please. And if you've got a s-snapshot of Max to leave with me, that'd be swell."

"You know, Em, the key to a successful burn is keeping a straight face. Or short of that, stifling the snort laugh."

She gaped, her eyes locking with his, and damn it, more laughter bubbled up in her chest. "I did not snort."

His brows raised in smug satisfaction. "Okay."

She leaned forward, amusement and indignation mingling in her next words. "I didn't."

She thought he was ready to deliver the next slam. She might even have been anticipating it, just a little. But instead of him waiting the mandatory beat and letting her have it, his brows drew forward, his gaze darkening.

She followed his stare to where his hands were cradling her leg. The long, thick fingers on one of his hands were splayed wide to cradle her calf, the other hand resting over her knee where her dress had piled up.

She hadn't noticed it before. Hadn't even been aware of where his hands had ended up when she shifted forward in her seat. But now, now she could feel his fingers like a brand. Feel that tingle of awareness, that low charge working its way outward. Riding the line of her leg, the bend of her knee, the length of her thigh. She could feel the heat of his palms, the press of each finger where it lay against her skin. God, she could feel her blood heating beneath them.

Her breath trembled.

Jase looked back to her. His eyes smoldered now with something she'd never seen in them before. They were close, only inches apart. A blanket of snow had already covered the windshield and driver-side windows, making this space they were sharing feel private, intimate.

She stopped breathing.

Because Jase wasn't looking at her like he wanted to insult her. Or carry on with the banter. He looked like he wanted something else. Maybe the same thing she'd only in that second realized she wanted too.

Jase frowned. Coming to his senses maybe, probably. Because this look between them was nuts. Wrong. Something she knew she shouldn't want, but couldn't seem to break away from regardless.

So it was good that he was. Because otherwise she didn't even want to think about what—

His stare dropped to her mouth. And with a shuddering breath, she realized, yes, she was already thinking about it.

About how big his hands felt on her leg. How strong his arms had been around her. How the lips she'd forced herself to stop speculating about in high school might taste.

"Just once," he said, his voice gone gravelly low. "Just to put an end to the curiosity."

She was nodding, sort of, her head moving the barest amount.

"No way will it live up to the hype," she replied. "I'll walk away disappointed. Probably feeling sorry for the girls with such high expectations."

Jase's mouth curved at one corner, a cocky addition to his words. "You'll walk away wishing for more."

She might. "Not a chance."

"Whatever." And then he did it. Caught the back of her neck in his palm and closed the distance between them, his eyes locked with hers, almost daring her to back out, until that last instant when she saw something flash in them besides challenge. But then, *contact*.

Contact that teased with a barely there quality, rubbing in a gentle, tasting exploration that shocked a trembling gasp past her lips.

Damn. She wasn't supposed to get caught up in it. She wanted to remain unaffected. Indifferent. But the skill with which Jase's firm lips moved over and against hers made indifference impossible. He was good.

Jase pulled back.

Shoot. She hadn't wanted it to end. Wasn't ready for the wanting more that he'd promised to become a reality so quickly. But the last thing she was going to do was beg, even if she could still feel that almost-too-light, somehow just-perfect press of his lips.

Her eyes drifted open, and she found Jase barely an inch away. A frown carved deep across his mouth. His eyes dark and fixed on hers.

"Jase," she whispered, barely managing the single

word before the fingers at the back of her neck tightened and she knew without question what was coming next.

More.

His mouth crushed down on hers. No tentative kiss this time. No featherlight tease. His mouth was firm, his kiss confident. Arresting. She opened beneath him, letting him lick into her mouth, breathe against her lips. Taste her tongue as she tasted his.

Her fingers were locked in the front of his shirt, pulling him closer. Because yes, please—*closer*. She needed him closer. And he must have been of the same mind because he'd wrapped his arms around her and was gathering her toward him as he kissed her again and again. Devoured her mouth, and groaned when she bit at his.

Her fingers were in his hair, the silky waves she'd spent too many study halls thinking about. Thank God she'd never gotten her hands into the stuff before now, or she wouldn't have been able to forget it. Even now, she wondered if she could.

His kiss was so hot.

Hot enough that her mind seemed to be flickering between satisfaction that this was Jase—her high-school fantasy fulfilled—and the certain knowledge that this had to stop because it was *Jase*. Jase kissing her like she'd never been kissed before. Jase thrusting into her mouth, his tongue sliding wet and hot against her own. Jase working one wide palm beneath her skirt and up the side of her thigh, his grip tightening and relaxing with every few inches he advanced. Jase making her burn and beg for his touch to extend just a little farther, just that much more, just—

A phone sounded but neither of them stopped, not until the third ring when suddenly Emily jerked back with a gasp, staring in horrified shock at Jase, who looked more stunned than anything else. Stunned and still wearing that sexy sort of frown on his face.

They were in the car. In the parking lot of the church, where they were both supposed to have been five minutes ago.

Jase snapped out of it, patting around his pockets and then retrieving his phone, all while keeping his eyes trained on her.

"Jase," he answered. Then, "Are you fu—" He broke off, closing his eyes as his free hand went to the bridge of his nose and a coarse sound worked its way past his gritted teeth. Slapping the wipers on, he asked, "They can't get anyone else?"

Emily sat up as her stomach began to sink. Over the dash she saw the first signs of activity. One bundled body after another leaving the church.

Oh no.

"Okay, man. Yeah, let me know." Clicking off the call, Jase looked down at Emily's feet still in his lap. "Priest slipped on the ice and broke his hip. They aren't sending anyone else out. The wedding will have to be rescheduled."

Passing the phone across the seat, he sat quietly as Emily dialed first one number, then another until finally she got through to the father of the bride.

Sally was okay but didn't want to talk. They were taking her home.

A moment later, there was a knock on the window. One of the other bridesmaids was holding up Emily's boots and coat.

"You want a ride home?" she asked, her stare flicking from Emily to Jase and then back again.

Emily was about to crawl out the window and into the girl's arms because she was so relieved to see her—because what the heck had she been thinking—when Jase pushed her back in her seat and reached past to grab her things.

"I'll take her home."

Oh man.

Chapter 10

THE RIDE BACK INTO THE CITY WAS QUIET, THE ROADS improving with every mile they traveled. Emily used Jase's phone to make a few calls, trying to distract herself. But when there was nothing left to do, she found herself simply looking at him. Watching the way he drove.

How his hands gripped the wheel.

The way the muscles in his legs flexed beneath his tux pants as he hit the accelerator.

The man was too good-looking.

Too confident.

Too much of an ass for Emily to have let him kiss her the way he had. For the *nothing* she'd had to say about him driving her home. For the questions running through her mind about what would happen when they got there.

Jase pulled up to her building and took a spot in the front. She had her boots and jacket now. Her purse. There was no reason for him to come up.

And yet, when he put the car in Park without a word, killed the engine, and hopped out, rounding to her side of the car without missing a beat, the flutter of anticipation within her was unmistakable.

Then they were inside the building. Riding the elevator up to her floor. She was unlocking the door with Jase a mere inch from her back. They were inside, the lock thrown, and his hands on the espresso-stained panels beside her head as he pressed into her with his hips. He was so much bigger than she was. So hot and broad and warm and, oh God, he was pushing her coat from her shoulders. Gathering her skirt as he pressed a hard-muscled thigh between her legs.

Hitting that perfect spot that had her lids dropping to half-mast and her breath leaving her lungs in a slow sigh.

"This doesn't mean anything," she panted, her fingers feeling for the studs fastening his shirt.

"Less than nothing," Jake assured her, bowing forward to let his hands coast up the backs of her thighs as he burrowed his face in the crook of her neck and groaned her name.

Her name. When he said it like that—like he was in heaven and hell at the same time, blaming her for both—her entire body ignited.

"Good. Just so we're clear."

Jase was rocking into her, his breath ragged, his erection thick and long between them. Positioned low against her pubic bone.

"You're so tall," she gasped, savoring the unique fit of this man moving against her body. Sure it wasn't the most romantic thing she'd ever said, but something told her Jase wouldn't have appreciated it if it was. This was, after all, a strictly physical release.

"Perfect fit. I fucking knew. From back—"

His words cut off as he buried his face in her neck and swore.

The coarse sound of it… *Yes.*

She wanted to hear it again. All night.

She rocked back into him. Meeting his rhythm as she turned into his ear.

Ran her teeth along the outer shell and felt his hands tighten on her ass as he swore again. Rocked harder. Just exactly *there*.

Emily started to shake, her fingers clutching at anything, everything, trying to get a hold on a world that felt like it was coming apart.

"Like that," she gasped, no longer caring whether she sounded like she was pleading or not. More than happy to let Jase have the upper hand especially if he was going to use it like… "Jase!"

"Are you close, Emily?" he growled, his body like steel around hers. Tensed, ready.

Another thrust rubbing against that needy, aching spot, and her answer broke against his lips. "Ye-es."

He hiked her knee higher, tucking it up against his hip. Then reached between them and, with what seemed a single flick of his hand, had his pants open, his cock free.

She looked down, her eyes going wide. Because wow. He was…a big man.

Everywhere.

Her tongue flicked out to wet her lip. She wasn't generally the drop-to-her-knees sort, but something about the sight of Jase's heavy cock between them had her mouth watering.

Her center clenching with a need to be filled.

Jase caught her chin in the crook of his finger, bringing her eyes back to his.

"Are you on the pill?" he asked, rocking into her again.

"Yes," she panted, moving into the press and slide

of his steely length against her sex. Wishing she had a magic wand to get this skirt out of the way. And her panties too. Because she wanted to feel him against her. She wanted the hot, wet friction of his skin… No!

Jesus, what was she thinking? This was Jase Foster. Pill or not…

The crinkling sound of a wrapper being ripped opened stopped her thoughts in their tracks.

"Good," he said, rolling the latex on with a deft move she never would have thought sexy before, but something about Jase's big hands moving up his length… "I mean, I'm safe, Em. And I know you well enough to know you'd tell me if you weren't. But I'm a 'no chances' kind of guy."

Was it hot?

Not in the traditional sense, but in terms of open communication and responsibility?

Definitely.

Especially when paired with the heated intensity in Jase's eyes. The bunched tension in the flexing muscle of his jaw. The way he raked his eyes over her and gathered up the length of her skirt, one hand after the other until all that remained between them was the pale-beige silk and white lace of her panties.

Jase smoothed his palm over the front of them, cupping her with his fingers. "Hot," he growled against her lips. Then pulling the scrap of lingerie aside, he stroked where she was already open to him.

"Christ, Em. You're so wet."

Her leg tensed around his hip, her body pleading for more of the contact her mouth wouldn't beg for.

Or she'd thought she wouldn't. But that was before

Jase slid a single finger inside her. Pushed deep and then, on the withdrawal, stroked forward, making contact with that spot deep, deep inside her that no one got right.

"Jase. There," she gasped, her eyes locked with his, her lips open as her breath sucked in when he did it again.

"What? This?" he asked, that heated look in his too-blue eyes going supernova.

So sexy. And combined with the cocky half grin on his gorgeous mouth, she might not need him to do anything at all but look at her that way.

"Yes!" she gasped, rocking into his hand.

"Ask me nice, Em. Say 'Please, Jase.'"

His finger grazed the spot again, only this time, too lightly for it to be anything more than exactly what he'd meant it to be. A tease. Torture.

Another play for control.

She wanted him to touch her. To take her over the edge. She wouldn't need much. He could do it with another single touch, if he touched her the way she needed him to.

But something inside her wouldn't let the "Yes, please, please, please, Jase!" poised on her tongue go free.

Instead, she leaned her shoulders back into the door, tipping her hips into his touch as she met his eyes, taking a little of her own control.

Something had happened in the last three and a half seconds Jase hadn't seen coming. He'd thought he had Emily ready to beg. To plead. To offer up home-cooked baked goods and a back rub if he would just finish her off.

Yeah, not gonna lie, it was hot as hell listening to

those breathy, desperate noises coming from her. In fact, thirty seconds ago, he would have ventured to say there wasn't anything hotter.

But that was before Emily Klein realized she wasn't interested in giving up the upper hand. At least not without a fight.

And holy hell, what she had in her arsenal.

She'd tipped her hips into his touch and given him one of those seductive looks from beneath the ashy fringe of her lashes. A look that said she liked what he was doing, enough to maybe let him keep it up a while. Yeah, it was the kind of look that lesser men embarrassed themselves over…because *hot*.

Where had she learned that, anyway?

He didn't have much time to ponder, because then her lips parted on a soft sigh. It was the precursor to the pink tip of her tongue wetting the inner flesh of her kiss-swollen bottom lip. Followed by her neat teeth pressing into that same flesh as she slowly rolled her hips from one side to the other, tracing her fingertips across her neckline.

Jesus, someone had been watching too much porn to be pulling moves like this.

To have him ready to drop to his knees and give her just about any damn thing he could think of.

And then she did it. Low and breathy and infinitely confident, immeasurably sexy, she murmured softly, "Please, Jase."

Damn. Those words, delivered in that tone, with that look.

He could feel the tightening at the base of his spine. His body reacting like he'd been pumping inside her for the past hour, not like he hadn't even had a taste of what she'd be like yet.

Every man had his limit.

Mouth crashing down on hers, he thrust his tongue past her lips, needing to be inside her more than he could remember needing anything else. Knowing it was going to be mere seconds before he was thrusting deep, but not being able to wait for that last bit of realignment.

Not that Emily seemed to mind. She was moaning around his tongue, licking at him with small flicks as he spread her wide to him, positioning himself until he was just exactly *there*.

The frantic hunger of their kiss eased.

Time slowed and their eyes met as he pushed into that spot of soft give, groaning at the tight passage gripping him. At the breathless mewls against his ear. At the feel of Emily's hands clutching at his neck, his shoulders, his arms and chest. Like she desperately needed to hold on to something, to him, but she didn't know exactly how or what would be enough.

Inch by inch, he pressed inside her, working himself deeper and deeper, pulling back only to give her body a chance to adjust, then pushing forward again until he'd taken her completely and they were staring into each other's eyes.

Her hands were still on the move, still restlessly roaming from one spot to the next. Clenching and flexing. Doing things to him he couldn't handle if he wanted to last.

And Jesus, he did. Because this was never happening again. Which meant he didn't want to rush. He wouldn't risk Emily not having a good time.

No way.

He'd never hear the end of it if he did, and while the idea of her ruthless insults were maybe making him even a little harder than he'd already been, the part of him that didn't like to lose had plans to make it so good that she would have to think of him if she ever wanted to come again.

Yeah, definitely harder still at that thought.

She'd be so pissed.

Lips parted, she narrowed her eyes on his mouth.

"What's that look?" she demanded breathlessly, her voice barely holding although he sensed that steel in her spine was as strong as ever.

"Just thinking about how pissed you're going to be when I ruin you for all other men."

Her mouth curved, a sexy little laugh escaping. "Good luck with that."

"Don't need luck," he growled, starting to move within her. All he needed was the promise of Emily cursing his name every time another man tried to satisfy her.

"Jase!"

"You what?" Lena gasped, as Emily paced back and forth across her best friend's office floor.

"I think I might have let him ruin me for all other men." Emily stopped, glared at the ceiling, and shook her head, cursing her own stupidity. "He warned me. Actually warned me what he was about to do. And Lena, you should have seen the look on his face. Like he didn't have a doubt in his mind that he could. But did I heed the warning?"

There was a little too much delight in her best friend's eyes when she answered, "I'm guessing no."

"No! And not just a simple no. I *dared* him to do it. I basically challenged him, Jase Foster of all men, to do his worst."

"And he did." Lena's expression was something between sympathy and amusement, one seeming to break through the other in regular intervals.

She really wasn't taking this seriously enough.

"Yes, he most definitely did."

Being the pragmatic sort that she was, Lena leaned back in her too-big executive chair and steepled her fingers.

"Okay, I don't want to minimize what you're going through here. But Em, it's only been two days. I think maybe you're giving him more credit than you should just yet. I mean, how many other guys have you been with since Saturday morning?"

"None," Emily grudgingly admitted. It was only Monday at noon, and honestly, her average was probably one sexual partner every two to three years. So chances were good it would be a while before she actually got to prove what she knew deep in her heart to be true—that she'd been ruined. Completely.

Because nothing had ever even come close to what Jase had done to her against that front door. And then on the back of her oatmeal linen sofa. She was pretty sure that the point where she had nearly lost consciousness…yeah, that had been on the buffet cabinet in her living room.

"Three times, Lena. To his once."

Her friend's brow pushed up slowly. "Three times in a row? Or with breaks? I mean, did you guys stop for some water or—?"

"No water. No breaks. He just… He was… I don't even know how…and then…"

Lena was up out of her chair then, rounding her desk, concern—genuine this time, thank you—filling her eyes. "It's okay. It's okay. Just sit down, Emily."

And then Lena winced, looking from the club chair to where Emily was standing beside it. "I mean, *can* you sit down?"

"Yes, yes." Just not without thinking of Jase. Which was all part of the same problem. She hadn't been able to stop thinking about him since she'd thanked him for the good time—drawing on every bit of false confidence and composure she could muster—and walked him to her door.

Where he'd looked like he might kiss her good-bye, but then she'd known she was already in too deep and had simply laughed like she was still the one in control and waved him out.

"Okay, I know that there are guys capable of making women climax more than once at a shot. But, Lena"—she met her friend's eyes—"it was more than just your run-of-the-mill orgasm. It was a really, really good one, and then another, and then"—when she had well and truly been begging—"another. *Who can do that?*"

Lena shook her head. "No. There's always someone else. At least until you meet *the one*. But from the way you talk about Jase—and I really wish I'd known before the wedding how you felt about him—he's not."

Emily agreed. "Definitely not. Which is why thinking about him like this is making me all the more angry." Just like he'd known it would.

God, she hated it when he was right.

Lena was waving her hands in front of herself in that

way she did when she wasn't interested in hearing something that was probably the truth.

"No. We'll give this another week or so, and then you'll take matters into your own hands. Buy an incredibly complicated vibrator with all the bells and whistles and set yourself up with *Magic Mike XXL* or something. You won't be thinking of Jase Foster when it's done. You'll be cured."

Emily wanted to believe, but the fact that she'd gotten chills at the mention of Jase's name—and not the prospect of Channing Tatum doing those incredibly erotic dance moves—didn't bode well.

———

Jase walked up to the freshly shoveled stoop and, kicking as much snow from his boots as he could, let himself in the front door.

"Hey, Dad," he said with a nod, unbuttoning his coat as a wave of warmth enveloped him.

"Jase." His father grinned, straightening from where he'd been leaning over a sea of tiny screws, nuts, and bolts spread across the tabletop. He rolled his shoulders, making Jase wonder just how long he'd been sorting all that crap, and strode over for the bear hug that always put a smile on Jase's face. "I didn't know you were coming by."

"Few errands in this neck of the woods and thought I'd take my old man out for some grub. You eat yet?"

Joe shot him a sideways look. "Worried I've started hitting the senior specials at four?"

Jase knew he hadn't. If there was one thing he could count on in this life, it was the sanctity of his father's routine. From as far back as Jase could remember, the man had worked Monday through Friday, leaving the house at 8:15 a.m. so while Jase had still lived there they could have breakfast together. He was back in the door by 6:05 p.m., and though dinner occasionally ran late around Jase's practices or games, it never, ever happened before 6:30 p.m. Just one of those things. Like Joe bowling on Wednesday nights, poker on Fridays, and Jase coming out for a few hours in the afternoon and staying through dinner every Sunday.

It was nice. Comforting, like the smell of banana bread right out of the oven.

And Jase liked knowing that whatever kind of shit storm was brewing in his life, home would be as constant as ever.

They decided on the brew pub they'd been going to for years and folded themselves into Jase's SUV. But before Jase had even gotten his seat belt on, Joe asked, "So what's got you so spun up that you're making up excuses to come all the way out to see your pops in the middle of the week?"

Jase shot his dad a look, but the old man had his number. Better even than he had his own, because it wasn't until he heard his dad say the words that he realized they were true. Yeah, he liked to get his running shoes at the place where he'd been buying them since he was six, but he lived in Chicago. And while there were probably a hundred stores he could have chosen that weren't an hour away, he'd gone to the one in Oak Park because he'd wanted to talk to his dad.

"Brace yourself. It's about girls."

"Hell, didn't Ray teach you about that stuff when you were fourteen?"

He had. And then Bear and Mick too. It had been an awkward evening, to say the least. Memorable and informative beyond anything Jase had been ready for.

Letting out a low chuckle at the memory, he joked, "Yeah, well. Maybe I need to brush up."

His dad huffed out a laugh, muttering something about being fairly certain that if one of them needed a brushup, it wasn't Jase.

A few blocks from the house, he just said it. "I slept with Eddie's girl."

His dad's eyes stayed trained on the road ahead as if he were the one behind the wheel, a small smile at the corner of his lips. "Eddie has a girl?"

Had he really driven all the way out to Oak Park for this?

"Emily," he clarified.

"Ahh, yeah. I remember you mentioning her a few months back. What did you say, she gets to you 'like nails down a blackboard'?"

Jase blew out a breath. "I didn't mean for it to happen. I didn't want it to happen."

"Why not? You had a thing for her, if I'm remembering correctly. Before she was Eddie's girl. Isn't that right? You were thinking about making her yours?"

Jase cranked around to check out his dad, who was unwrapping a stick of chewing gum. He offered it with a guileless look and, seeing Jase's confusion, shrugged. "You were pretty obvious about it."

Maybe to his dad. And he was fairly sure Emily had a sense of it—for a while, anyway. But not anyone else. Not Eddie, or he never would have called dibs.

'Course, way back when, Jase wouldn't have thought

that Eddie would do half the shit he ended up doing. The car, the booze, the drugs.

"So you and Emily? I'm guessing the fact that you're referring to her as 'Eddie's girl' and sleeping with her versus dating her means you won't be bringing her around for dinner anytime soon."

Jase let out a short laugh, thinking about Emily's assurance that what they were doing meant nothing. And the way hearing that had actually made him feel better.

And yet, some part of him that he really didn't want to deal with was thinking, *Yeah, my dad would like her a lot*. Especially that laugh of hers—the one she gave so freely to everyone except him.

"No, not that kind of thing."

Joe folded a rectangle of gum into his mouth and nodded.

"So why are you telling me about her? Again."

It made sense that he'd ask. After all, it wasn't as though Jase brought home the tales of his every conquest and hookup. In fact, he rarely talked about the women he dated. Sure, his dad knew about them because of the guys. Once every month or so, they'd all get together and his dad would demand updates on his boy. Jase would joke about the fact that Joe saw him every week, and the old man would counter that he wanted all the dirt Jase never ponied up. Dirt Brody, Sean, Max, and especially Molly loved to dish.

So his dad knew he wasn't a monk and never would have expected him to be.

But this, him coming out to talk about Emily… Yeah, it had to mean something. Though he had no idea what. And maybe that was just it.

"I don't know what I'm doing with her. I don't know why I just couldn't stop."

They pulled up to a stop sign and Joe shifted in his seat, crossing his arms over that big chest of his. "You feeling guilty? Like maybe you took something you shouldn't have?"

"What, because she's Eddie's girl? No. It's been, what…eight, nine years since things ended with them? I haven't even seen the guy in three." And when he had, the kid he'd loved like a brother had been a shadow in the bloodshot eyes Jase barely recognized. The eyes that said that last stint in rehab hadn't done the trick. Jase had talked to Eddie's parents, but Eddie didn't want help.

"I was thinking it might be more about having sex with a woman you don't like. Wondering if maybe that's what was getting to you. Your conscience."

Jase was about a hairsbreadth from saying hell no, when something inside him yanked that knee-jerk response back. Made him sit on it a second longer and really ask himself what he thought.

They drove in silence another block before he looked over at his dad and told him the truth. "She makes me furious. And I can't get along with her to save my life. And every single thing out of her mouth grates over my nerves like nothing else. But aside from all that, she's actually a really good girl. Cares about her friends. Cares about everyone." Except him, probably. "She's smart. Funny."

Gorgeous.

"If I'm really being honest with myself, yeah, I like her a lot. Just not in a way where—"

"Where you can do anything but take her to bed."

Jase gave in to a weighted sigh. "Pretty much."

"And you feel okay about that?"

The answer was obvious. If he did, he wouldn't have made the hour-plus drive to get his dad to help him figure out what he already knew.

Yeah, it definitely couldn't happen again.

Chapter 11

January

THE NEW YEAR CAME AND WENT, AND JASE'S RESO-
lution to get his head out of Emily Klein's panties was
a complete bust. Not good, since he was about to see
her for the first time since she'd shooed him out of her
apartment approximately twelve and a half minutes after
they'd collapsed on the floor beside her bed.

Sally and Romeo's wedding had been rescheduled
and pared down even more. The service was taking
place at five that evening with a priest they hadn't met
who'd come to take over while the man who'd baptized
Sally recovered from surgery. And from there they were
going to some bistro they'd managed to rent out for the
reception. The guest list had gone from the initial seven
hundred and fifty of their closest friends and family
down to three hundred and now down to fifty-seven.
But it didn't matter. There was bound to be at least one
available beauty on hand that evening to keep him from
any more wayward thoughts about Emily.

Yeah, all he needed was a new pretty face, and he'd
be done thinking about the curve of Emily's leg in his
hand. The breathy sounds she'd made when he was
inside her. The way she'd gasped his name when he
made her come. How soft and wet and tight—

Jase groaned, bracing a hand against his fridge door.

Enough.

A message popped up on his phone, and Jase saw the guys were out front waiting for him. The weather had mellowed back to Chicago's more typical winter, with the temps hovering just above freezing. So they'd lost a good portion of the snowfall, and the roads were still clear.

No more monkey wrenches courtesy of Mother Nature. At least not tonight.

Jase locked up, being sure to engage both dead bolts, and then took the elevator down to street level, where the "security" door was propped open with a broken piece of concrete and had a sheet of paper taped to it regarding the party happening on seven. Outside, Brody was double-parked. With Max in the front, Jase hopped into the too-small rear and clapped both men on the shoulder. "Sure hope I don't get carsick back here," he warned, making a last-ditch effort to score shotgun.

Brody shrugged. "If you hurl, you'll be the one covered in it for the wedding. Max and I are just guests tonight. So maybe crack a window, because I'm not letting you drive the Bentley and Max is packing under his suit."

Jase shot a skeptical look his buddy's way, but all he got was the guy's blank cop stare. "Don't even think about it."

It had been worth a shot.

"So you guys know who's going to be there tonight?"

Brody pulled into traffic and kept his eyes on the road. "Sally's got three single bridesmaids. But one of them is Emily, and then there's Peg, who's pretty and looks like she might have a bit of a wild streak if you get her out of her mother's line of sight."

Max was shaking his head. "Don't go there. Peg's cute, but she's got some growing up to do. Don't think you really want to be a part of that."

Brody's mouth pulled down as he tipped his head from side to side, seeming to consider. "Probably right. Which leaves us with Leslie who was at the Skolnics' wedding, so you already know her. Also Romeo's got a slew of hot cousins. Just keep an eye out for their brothers. Tight-knit family, you know."

Jase listened as Brody and Max speculated on which women they'd met from the engagement party would be making the short list for this third go at the wedding. They all had their merits, he was sure, but for whatever reason, with each name they brought up, Jase mentally scratched her from his rapidly dwindling list of potential distractions.

Too quiet.

Too tiny.

Too serious.

Too hard.

Too much like Emily or, damn it, not enough.

And great, now he was thinking about her again. The soft curve of her mouth when she smiled at anyone other than him. The way her hair spilled past her shoulders, just begging him to reach out and play with one of those loose spirals. What it did to him when she let him look into her deep brown eyes—

He was so screwed.

She'd gotten to him, all right. Because that unapproved mental field trip hadn't even been about the naughty, good-times bedroom stuff. Okay, the eyes maybe. Because the more he thought about it, the more he remembered that deep, soft eye contact had been pretty heart slamming when he'd been pushing inside her—which made him feel only marginally better, but he'd take what he could get.

If he didn't get it together, and fast, she'd know exactly what kind of messed-up bullshit was going on in his head. She'd be able to see it in his eyes. Hell, maybe she'd even be able to smell it on him. And that was the dead-last thing he needed, because they'd already agreed what had happened between them would be a one-time thing. And despite the way she'd gotten under his skin, he didn't want any more than that.

The church parking lot was empty compared to what it had looked like two weeks ago. He walked across the asphalt, his eyes scanning the section at the far end where he'd found Emily scrambling to get to the church. The girl had been determined, for all the good it did her.

A hand slapped him on the back. "Dude, get in there."

Yeah, no sense lingering outside in the hopes of putting off the next inevitable interaction with Emily.

Inside the church, Jase found Romeo with a handful of relatives and the other two groomsmen. He greeted his friend with a hug and then rolled through the lineup of Romeo's relatives, doing his best to keep everyone's names straight while the bulk of his brain power was alternately reliving being with Emily and trying to put her out of his mind.

Finally, it was go time. Jase bumped knuckles with Romeo, who headed to the front of the church with his best man, and Jase moved to the back to line up with Emily.

But she wasn't waiting where she was supposed to

be, and a slice of concern skewered through him. Had she not been able to make it? He was sure someone would have told him if that was the case. Hell, after what they'd done, he couldn't believe she wouldn't have called him herself.

What if she'd had another accident? What if this one had been more serious? Something in his gut twisted hard. What if she was hurt somewhere, and they were all lined up like a bunch of jackasses when they should have been out looking for—

She was there. Stepping out of the bride's chamber, holding hands with Sally while she whispered a few words. Words of encouragement maybe, reassurance, he thought, watching as Sally's anxious face seemed to soften, her eyes filling with hope and joy as they found the doors she was about to walk through.

Sally looked every bit the beautiful bride, and Jase realized that was in no small part because of the woman standing beside her.

For one insane moment, he was filled with a sense of pride.

Intense pride. But then Emily's eyes came up and met his. Cool and distant. Exactly what he'd hoped he would get from her. Precisely the reminder he needed that she wasn't his to be proud of. She wasn't his for anything beyond the few yards down this aisle, and even that was limited to keeping her from stumbling.

Really, it was perfect. Because despite this mess happening in his head, he didn't want anything more than that. He knew better.

She walked closer, the skirt he'd had bunched up between them two weeks ago swaying in wrinkle-free perfection. Each step bringing her that much closer to him. To the moment when she would tuck her hand around the crook of his arm.

And now he needed to stop thinking about the way her fingers had felt clutching at him two weeks ago, and the punch to his gut when he'd looked up to where he'd pinned her hands above her head and realized their fingers had woven together. He looked at Emily, a question pushing at his chest. She met his stare, unfazed. A pleasant, plastic smile on her lips. Just the way she was supposed to be. Just the way they'd agreed.

―⁓―

Emily was never going to get through this. Not without giving away how screwed up her thoughts had become.

As if it wasn't bad enough that the man was in her head every time she closed her eyes. Every time she closed her front door for that matter, and now…having him here in the church? She'd about tapped out the reserve of resistance keeping her gaze from raking over every inch of Jase's hard-muscled body. Denying the suddenly desperate need to wet her lips and lean into his space and draw a deep breath of that subtle cologne she couldn't quite get enough of.

Yeah, she was about to blow it big time by eyeing every semi-dark alcove and closed door within the sacred space like they were rife with sexual promise.

Lightning was so going to strike her down.

Which would be totally fine if it meant keeping the fact that Jase had been absolutely correct in his statement that he was going to ruin her from coming to light.

He'd gloat.

And while that wasn't totally unsexy in and of itself, she really didn't need the guy taunting her with more of what she couldn't have. And based on the hard scowl he was giving her, any secret hopes she might have had about the two of them turning just once into just *twice* were dowsed completely.

Just be cool.

The doors opened and the music changed.

"Em?" Jase murmured, offering her his arm.

She slipped her fingers around his elbow, and her breath caught at the low jolt coursing through her hand and the quiet stir in her belly.

Jase's eyes were locked with hers, the same kind of inconvenient shock she was experiencing from that single point of contact morphing into a look that was charged, dark, and intense.

———

Jase should have been stripped of his groomsman stripes.

The wedding was the longest he'd ever experienced. Whether the stand-in priest was just trying to give these kooky kids their money's worth or whether Jase was imagining the man's words dragging on and on, he didn't know. What he did know was that the ceremony itself had been a torture unique in his life. And through every minute of it, he'd tried—really, really tried—to focus on the couple he was standing up for. He tried to pay attention to the passages they'd chosen to share that day. And above all, he tried not to look at Emily.

On all counts, he failed.

She was gorgeous.

Fine, what else was new? Well, that look in her

eyes when they'd touched and the room had practically caught fire around them. Yeah, that was pretty new.

And once he'd seen it, the hot need that matched his own, he'd been ready to pull her straight out of the church and back to… Well, shit. Brody's car.

Unfortunately that's when they'd gotten the hissed "Emily and Jase, go!" along with the firm shove propelling them toward the doors and down the aisle…barely a beat out of step.

But the whole way, they'd been casting sidelong looks at each other. And at one point, Emily had needed to duck her head when her cheeks turned a particularly satisfying shade of scarlet.

Oh yeah, *just once* was off the table.

He was having her again. As soon as this wedding was through.

Mr. and Mrs. Romeo Santos retreated from the church amid well wishes and congratulations from those able to attend. They'd been quickly ushered away in their black Rolls Royce limo, gleaming beneath the unavoidable salt and sludge splatter of a Chicago winter.

Emily's heart was filled to overflowing with happiness for Sally and Romeo, but still that wasn't foremost in her mind. It was the escalating sense of anticipation causing the flutter in her belly she couldn't ignore. The nervous tension building within her.

Because of Jase.

Because of the way he'd been looking at her and the near-electric charge she'd experienced wrapping her hand around his arm.

Because of that last quiet word—"After"—spoken low enough that it had only been for her as they went to their opposite sides of the church.

Well, it was *after*, and now she could feel Jase's eyes on her. She knew he was close.

Knew he was there the second before he made contact, settling his palm at the curve of her waist and gently but firmly guiding her back from the press of family and friends clogging the hall leading out of the church.

She turned to him, thinking he would drop his head to her ear and whisper something about when they would meet. But all she got was a fleeting glimpse of the heat in his eyes as he positioned her in front him, keeping one wide hand around her waist, and the hot press of his body at her back.

He was leading her back into the church. Reaching past her to open the door to the bride's chamber and then ushering her inside.

"Jase, we'll have to be quick," she whispered in a rush. Whatever plans he wanted to make—Her hotel room or his? What time? How best not to get caught, because this was one dirty secret she wasn't ready to share—that's all they'd have time for. They were a part of the wedding party, and people would be waiting for them.

But instead of Jase asking her anything, instead of looking over her face like he wanted to kiss her but letting out one of those frustrated growling sounds he made and then taking a step away, he answered with a gruff "Okay."

And then the hand that had been at her waist slid forward, spanning wide and low across her belly. His mouth opened over the curve of her neck, sending her senses spiraling, and he pulled her back into the startling heat and hard-muscled expanse of his body.

"Jase!"

His teeth scraped over the sensitive stretch of skin and Emily's knees went loose, her breath rushing out on a hiss.

But Jase had her. He wrapped his arm around her torso so the strength of his arm held her tight against him, leaving one hand to cup her breast and his other to rub lower down her abdomen and pelvic bone, until he was between her legs.

A deep guttural sound rumbled against her ear as he stroked her again. "I can feel how hot you are, Em. Even through all this skirt, you're practically burning up my hand."

And oh God, it was good. She was so sensitive from the weeks of thinking—obsessing—over everything Jase had done to her.

"I-I've been thinking about you," she admitted, angling her head to give him more access to her neck.

"Bet that torqued you off," he said, the jab sounding more playful than antagonistic.

She laughed quietly, melting back into Jase so her bottom met the hard ridge of his erection. Nice. Even more so when he pressed into her from behind as he petted her through the fabric of her skirt in front.

It was too much.

"Jase," she whispered, her hips moving with the rhythm he'd established.

"Tell me you want this." His voice was gravel rough, as low as she'd ever heard it. "Tell me you can't wait either."

The answer would have been yes to both. But coupled with that last telling word, *either*, her need skyrocketed toward critical.

Eyes closed, she turned her face toward his. Felt the hot wash of his breath beneath her jaw, over her cheek. And then he was kissing her, his mouth devouring hers as he guided her to the low vanity where Sally had applied the last touches of her makeup and whispered the name Sally Santos like it was a prayer.

They shouldn't be there. They shouldn't be anywhere near a spot touched by so many tender moments. The beginning of so many lives together.

But then Jase was pressing her hands into the top of the counter, meeting her eyes in the mirror as he gathered her skirt until he had it above her waist. Until she could see the bare skin of her thighs and the coffee and cream of her panties.

Reaching between her legs, he slid the silk and lace garment down her thighs until it fell around her feet. She stepped out of it and, at Jase's gentle urging, widened her stance. His fingers brushed over the swollen, too-sensitive folds of her sex, making her moan and tremble from that grazing touch alone.

And then he was pushing inside her.

"*Oh God.*"

One finger, deep and deeper. Hitting her just right. A second, stretching her as his palm cupped and rubbed against her.

"I can feel how close you are, Emily."

The sound of his voice rumbling against her ear pushed her even closer.

His teeth closed in a gentle clasp on the lobe of her

ear, as he stroked once more across that needy little bundle of nerves no one had ever found but him and—

His free hand closed over her mouth as her moans turned to cries of the most telling variety. She couldn't stop, couldn't do anything but ride out the pleasure Jase had given her until it was done.

And then Jase released her, leaving her to support herself where she'd planted her palms on the vanity and stood staring at her breathless, wanton reflection.

Who was this woman?

She didn't know, but she most definitely recognized the hard-jawed, steely-eyed man behind her. Jase looked like every fantasy she'd ever had mixed with all the ones she'd never dared to dream about.

His eyes were blazing with need, raking down her reflection as he rolled on a condom. And then he was lined up behind her, their gazes still locked in the mirror.

A muscle jumped repeatedly in his jaw, and then he was pushing inside her. Sliding in with one deep, earth-shattering stroke that seemed to push the breath straight from her lungs.

"Fucking beautiful," he bit out from behind her, his thick fingers flexing against her hips, his throat moving up and down.

She felt beautiful. Sexy.

And when his focus switched from her eyes to where he was thrusting inside her, the heat of that visual pushed her past any state of arousal she'd ever been in before.

Her body pulsed around his thrusts. *Closer.*

She watched in fascination as the strain built in his features, as his need escalated with her own. She wanted to push him harder, take him further. Make him lose control the way she couldn't seem to stop doing around him.

Arching her spine, she rocked back into his next thrust, earning the satisfaction of his eyes snapping up to meet hers in the reflection.

"Emily," he ground out as if in warning, but of what she couldn't imagine. Again she arched, pushing back into him as he thrust deep and hard into her.

"More," she panted, wanting to see him come undone. Wanting to be the reason why.

Heck. Maybe she wanted to ruin him for all other women the way he'd ruined her.

The nod he gave her was tight and strained, a visual that made her clench in need.

And then he was giving her what she'd asked for. Pounding into her hard and deep, again and again. Filling her so completely that she could barely find room for a breath.

Faster, he hammered into her over-sensitized flesh. Then he pulled her up against him, her back to his front, and buried his face in the crook of her neck, as he quaked through his release within her.

It was hot like she hadn't known existed. And that was before he reached between her legs and gently squeezed while he was still pulsing within her.

Starbursts filled her vision as she bucked, coming from that single touch. Because he was just that freaking good.

After, Jase took care of the rubber by tying a knot in it, wrapping it in a tissue, and tucking it in his pocket. Emily had found her way into the chair where the brides sat and watched, intrigued by his every action.

In awe of his mad skills.

Not caring a lick if he'd well and truly ruined her for everyone else. Forever.

She was pretty sure today would get her through the next few years. At the least.

Or she had been until Jase leaned back into the vanity and, crossing his arms, looked her over like he was thinking about what he wanted to do with her next.

And yeah, just like that, she was ready to go.

"Em," he said, pinching the bridge of his nose. "Stop staring at me like that, or we aren't going to get out of here at all. And something tells me it's just a matter of time before they miss us enough to come looking."

Chapter 12

EMILY WAS THE WORST BRIDESMAID IN THE HISTORY of bridesmaids.

She'd had sex. And not just straight, horizontal, quick, and clean sex.

It had been legitimately dirty.

Dirty like a girl like her never saw.

From behind, in front of a mirror, literally feet away from more than fifty guests. Even if Jase had pushed the thumb lock on the door, they'd been in a house of God when she'd cried his name.

So shady.

And then Jase had straightened her skirt, tucked her panties into his tux pocket, and pushed a few strands of hair back into place before giving her a light swat on the rear on her way out, murmuring "Think fast" as she walked back into the belly of the beast. A beast that had thinned out considerably, leaving her with just a few stragglers in the church entry.

"There you are," Peg said on an exasperated sigh, slipping back in the front doors with Leslie on her heels.

Emily put her hands up, pasting on her most unfazed smile. "Sorry, I thought I'd left my purse."

Leslie raised a brow. "Already out in the car with Harold."

Offering the requisite noises of relief, Emily headed out to the waiting car for the trip to the restaurant—looking back only once and finding Jase's eyes on her when she did. He was smiling. It wasn't like the smile of a cat who'd gotten into the cream either. Some telling grin that would have everyone speculating what had put that look on his face. It was subtle, quiet. It was…nice.

It was a smile like she hadn't seen from him since high school, and the sight of it threw her off more than everything else that had happened between them. Had her looking back more than once. A concern she couldn't exactly name building inside of her.

The bridesmaids rode out to the restaurant together, Peg and Leslie chatting about the groomsmen who'd gotten away. Club Bromance seemed to be getting the bulk of the conversation. Mostly Max and Brody, which was odd because Jase was clearly the front-runner in looks and size. Not that she was going to point that out to them.

But then Peg did mention Jase, barely getting his name out before her voice cut off into an awkward silence that pulled Emily's attention from the snow-covered fields and gray-washed sky back into the car. To where Leslie was giving Sally's little sister a meaningful look.

"What?" Emily asked, heat pushing into her cheeks before they even had a chance to answer. *They knew.*

"Okay, so we get that you don't want to admit it, but it's totally obvious there's something going on with you and Jase," Peg said in a matter-of-fact tone. "To most everyone, anyway."

Emily's lips parted, her protest perched on her tongue. And then she softened back into her seat. "I don't know what's going on with Jase. But it's nothing serious. That much I can assure you."

When they pulled up to the restaurant, Mrs. Willson

was standing by the front door with a few ladies wearing pinched faces to match her own, still harping on Sally's failed wedding attempt from the previous month. "But what did they think would happen with a December date—"

Emily breezed past with a polite smile, relieved for Sally that all the anxiety this day had brought would finally be behind her. The important parts—where she and Romeo had exchanged their vows and sealed them with a kiss—those she would hold on to forever. The rest didn't matter.

The location wasn't as glamorous as the hotel ballroom Sally had been dreaming about from the time she was a girl. It wasn't as cool as the location Emily and Jase had picked together. But it was intimate. And it was all theirs for the night.

Stopping at the coatroom, Emily felt her spine begin to tingle in what was becoming a familiar way. She glanced over her shoulder as two large hands reached around her to help her with her coat. Jase. Watching her with a look on his face that wasn't antagonizing in the least. It was warm, rather than hot. His knuckles briefly smoothed down the lengths of her arms, and then he was reaching past her to hand her coat to the check clerk.

"Thank you," Emily murmured, suddenly feeling shy. Like she didn't know exactly where she stood with this man anymore.

His hand settled at the small of her back, spreading more of the warm heat and tingles, as he led her into the reception.

"We need to talk, Em," he said, guiding her through

several clusters of guests on their way to the wedding party's table.

"I know." What happened between them had been… well, nothing short of the total ruination she'd been promised. But still, now that it had happened twice?

Jase held her chair for her and then dropped into the seat to her right. Because of course they were seated together.

Pushing his chair back for more room, Jase leaned forward, resting his forearms over his legs and making a mesh of his fingers where they hung between. "I wasn't planning what happened after the wedding."

She raised a brow at him, and he looked away with that gruff laugh that made everyone wish they were in on the joke. She had to admit, it felt pretty good that she was this time.

When he looked back, it was with a devastating mix of amusement and heat in his eyes. "Okay, I wasn't planning it before I saw you."

"And then?" she asked, keeping her body language as casual and unobvious as she could, considering Jase had just owned up to plotting to get her alone after the ceremony.

His jaw shifted out of line. "Fishing? Em, a girl like you?"

She felt her own smile slipping free, and Jase's eyes locking on it.

"*And then*," he added, "I saw you. And I knew I'd be lying to myself to think that once was going to be enough."

Her belly was doing that fluttering thing again, the beating of her heart feeling heavier with every beat.

"But twice will?" She really was fishing then, but she needed to know.

Jase sat back, that too-sexy grin going full tilt. "You tell me."

"I think it needs to be," she said. "Nothing's changed between us, Jase."

"Hiya, Jase," one of Romeo's brothers called from somewhere behind her. "Stop working the bridesmaid and come do a shot to celebrate."

Emily rolled her eyes and then cast him a sidelong glance. "Your people await."

Jase nodded and pushed up from his chair. Still holding her eyes, he brushed his thumb across the corner of her mouth. "I wouldn't say nothing's changed, Em."

And then he was gone, the hoots and bromantic exclamations ensuring the lost one had been safely returned to the fold. Emily sat, her fingertips tracing the spot where he'd touched her. The upturned corner of her mouth.

―――――

"So, you and Emily?" Brody asked over the brim of his bourbon, eyes glittering with amusement.

Jase shoved a hand through his hair, scanning the reception in progress. Dinner was over, and a small dance floor had been set up where a DJ was playing a selection of Sally and Romeo's favorite songs.

"Don't go there."

"No?" Another savoring sip of his drink. "After you all but lifted your leg, marking her as your territory tonight? And funny thing, but back at the church, I could have sworn—"

Jase locked him with his most lethal glare. The one

he used to pull out during face-offs back in his college hockey days.

Sadly, he'd known Brody long enough to realize the guy wasn't intimidated by the usual fare. Still, he got the message and let the rest of his statement drop. Almost.

"I thought so."

Jackass.

"You don't know what you're talking about with this marking thing."

"Right." Brody nodded. "You weren't helping her out of her coat like you were unwrapping the biggest present under your tree. And the fact that you've had your hands on her, in one way or another, pretty much since she walked in the door…no one would read into that. Or how about the way you put your arm around the back of her chair while you leaned in and whispered into her ear all through dinner? Or that dance with the wedding party when you nearly threw an elbow into Romeo's brother before he could ask her?"

Jase pulled at his suddenly too-tight collar. Because… Fine, maybe he had done all that.

Then Brody really stuck it to him. "Definitely nothing suggestive about the fact that when you aren't within touching distance, you can't seem to take your eyes off her for more than a second. Jase, man, you're watching her right now."

He was. But so was every other chump in the place.

How the hell could they stop when she was laughing like that, with her eyes closed, her head half back, and the long slender column of her neck just begging for a mouth to cover it.

To tease that spot that made her beg. To suck and—

Jase was out of his seat before he realized what he was doing. Crossing the floor until he was close enough to lean in behind her, whispering low in her ear before he passed. "Three times. And then we'll be done."

She was still stammering, a hot flush burning through her cheeks, as he headed over to Sally's dad.

Emily lay staring at her hotel room ceiling, her breath still not returned after… She turned her head on her pillow to look at Jase's profile. "Was that three times or four?"

"Four." His skin was dotted with sweat, his cheeks darkened from exertion. His mouth curved into a satisfied grin. "Why? Trying to figure out how many notches to carve into the bedpost?"

"For Facebook," she replied, as deadpan as she had in her.

Deadpan enough, because Jase coughed, pushing abruptly up to his elbows. But then he must have seen her face, seen the amusement in her eyes, because suddenly he rolled on top of her, caught her weakened arms above her head, and growled down at her, that smile still tempting her to lick it.

"Got you," she murmured, completely at his mercy.

His eyes darkened, and he lowered his mouth to hers, murmuring "Guess you did" just before contact.

Jase stepped out of the steamy bathroom to find Emily propped against the headboard, the hotel robe she'd wrapped up in making a loose vee that revealed more of her beautiful body than it covered.

The sound of explosions emanated from the TV, alternating with her bouts of laughter.

"*Guardians of the Galaxy*," she said with a wave toward the screen.

He'd been thinking about leaving after the shower. Half expecting those Cold War walls to be back up between them, but seeing Emily still looking so soft and sexy and accessible... Hell, he was in the bed, tucking her against his chest before he had a chance to think about why he shouldn't.

And then they were laughing together, sinking lower into the bed as the movie progressed. Emily confessed to a deep and abiding love of Chris Pratt that had begun when she'd seen some picture of him posing suggestively with the Washington Monument, while Jase owned up to being a hard-core Groot groupie—just so he could see one of those smiles she had for everyone else finally break *for him*.

It should have been weird, the two of them together like that. Sure they'd had sex a number of times. He'd had her on the bed twice, on the bathroom counter, and in the shower, but this...this hanging out *snuggling* wasn't something they did together. And yet, he couldn't stop gathering her closer, wrapping his arms around her so her back and his front were in perfect alignment and he could rest his cheek against the soft waves of her hair.

The credits started to roll, and Jase knew better than to think there'd be another movie. More cuddling. It was already after three a.m.

Emily shifted within the hold of his arms and peered

up at him. "Last time?" she asked, her words stroking over him as effectively as a hand, while also making something deep in his chest thump to life.

"And then what?" he asked, pulling her over him so she was straddling the place where he'd gone hard for her already.

"And then we sleep," she said quietly, almost shyly. "And tomorrow we put this behind us."

This was the part where he said yes. Where he grasped her generous offer of another round with both hands and thanked his lucky stars for the easy out that came attached. Because what more could he ask for, really?

"That's what you want?" he asked instead. His fingers curved around her hips to hold her in place as he rocked into her from beneath.

Her breath hissed out, her eyes going hazy above him.

He didn't know what he was expecting. A pause, a confusion-filled look. Hesitance?

Whatever, it wasn't what he got. "Yes. Jase, as much fun as this has been, you're the kind of bad habit I can't afford. This isn't going anywhere. Neither of us would ever think it could. And while I'm not actually looking for Mr. Right, making a habit of playing with Mr. Wrong can't be a good idea."

She was right, of course. Which was why he shut down that quiet voice asking questions about another shot, tamping it down deep and burying it beneath a heap of sensual intent.

Chapter 13

EMILY LET OUT A SIGH OF RELIEF AS HER CAB PULLED to a stop in front of her building and Lena waved from where she was waiting in the main lobby. Throat going tight with emotion, Emily paid the driver. This was what friends were for. Real friends showed up in their pajamas, Uggs, and down parkas at ten thirty Sunday morning when they got dirty hookup exit texts.

She'd barely made it through the lobby doors when a bottle of pinot grigio and a duty-free-size Toblerone were wagging in front of her face, Lena grinning from beyond.

"Details, Emily. Every sordid one."

Emily let out a weary laugh and waved her friend through the security door. "Mind if we get upstairs first, or should we just crisscross-applesauce it right here in the lobby? Drink straight from the bottle and go all *Lord of the Flies* on the chocolate?"

Lena was nodding. Apparently, either scenario worked for her.

Forty minutes later, Emily had exchanged her bridesmaid dress and heels for her own pj's and was toasting her toes in front of the fireplace as she licked Swiss chocolate, honey, and almond nougat goodness from her thumb.

"Oh, come on. *Over*, over? Like, for real done?" Lena cried, topping off Emily's glass with a generous pour. "But he was *so* very good at ruining you. Again and again and again."

"That he was. But yes, it is."

Offering up a pout that would put a six-year-old princess to shame, Lena slumped against the chair behind her. "Then what? Did you guys have a fight? Was he a jerk after?"

"No," Emily grumbled, waving off her friend's concern. "Actually, we fought less than we ever had before."

"So the spark is gone?"

Emily's thoughts drifted back to that last time in the hotel room, to Jase moving inside her, the look in his eyes so hot and possessive that she'd nearly combusted on the spot. Or maybe she actually had. Keeping track had gotten difficult.

"Never mind. I can see from the way your eyeballs are fogging up that it's not." Lena raised a brow. "Seriously though, why not give it a shot?"

"Because it's just not like that with us."

She'd trusted Jase Foster with her heart once, only to have him crush it. She'd given him her friendship, only to have him toss it aside like trash. And even though those things had happened over ten years ago when they'd both been young and both had made mistakes, she still wasn't interested in setting herself up for the disappointment—or hurt—that continuing with Jase would all but guarantee.

"Look, we've set aside our differences for the sake of lust, but we're not friends. We're not on the same page—ever."

"Seems like maybe you're on the same page sometimes. Just sayin'." Then Lena flashed a wicked grin. "I mean, cripes, Em. I'm starting to think maybe you should marry this guy. Because that look you get talking about him…" She shook her head and took a hearty sip of her wine. "I'm still in the honeymoon stage, and even I'm jealous of that look."

Emily tried to muster some resentment toward Jase, wanting to blame him for not just ruining her, but also tainting that sacred honeymoon bliss for Lena and Dean. Only all the unreasonable wrath she'd usually been able to draw on at a moment's notice was nowhere to be found.

"Don't even joke about the marrying thing. The way you girls are dropping like flies, I'm starting to think it's something in the water. Besides, Jase and I agreed. We're done."

"We'll see." Breaking off another obscene chunk of chocolate for Emily and then one for herself, Lena shrugged. "I mean, this isn't the first time you thought it was *over*, over…right?"

———

"*Come on.*" Jase slugged his pillow, trying to get comfortable, but tired as he was, sleep remained just out of reach.

He knew who to blame.

Emily. She of the long legs and fractured breath at his ear. The one he wasn't even dating, but hadn't been able to get out of his head since he'd woken up with the scent of her hair on the pillow beside his. Writer of the note telling him to be out of the room before eleven.

He'd thought he was in the clear. Hell, he'd been ready to do cartwheels over how easy she'd made it for him to get back to non-Emily living. Only then it had started.

The stray thoughts—Had she worn that dress home? Was she feeling the effects of their marathon night together the way he was? Was it making her smile?

The impulses—Maybe he ought to text and make sure she got home okay…or call just to check that they were good after last night.

No. No way.

No phone calls. No texts.

He'd gotten through the whole day, but now as he lay in bed, nothing to keep his thoughts on the up and up, she was there again. Whispering his name, biting his shoulder, laughing in his arms.

Christ.

Grabbing the remote, he sat up and turned on the TV. Flipped channels until he landed on *Jurassic World*.

There she was again. Emily. Pushing into the front of his mind. Making him wonder whether she'd like this one or not.

After all, it had the thrills and big-budget appeal. The snappy dialogue and the added bonus of starring her screen boyfriend, Chris Pratt. He was pretty sure it would be right up her alley. Before he knew it, he had his phone out, her contact pulled up, and his thumb twitching in readiness to hit Dial.

Enough.

He didn't care what movies she liked.

He wasn't interested in a repeat of those few hours where he'd been able to hold her and laugh with her and… Shit.

He didn't want to watch a movie with Emily. End of story.

Except it wasn't. Because even when he'd switched

to hockey, the Blackhawks beating the snot out of the Penguins wasn't enough to keep him from thinking about her. About whether she still liked hockey. If she ever got to a game. And if he took her to one, whether—

Okay, the idea of accidentally falling into bed with her again wasn't horrible. But based on the regularity with which those soft, brown eyes had been popping up in his thoughts throughout the day—and if he was totally honest with himself, before that—he knew better.

He'd read somewhere that doing something once could be considered an accident, twice a pattern, and three times meant you were looking at a habit. Emily had become his habit. His addiction. And like a junkie, he wanted another fix.

Which wasn't going to happen.

Finally, he turned off the TV, punched his pillow again, and told himself to chill the hell out, while reminding himself of all the reasons he wasn't interested in Emily Klein.

The thing about Janice Sagal was that not much got past her. With her no-nonsense attitude, intolerance for bullshit, and acute attention to detail, the wiry brunette was indispensable as Jase's assistant. One catch. Those keen powers of observation weren't limited to assisting Jase with private banking. Janice wanted in on his private *life*, a right she'd assured him she'd earned after taking down a certain unsavory message from one of his less-discreet girlfriends. And over the years they'd come to an understanding: Jase dished gossip and Janice ate it up, gave him nonstop flak about it, and did a phenomenal job on everything he asked her to and more.

What they had worked, and she'd become a confidante and true friend. One who took exception to being left out of the loop.

And Jase had definitely left her out of this one. For months, though it was really the last week that would have him in hot water.

Hence his use of the break room on sixteen instead of the one on seventeen, which was just down the hall from his office but frequented by Janice. Whom he'd been avoiding.

Downing the dregs of the coffee he'd been chugging since he arrived at quarter to eight, he sent up a silent prayer for his stomach lining and then headed back to his office. He had a meeting scheduled with the VP in twenty, so blowing past Janice without stopping to talk shouldn't trigger any alarms.

God, he was a pussy, but this stuff with Emily… Hell, he didn't need anyone reminding him about it when nearly a week after the fact he could barely go a half hour without thinking of her himself.

Janice was on the phone chewing some poor schmuck out over a screwup with the weekly reports when he walked past with a nod. She rolled her eyes at him in what was a pretty typical greeting, and he grinned as he slipped through his door.

Safe—or so he'd thought.

He'd barely sat down when she waddled through the door toward one of the open seats across from him.

He swallowed as guilty tension settled in his gut.

He was allowed to have a few secrets. He was a guy, for fuck's sake.

"Hey, Janice, what've you got?" he asked,

watching uneasily as she lowered herself into the chair, her big baby belly making her movements more awkward and adorable every day. Not that he'd dare tell that to her face.

"Your meeting got canceled," she announced, like the information he could have gotten by phone, email, or text was worth her making the trip into his office.

Not likely.

He waited, his tongue tucked against a molar, pretty sure he knew where this was going.

"So," she started with a lengthy exhale he wasn't entirely sure was just for effect. "What's with the skulking around and dodging behind corners every time it looks like our paths are going to cross in the hall?"

Forcing a laugh, he shook his head. "*Skulking?* What?"

He'd totally been skulking.

"That's how you want to play it?" She made a gruff noise, pressed a hand to her belly, and readjusted in her chair. "Okay, fine. I heard someone saw you crawling out of a dark corner of a certain *church* this weekend... with the flames of hell licking at your feet, Jase. And yet, when we spoke *at length* about the wedding, you neglected to mention anything about a girl. The best part, Jase, and I have to hear it thirdhand."

"That might be a little on the dramatic side." Christ, who were her sources?

For a while he'd thought one of them was Sean. The guy was such a chronic kiss-up, and it gave him hives that he hadn't been able to win Janice over. But he hadn't even been at the wedding.

And neither had Molly, whom Janice adored and even met for lunch from time to time.

Brody and Max were possible, but he just couldn't see either of them calling Janice to whisper salacious somethings in her ear.

"Is it?" She looked like she was about to say more—really dig into him—but then she sort of froze up, her face going from white to red.

Oh no.

He knew better, but just couldn't help himself. "You okay, Jan?"

It was only a matter of time before that baby refused to settle for the tight quarters he'd been camped out in for the past seven months, but it was too soon. Jase had done a little reading and—

Narrowed eyes snapped to him, and he forced himself not to shrink back. "Don't you think I'd tell you if I wasn't all right?"

"How about I get you a glass of water or something?"

Her head turned from side to side in a slow warning he wasn't going to ignore. "How about you tell me who the woman at the wedding was, and we forget this whole thing?"

Christ, she knew how to play hardball. And he knew better than to resist. "Emily Klein. Bridesmaid for Sally Willson. We went to high school together." And then, because he had to admit it to someone, he added, "We used to hang out."

Janice suddenly looked a whole lot more comfortable. Still, he reached into his desk drawer and grabbed the bottle of water he had tucked inside. Cracking the top, he walked it around to Janice and then sat back on the desk, arms crossed. Waiting.

A shrewd smile stretched across her lips as she took

a sip and nodded for him to go on, rubbing her belly like it was some kind of hairless cat.

Again. Not something to share.

But there was no getting out of this business with Emily. Not entirely.

"Anyway, you've gotten in too late in the game on this one, Jan. It's over."

"That's too bad. Sounds like she was giving you a run for your money. Would have liked to see that, for a change."

Jesus, who was feeding her this stuff?

"So you won't be seeing her again?" she asked, giving him that helpless-pregnant-lady look.

This time, Jase was shifting like he was the one with seven pounds of little human taking over his insides.

Janice's brow rose. "Jase?"

"Not exactly. I mean, I'll be seeing her at a wedding coming up. And I imagine there will be more after that. She's got about a million girlfriends. And somewhere along the line, they started marrying my guys. But that doesn't matter. Seeing her won't change anything."

Janice just stared at him a moment with an expression on her face that he hadn't seen before. Didn't care for.

"We agreed, Janice. She's no more interested in continuing than I am."

"Sure," she offered, that look not budging a bit.

He wanted to demand to know what that look was supposed to mean, but he already did. She was calling him an ass and asking him what kind of fool he took her for.

"Nice," he grumbled as Janice pushed awkwardly from her seat, then scowled at him as he helped her the rest of the way up.

"So when's this wedding?" she asked, making her way stiffly to the door.

"Three weeks. And in the name of full disclosure, I'll be seeing her at the rehearsal dinner too. But before you start watching the phone, waiting for your sources to dish, it's a plus-one thing. So we'll both have dates for both nights."

"Oh, a date, like you took to Romeo's wedding… because that was a plus one too, wasn't it?" she asked, knowing full well it was and he hadn't.

"Doesn't matter. I'll take one to this. Just so Emily doesn't get any ideas."

Chapter 14

February

"Whoa, look who managed to claw his way free of the bedroom."

Jase glanced up from tying his Nikes to see Max clapping Romeo on the shoulder across the locker room.

"Good to see you, man. How's the better half?"

"The morning sickness is gone," Romeo said, grinning. "Sally's appetite is back, and baby's been asking for cake. Lots of cake. Like, we've gone through four since we got back from Florida."

What Romeo didn't mention was that he'd been baking the cakes his new wife had been craving from scratch for almost two weeks now. A fact Jase knew, since he'd been the one Romeo called from the grocery store in a panic about whether the cake from the bakery department was going to be good enough. What exactly they put in it, and whether a box mix would be better. He'd been going off the deep end over cake—and friends didn't let friends go down that way.

So Jase had called Janice, gotten a recipe, met Romeo at the store, and taken him back to Chez Foster where they'd muddled through the cake-baking process together like men. Meaning, it took three tries, a second trip to the market, and a refusal to call for directions... but in the end, that was one fine cake Romeo took home.

Janice to the rescue again.

"You here for the game?" Jase asked, joining them along with Dean and a couple of the other regulars they'd been playing ball with over the past few years.

"Yeah, man. I need it," Romeo said, patting a stomach as flat as Jase's. Probably more so. "Don't want to get soft."

Max snorted, cutting a glance at Jase. "Come on, man. I know he just got married and has a baby on the way, but no way can I let that one go."

Never.

"And this was the only place you thought you could get *hard*?" Max asked, eyes gleaming, hand over his heart. "Man, I'm flattered, but I respect the institution of marriage far too much to—"

"Aww, shit," Romeo groaned, shaking his head. "Bite me, Brandt."

"That's what I'm saying... I *want* to. You know I do. But it's over, lamb chop."

These guys. Gotta love 'em.

A few minutes later, the other guys headed out to the court, while Jase stayed behind as Romeo finished getting changed.

He looked good, relaxed like he hadn't looked since before the engagement party. "Married life looks good on you, man," Jase told him.

Reaching into his gym bag, Romeo nodded. "It's been good." Then checking to see who was left in the locker room, he added, "Having that wedding behind us, man... What a difference. Suddenly, it's just Sal and me, you know? No more town hall meetings about the big day. No more worrying if this one will fall through too. No more Willsons looking at me like they wished they could scrape me off their shoe."

It had been rough with them, for sure. "They coming around now that you guys are official?"

Romeo laughed. "Not likely, but the wedding is over. It was like you said—they just sort of faded back into the woodwork. Yeah, they'll be around with the baby, but in small doses. Not like my folks."

"Glad to hear it."

Romeo pulled a fitted sport shirt over his head and closed his locker.

"Being honest here, you look worse than you did two weeks ago. What's going on?"

Jase shook his head but then shrugged, because it was Romeo, and the guy had divulged his darkest secrets and worst fears to him over the years. Jase could trust him, and maybe he just needed to say it.

"Emily."

Romeo raised a brow and lowered his voice. "I thought that was nothing. She isn't suddenly looking for more, is she?"

Running his palm across his mouth, Jase shook his head.

"Then what… Oh, shit—are you the one who's falling? Because seriously, if that were the case, you'd have just made my wife the happiest freaking woman on the planet. She worries about you, Jase, with that string of 'girlfriends' but never anyone special. And Emily… She's special. Dude, let me tell Sally."

Jase almost choked on his tongue. "No! You've got it wrong. I'm not falling into anything, especially not with Emily."

He liked women. Respected them. But when it came to romance, there were rules he lived by, and *falling* went against them. Jase liked to date. Exclusively. But on a limited basis and always on his terms. Girlfriends. Brief relationships that were casual and fun, with minimal chance of drama or expectations getting out of hand. And it worked.

"So what is it?"

It was the sizzle-and-pop chemistry between them. Her long legs and soft smile. That sharp wit and wicked, sweet tongue.

"She's going to be there for the rehearsal tonight. Marcos Nicks's wedding. We're paired up as attendants for tomorrow, which means we'll probably be partnered for the meals."

He'd have to dance with her. Feel her in his arms. Close enough to touch in all the places he knew he shouldn't.

"If you're worried about it being weird between you, or her expecting something from you, just call her up, man. She's cool. I think you're stressing about nothing."

Romeo didn't get it. And even though the words were there, Jase couldn't make himself say them out loud.

He was the one who wanted something. He was the one who hadn't been able to get Emily out his head. And even as he stood there sweating about the night to come, a part of him knew it was because he'd already accepted the inevitable.

"Jase, chill. Shake out your arms, loosen up your shoulders. It's one night. Look, if you two hook up again, whatever. If not, then no big deal. But relax about it and just…hell, let life happen, you know?"

He was right. Besides, there was always the

possibility—the *good possibility*—that once Jase actually saw Emily tonight, he'd take one look at her and
realize he'd been worked up over nothing and he wasn't
interested anymore. Okay, so maybe it was more like a
slim possibility, but a possibility just the same.

"Yeah, thanks, man."

Romeo smacked the back of his hand into Jase's gut
and flashed him a mouth full of pearly whites. "Then
enough of this chick business. Let's play some ball."

—◊◊◊—

By the time Jase pulled into the lot of the squat Episcopal
church that night, he'd almost convinced himself that
seeing Emily again was all it would take to get his head
back on straight. Like some kind of contagion, she'd be
the key to a cure.

But as he approached the red-painted double doors,
his heart started pounding the way it used to before a big
game. When all the guys would be chest bumping into
each other, rattling helmets, and smacking the glass with
their sticks—and he'd be staring at the scoreboard, his
blood pumping hot, all thoughts zeroing in on that one goal.

Emily's laugh reached him the moment he stepped
through the doors to the vestibule. That heavenly sound
echoed through the open space, playing in the rafters
before slipping softly around him.

He wanted her.

And cue the not-so-soft physical reaction. Great, he
was already scanning for the closest closet. A month had
been too long.

Crossing into the nave, he saw her. She was wearing a classic black dress that clung in all the best ways,

leaning casually against one of the pews and talking to another bridesmaid. Emily's hair was pinned up in some kind of twisty thing that was sexy enough to have him wondering what it would take to get it down again.

What it would take to get her alone again.

And then she stalled where she was, turning to look over her shoulder his way.

His pulse jacked.

One look and he'd know whether a coatroom or closet visit was off the table or not.

"Hiya, Jase. You made it," Brody announced, clapping him hard on the shoulder and effectively yanking Jase's attention around to him and Max. Whom he hadn't even noticed walking in.

"Guys, good to see you." Or normally it would have been, but they'd just cost him the answer to a question he'd wanted very badly. A glance back to Emily, and she was fully engaged in her conversation. Turning back to the guys who were watching him a little too intently, Jase asked, "We know when they're starting?"

The sharp clapping of their wedding coordinator, followed by the command that they begin, had everyone turning back toward the front of the church, and all attention was on the rehearsal at hand. Jase's too. It was either that or pull a fire alarm and lure Emily into another dark alcove, and he wasn't sure either of their eternal souls could take the hit of a second infraction.

So he focused on the front of the church. Without so much as a glimmer of humor in her eyes, the neat-as-a-pin little woman directed them through a routine Jase could manage with his eyes closed, considering the number of times he'd been through it already.

For a moment he thought he might be able to get some satisfaction if they lined the attendants up for a walk-through, but even then they were crowded with the other attendants, the coordinator snapping in everyone's faces until finally the rehearsal was over and they were all being shooed out into the night.

Jase watched as Emily left with a couple of the girls before he had been able to score any deep eye contact. But it didn't matter. They were all heading over to the restaurant Greek Islands from there. He'd have time.

—⁓—

Waiting by the bar in the rustic-style Greektown staple, he replied to a few work emails and then basically faked "busy" until she walked through the door, laughing with one of the other girls in a way that had his heart thudding heavily in his chest.

Emily's steps slowed when she saw him, her smile fading just enough for him to see the nerves she usually hid. He got it. They needed to talk. But not wanting to draw too much attention, or be completely obvious or a total ass, he helped the other girl with her jacket first and directed her toward the back of the restaurant. And then he turned to Emily, the sense of smug satisfaction she brought out in him rushing through his veins.

"No date tonight," he murmured close to her ear as he helped her out of her coat. His thumbs trailed down the bare skin of her arms and he drew a slow breath, taking in the scent of her.

Emily stiffened, then turned to him, alarm in her eyes. "Jase, we agreed. It's over."

She really was a good girl. "We did. But—"

"I have a date," she cut in, sounding almost…apologetic?

No way. She'd shown up alone. And the way she wasn't letting her eyes connect with his was perhaps even more telling than if she'd been staring straight into them. Because *he could feel it*. He could feel the resistance and the draw and that same *something* lighting up the air between them.

"So where is he?" he asked, running this thumb along the bend of her elbow.

"Caught in traffic. He's just late. Jase…" she said, whispering his name, but he didn't need to hear whatever was coming next.

"Sure," he said, stealing Janice's most nut-crushing line. Emily was trying to save face, even though they were beyond that. He got it. She didn't want to be the one who made the move. She didn't want to be obvious. So she claimed a date. One who conveniently wouldn't show. Whatever. As long as she left with *him*, Jase didn't care how it happened.

At the table there were three open seats remaining. Together.

Jase pulled out the middle chair for Emily before taking the seat to her right. Leaving the chair for her imaginary date available on the other side.

Everyone was chatting about the church and how beautiful the ceremony was going to be the next day. Jase joked around with the guys. Teased the bride-to-be, flirted with her grandmother. Basically made sure he'd done his small-talk best before doing what he'd been wanting to do from the start. Turn his attention to Emily.

As if sensing her reprieve was over, she met his eyes.

"So how have you been?" she asked politely. Stiffly.

Which only made him think about what it was like when her body went soft and lax beneath him.

"Jase," she said so quietly that it snapped his attention back to the now. To where he was staring at her mouth.

Right.

Eyes up here. Got it.

"So tell me about your date," he said with just a pinch of malevolence, because this was Emily after all. Old habits and all that.

She seemed duly uncomfortable.

He liked it. She could squirm a bit for making up a date. And he'd make it up to her later.

When she didn't volunteer any information, he prodded again.

"What's his name? Have you guys been seeing each other long?" He smiled wickedly. Knowing it hadn't been that long since she'd been with him. "Getting serious?"

Emily stared down at the empty spot beside her and took a long, deep breath. Bracing, maybe. Time to come clean?

"His name is Mitchel. We've been out a few times."

Emily, Emily.

"A few times." Suggesting *three* or more. Which suggested something else altogether. Something that tightened his gut and left a sour taste on his tongue. Because the third date usually meant—

No.

She was screwing with him.

So he'd screw back. "And what does this Mitchel do for a living?"

"Investment banker," came the answer in a register octaves too low.

Jase froze, his eyes locked with Emily's as it hit him.

Mitchel wasn't just the product of Emily's imagination. He was real. *Mitchel freaking Beekman*, the guy who'd been all over Emily at Romeo's engagement party.

And, motherfucker, *he was there*.

A pair of broad shoulders in a navy wool overcoat brushed past him.

"Hey, Sunshine. Sorry, I got held up," Mitchel offered jovially before rubbing a hand over Emily's upper arm and dropping a kiss on her cheek. An appreciative sort of grunt left the guy as he stepped back and raked a look over her that had Jase's hands balling at his side. "You look amazing."

Emily ducked her head and brushed a few strands of hair from her face, obviously flustered by the compliment.

Mitchel turned to Jase then, a wide smile in place as he shoved out his hand. "Jase, man, good to see you again."

Jase pulled it together and did the whole polite thing, not entirely sure whether the guy had picked up on what was happening before he walked in.

If their roles had been reversed, no way would Jase have missed some asshole putting those moves on Emily. And he sure as hell would have let the guy know *he knew* what was going on. But that was just him.

Not Mitchel. Emily's not-fake date, who was barely six feet.

An uncomfortable weight landed in Jase's gut. He looked away, then back, as an ugly, unfamiliar part of him started to pound at the inside of his chest.

What was this?

Jealousy? Not just the funny, no-big-deal kind, but the real, gut-wrenching, bad-decision-making, caveman kind?

Jase didn't get jealous—at least he hadn't with the women he'd dated in the past. But now that Emily was in the picture, yeah, jealousy.

He was so screwed.

His eyes cut back to where she was smiling at Mitchel. Whom she'd been out with a few times. Did that mean they'd already had three dates and this was the fourth? Or was tonight—the night she was wearing that killer dress with her hair all wound up so there was no missing the sexy length of her neck—date *number three*?

Not. Going. To. Think. About. It.

He needed a distraction.

An emergency. Why hadn't he gone to medical school? He could be faking a call from the hospital right that minute. Skating out to go save some critical pretend patient in immediate need of his expertise. Only then he wouldn't be able to scrutinize every subtle touch, breath, look, or word shared between Emily and Mitchel for the rest of the night. He wouldn't be able to make an educated guess on where this date was going after the flaming saganaki and cheers of "Opa!"

It didn't matter. He didn't need Emily.

There were at least a dozen women he could call and have waiting at his doorstep when he got home.

Only he didn't want any of them. He didn't want anyone in his bed except Emily. And there was every likelihood that she would be going home with another man.

Flagging the waitress, he ordered a drink. A stiff one.

The night wrapped up not a minute too soon. Two grueling hours of Jase pretending he didn't care about the conversation taking place beside him. Trying not to react to the occasional brush of some soft bit of Emily he wished he didn't know quite so intimately. Trying not to think about what *a few dates* constituted for a girl like her.

And then trying not to think about what Emily—no matter what kind of girl she was—had let him do to her in a church after exactly zero dates.

He'd wanted more than the one drink he nursed all night, but better judgment and the all-too-real fear of putting a serious move on another man's date—in front of two dozen friends and family—kept him from giving in.

Standing with the rest of the group, he leaned in and dropped a kiss on Delphine's cheek, promising her a perfect day tomorrow. He toughed out an extended good-bye with Marcos's great-aunt, who liked to hold hands while she talked about the new medicine she'd started taking, and passed on Brody's invitation to take it back to the bar.

There was no way he could sit down with his friends and be cool while his thoughts were wrapped up in the sound of Emily's soft laugh for some other guy.

No, he needed to be alone.

Shrugging into his coat, he'd thought he was in the clear when Emily stopped beside him.

"Jase," she started, not able to meet his eyes.

"I'll see you tomorrow, Em." He thought about catching her chin in the crook of his finger and bringing her eyes to his, but if he let himself do that much, he wasn't sure he'd be able to stop. So instead, he said the words a bigger man might have actually meant. "Have a good night."

Twenty minutes later, he was stalking across the entry to his apartment, the echo of his door slamming harder than it should have still ringing in his ears. He threw his coat over the back of the couch and went straight for the bar, thoughts of Mitchel asking Emily if she'd ever been to France swirling through his head as the first gulp of scotch burned its way to his gut. *Provence*. Like, maybe they ought to go together. Because Emily would *love* the lavender fields.

Yeah, she probably would.

She'd probably find it romantic and be full of those soft, sweet smiles he hadn't had enough of since high school. Since he'd started putting up the walls between them so his friend could have the girl he'd announced he wanted to marry. Since he started blaming her for—

He swallowed past a lump that tasted an awful lot like regret.

Since he'd stopped deserving those smiles that it always killed him just a little to see.

Throwing back another swallow, he had one consolation to keep him warm that night. If she married stupid Mitchel, at least Jase wouldn't have to worry about being paired up with her for that wedding. Even if he was the right height.

Hell, he wouldn't even be invited.

Because they weren't friends.

Walking to the living room windows, he stared out at the night, the dark swath of Lake Michigan beyond the Drive. He threw back another slug.

A few dates.

Did she love that guy?

A knock sounded at his door.

Checking his watch, he saw it was after eleven.

Maybe one of the guys? They usually just let themselves up if the security door was open—and about half the time it was. But they'd have called first, and his phone was silent.

His steps slowed halfway to the door. It could be Lorna. The curvy brunette from upstairs who had a knack for knowing when he was in the mood for company.

Except tonight, he just wasn't.

Walking the rest of the way to the front of the apartment and working out a friendly put-off, he swung the door open—and froze.

His heart slammed against his ribs.

His vision narrowed to one singular point before him.

The strawberry blond with the Audrey Hepburn style, standing in front of his door.

Alone.

"Emily," he finally managed, her name coming out rough and low. His relief in seeing her there was disturbing in its magnitude.

"I didn't know if… Maybe I shouldn't ha—"

She didn't have a chance to finish whatever she'd been about to say, because he reached for her, wrapped his hand around the back of her neck, and pulled her into the kiss he couldn't wait for. The kiss she eagerly returned, opening beneath him like she was as starved for the taste of him as he was for her. They'd barely closed the door before he had her pressed against it.

Chapter 15

IT WAS JUST AFTER DAWN WHEN EMILY WOKE. PUSHING up on one elbow, she swept the hair back from her eyes.

She hadn't meant to fall asleep in Jase's bed. But then she hadn't meant to end up in his bed at all—at least not when she'd been getting dressed for the night before. When she'd had her date with Mitchel all lined up as defense number one against this thing with Jase they'd agreed shouldn't go any further than it already had.

Mitchel was supposed to be a nice distraction. He was decent looking. Interesting. Successful and sort of funny. An overall good guy who wasn't throwing off any of the signs that suggested he might be the type to get too attached, too possessive, too dependent. The signs that he might have a little bit of the crazy running through his veins. The signs that made her break out in a cold sweat and swear off all guys for at least the next thirteen months every time she caught even a whiff of it.

Mitchel had seemed like a good fit, which was what she'd been thinking when she ran into him at the coffee place around the corner from work and he'd asked if she wanted to share a table for a few minutes, teasing that he'd gotten gypped out of her company when he'd been out of town for Romeo and Sally's rescheduled wedding. She'd laughed politely, silently thanking her stars he hadn't been there. He was one guest who might have actually noticed when she'd disappeared.

The conversation was comfortable, just like it had been that first time they'd met. And when she was done with her coffee, he asked if he could take her to dinner that weekend. She'd been hesitant. On the brink of saying no when she asked herself why.

And the only answer was because of Jase Foster.

So she'd said yes, thinking the timing was perfect. If she had dinner with Mitchel, then she could bring him as her plus one for the rehearsal. And once and for all stop obsessing over what would happen when she finally saw Jase again. Take her destiny into her own hands and ensure the right thing happened when she saw him. *Nothing.*

Good plan. Except for one thing.

Mitchel wasn't Jase. And no matter how much she'd wished that he would distract her from the man she shouldn't want, he couldn't. She'd spent the rehearsal dinner in a heightened state of awareness—her body in tune with every move Jase made. Every inadvertent touch nearly setting her aflame. It took everything she had to pay attention to her date. To smile at the right times. To respond to his questions and not give away the fact that she was hanging on every word the man she wasn't with was saying. That all she could think about was the fact that Jase was there alone. And the way he'd looked at her before Mitchel had shown up. The way he'd looked at her after. And then the way he hadn't looked at her at all.

Which was why once the night was through, she'd thanked Mitchel for a lovely time and told him good night outside the restaurant, passing on his invitation to find somewhere quiet to grab a drink. And then she'd tossed all better judgment aside and hopped in a cab and gone straight to Jase's apartment—because she simply couldn't stop herself.

But now, as night turned to morning, this stringless little hedonistic reprieve was over and it was time to scoot. To spend the day wiping the stupid, satisfied grin from her face before heading over to Delphine's around four to get ready for the wedding at six.

Jase had fallen asleep with his arm slung loosely around her, so step one was extracting herself from that too-tempting hold.

Shimmying to the side, she'd made it about halfway clear of the bed when Jase's breathing changed and then she found herself scooped back into all that solid warmth, held tighter than she had been before.

"Trying to sneak out on me?" he asked, his sleep-rough voice rumbling low against her ear.

It seemed too early to smile, but the playful tone in his voice triggered that slow spread across her lips just the same.

"No way, *darling*," she replied, covering his hand with hers. "I was just going to check with the movers about getting my stuff moved in while we're at the ceremony. Maybe see if Delphine minds if we piggybacked their wedding."

The snort against her ear shouldn't have given her any kind of warm, fuzzy anything. But for whatever reason, it did. She liked that she could make Jase laugh. She'd always liked it.

And that last thought was the one that had her prying up Jase's arm and wiggling her way out. Because this wasn't about warm fuzzies. It wasn't about her heart pounding a little faster when she thought of him. It wasn't even about the two of them being friends—and that was something she'd do well to remember.

Standing beside the bed, she scanned the floor and scowled. No panties or bra. No dress. Just her four-inch black heels—at opposite sides of the room where Jase had tossed one, then after kissing his way from bare ankle to bare ankle, he'd discarded the other.

Good times.

Jase pushed up on one well-toned arm, the sheet pooling around his lap so he was decent but just. He scrubbed a spectacular bedhead and gave her a long, appreciative look. "The wedding isn't until six, and you've got until noon before you need to be at Delphine's. Come back."

Tempting. Definitely tempting.

Snagging a corner of the slate-and-charcoal comforter, she yanked it off the bed and tucked it beneath her arms. "Not that early. I have a few errands I need to take care of before meeting Delphine."

She needed to get out of there before they found themselves in one of those awkward silences that would demand she say something about what brought her there the night before. What it meant about the night to come.

Stuffing her foot into one heel before hobbling over to the other and doing the same, she flashed him a restrained smile. "See you at the church."

It seemed like the right thing to say, until Jase's brows shot up and then he was out of bed, wrapping the sheet around his hips as he followed her down the hall.

"Hey, wait a minute, will you?"

Scooping up her panties at what was now her favorite stretch of wall, she glanced back. "Hmm?"

He shouldn't be following her. He shouldn't have done anything more than maybe holler to her from his bed that she should lock the door on her way out.

That would have been the cool thing to do.

"Emily, you don't have any errands to check off your list at 6:47 a.m."

Her bra was dangling from the arm of a steel-frame dining room chair. Which left her dress. The most critical element in her escape plan. "No, but I should get home and showered. I have a lot to get done today."

Not in the kitchen either. Which meant…sure enough, there it was, a splash of black against the blond hardwood of Jase's entry. And bonus, her coat was right beside it.

Hopping around, she managed to get into her panties and work them up to her waist beneath the comforter. "Just give me a minute to get dressed, and I'll be out of your hair."

It was a solid plan, but then Jase was right there beside her, his big hands curving over her shoulders as he pulled her around to face him.

Would she ever get used to looking up into those blue eyes?

No, she wouldn't. That's what leaving was all about.

"Emily."

"Jase?"

"I don't want you to go. I…" He shoved a hand through his hair and swore. Only this time, it didn't sound like he was cursing his own weakness where she was concerned; it sounded like frustration. "Damn it, Em, I have some things I need to say to you. Some things I should have said a long time ago, but I didn't.

And now here we are in my apartment, and you're trying to skate out like this was just some one-night hookup and—"

"And?" she asked quietly, not sure where he was going with this or even where she wanted him to go.

"And I don't want you to leave. I want… I want to tell you I'm sorry, damn it."

She blinked. He was sorry. There were things she'd thought this man should have apologized to her for over the years. Big things. But never had he seemed to have even one iota of sympathy for her struggles. He'd never understood what she'd gone through with Eddie. He'd never believed her.

So those things she would have welcomed an apology for couldn't be it. Which meant he was apologizing for the business with her date last night. Or maybe for the whole twisted affair—was it even an affair? No, that sounded way too stringy for what she'd signed on for. *Fling* sounded about right. Actually, *hookup* was probably dead-on. It was just the four-night variety, not one.

God, she didn't want to hear he was sorry for what they'd been doing together. If anyone apologized here, it was going to be her…*for using him*.

"Whatever you're sorry for, don't be. I wouldn't be here if—"

"I'm sorry for Eddie," he said, and everything stopped.

Suddenly the silence in Jase's sleek, modern apartment seemed deafening. The rustling of bedsheets and clicking of heels and pounding of her heart had ceased with that single statement. The topic they'd been gingerly avoiding—only getting close enough to throw a subtle jab the other's way, for as long as they'd been on opposite sides of the mess that had defined their relationship—had just been broached.

The wound she'd become an expert at ignoring reopened.

She stared at Jase, too stunned to shield her emotions.

"Christ, the look on your face right now. Emily, I don't want to hurt you. I'm sorry. I just can't pretend it isn't there between us anymore. And I can't pretend I don't want there to be an *us* either."

"Us," she coughed out, clutching the comforter tighter against her chest, because that was one word she'd thought she was completely safe from when it came to this man. "You don't want there to be an *us*, Jase. You're just…tired and—"

He laughed then, wrapping one heavy arm along her back and using it to pull her in to him, to take a kiss that was, God help her, so damn good. But instead of pushing the kiss further, instead of backing her against the wall or picking her up so her toes dangled off the floor—a novelty that had yet to wear off—he dropped a kiss on her nose.

"I know what I want, Emily. And I know there are a few things you ought to hear from me before I can ask you for it."

Looking up into the deep blue of Jase's eyes, she shook her head.

"I don't want to talk about all that. For the first time, things are finally easy between you and me. Can't we just let last night be something we both wanted and not worry about the rest? I don't need anything more than this."

She didn't. She couldn't.

Except then this man who had been the first to make her feel too many things, who she didn't want to allow to have any sway over her whatsoever, went and said the one thing she couldn't defend against.

"But you *deserve* it, Em. And the truth is, I *need* to say it. I'm not a bad guy. I try like hell to do the right thing in my life, to be a good friend to the people around me, but with you, it hasn't gone that way."

"No. I guess not," she said quietly, too many years of resentment and questions and hurt suddenly weighing her down so that the shoulders she always kept tall and straight bowed beneath the strain.

There were questions she had. Explanations she wanted. But to ask would only make her more vulnerable.

Then she thought about it, and screw that. In this one thing Jase was right. She did deserve an explanation.

And vulnerable?

Not unless she allowed herself to be. So she pushed her shoulders back and stepped out from beneath Jase's arm to walk over to the couch in his living room.

Like everything else in the apartment, it was masculine to the extreme. A dark-roast leather cut in clean lines and built with a frame to fit a man of Jase's size. A woman of her height.

She sank into the corner and kicked off her heels, pulling her knees up in front of her. "I used to think we were friends."

Sheet still wrapped around his waist, Jase sat beside her. He braced his arms over the vee of his legs and folded one hand into the palm of the other. "I never thought of you as my friend."

It shouldn't have been a surprise. And it sure as hell

shouldn't have hurt, but his words hit her like a blow. Because she remembered those smiles. She remembered the laughter. The talking. The things that set what they'd had apart from anyone else. How could she have read it so wrong?

It didn't matter.

"Good to know." She moved to stand, but before she could even wrestle one foot from the thick bedding tucked around her, Jase caught her fingers.

"I never thought of you as my friend, because I'd always thought of you as something else. First, you were the girl I wanted. And then you were the girl I couldn't have. You became the girl my best friend loved, and turned into the girl who was screwing with his head and tearing up his heart. And then when it didn't look like it could get any worse, you became the girl who almost killed him."

Emily's breath rushed out in a whoosh.

She wanted to pull her hand away, but Jase was looking up into her eyes and she couldn't make herself move.

"Emily, that's how I saw it. But as I sit here now and look back at our history as a man and not the kid I was, I realize I was only right about one of those things. You were the girl I wanted. From the first day I saw that soft smile and those crazy long legs, I was a goner. You were so sweet and smart, and you made me laugh. And I wanted you. But for as cocky as I was about sports and grades and all that other meaningless shit in high school, I didn't feel so cocky around you. Around you, I was warming up to it. And the day I was ready to ask you if maybe you felt the same way, Eddie said it first.

"We were walking down the hall, and I was watching

you like I always did, instead of watching him, which might have clued me in a little earlier, but there we were and he puts his hand on my arm and stops me. And the look on his face is everything I felt inside when I looked at you. And he tells me you're the girl he's going to marry."

Emily's breath left her in a slow leak, her skin itching and muscles tensing at the mention of Eddie staking any kind of claim on her at all. This time, Jase let her go and she walked to the far side of the room where the windows overlooking the lakefront gave her an excuse not to have to look back at Jase.

To just breathe while she reminded herself that Eddie wasn't a part of her life anymore. That she was her own woman. Strong. Independent.

Another slow exhalation and she was able to think past Eddie's outrageous claim to what Jase had been telling her. To the answer to a question that had plagued her for ten years.

It hadn't been her imagination. It hadn't been her sixteen-year-old heart seeing what she wanted to see. There had been something there between them from the start.

For whatever that mattered.

"I told myself you were the girl I couldn't have. But the truth was, you were the girl I pushed away. I made the choice, no one else. You weren't Eddie's girl until I all but threw you at him. And even then it took months and months of me finding excuses to keep you close and telling myself it was to support Eddie in his quest to win you, but the truth was, I wanted you around. I liked how I felt when I was with you. Until the day you finally decided to give Eddie a shot—and suddenly it didn't feel so good anymore.

"So I put a little more distance between us. Tried not to keep track of what was happening between you and the guy who'd told me he'd share his mom with me because mine was gone. I tried to wall off the part of me that still cared about you more than I should have. And when Eddie started talking about things getting rough with you guys, it was easier for me to see you as the villain. It was easier for me to believe him than to believe in you. Because he was supposed to be my best friend, and you were the girl I wasn't supposed to let come between us."

She shook her head, finally able to make sense of at least a piece of that time when her world had started to fall apart.

The part of her still wounded by that time in her life wanted to rail at Jase. Point out how every one of his actions had hurt her. How *wrong* he'd been.

But why? The reason he was sitting in front of her, talking like this, was because he already knew.

"So you believed him when he told you I was messing around with other guys, and I was playing mind games to screw with his head. I get it." It wasn't cool and it wasn't fair and it was a million years ago, and Jase was telling her he'd made a mistake. "But what about when I went to you for help? When I told you I thought there was something serious going on with him. That he was talking crazy and he needed help. What about then? You didn't have to like me anymore, Jase. You didn't have to care about me at all to help him. To just listen."

That was the part that had killed her. The part that had

left her feeling so helpless, so alone, so *trapped*—no one would listen. Not her parents. Not his. Not Jase.

She returned to the couch and sat, leaving a few inches of space between them. Because in that moment, all she could feel was the weight of that burden she'd carried alone, like it was still there on her shoulders, making her work for every breath she took. Like somehow Jase's words were enough to take her back to that helpless time when Eddie's mood swings and desperation and threatening violence were as fresh as they had been that last day in his car. As suffocating.

"That was a mistake I'll never forgive myself for. But Eddie was starting to spin out of control, and all I could see was you at the center of it. You, the girl I'd been so sure was different. It pissed me off to believe I'd been wrong. It made me nuts that he wouldn't let you go, and it made me hate myself to know, deep down, there was more than one reason I wanted him to."

Emily's breath caught at that last admission. One she could see it pained Jase to make.

"I should have been there for you, Em, because you deserved it, and even if you hadn't…you're right, at the very least because it would have meant being there for him. But I was seventeen, and stupidly I *thought* I was being there for him. I thought I was supporting him by taking his side. By not listening when you wanted help because you coming to me instead of working things out with Eddie looked like the kind of manipulative bullshit I'd seen before and didn't want any part of again. Not with Eddie. Not with you. I couldn't handle it. It's no excuse, Em, and I'm so fucking sorry you didn't have anyone on your side."

Her eyes closed, her throat tightening with decade-old emotion. But as the seconds ticked by, the heaviness began to lift. The guilt and frustration and resentment—all those things she tried so hard not to let herself feel, but were always just below the surface—were suddenly gone. Because he was right.

She felt free. Tears pushed at her eyes, and she realized how hard she'd been working not to let those old resentments get in the way.

When she looked back at him, it was through watery eyes. "We were all kids, Jase. None of us knew what we were doing." Drawing a shaky breath, she offered a small shrug. "I made mistakes."

She could have ended things with Eddie at the first warning sign, the first day he looked at her with those eyes that weren't quite right—but she hadn't recognized that look for the coming train wreck it was. She'd thought "mature" relationships were about trying to work things out, and that maybe Eddie was as new to the relationship thing as she was so it was worth giving him a chance to get his footing. And then she'd thought if she could just bide her time until college started, no one had to get hurt.

She'd been wrong.

"Whatever mistakes you made, you were entitled to." Jase let out a heavy breath and looked down at his hands. "I should have said something to you about it before now, but it took a while before I could see the truth. And I don't know, maybe it was easier to stay on the opposite side of the fence than own up to my responsibilities—which just makes it worse. You had every right to hate me for the way I treated you, Em. I wish I'd been able to see you as a friend, instead of seeing you as all the things you weren't. But I'm telling you now." He met her eyes and held up his palms. "Emily, I'm sorry."

Beyond the windows, the deep, bruised sky was giving way to a vibrant orange-gold glow. The beginning of a new day. "Me too."

He let out a short laugh and rubbed at the scruff on his jaw. "For what? You don't have anything to be sorry for."

"I'm sorry for the million different choices I could have made along the way, and the lives that were never quite the same because I didn't. I'm sorry for Eddie—"

Jase's brows crashed forward and he opened his mouth, but she cut him off with a staying hand. "Not because I think what happened with him was my fault, but because I remember his smile, the mischief in his eyes. I remember that contagious laugh no one could resist—and it breaks my heart that good things didn't come to the goofy boy that laugh belonged to."

God, how long had it been since she'd thought about Eddie as anything but the nightmare he'd become in her life? It hurt in a way she wasn't used to, hadn't been prepared to defend against.

Jase swallowed, his eyes going distant. "Yeah."

The regret in that single word…

They'd been best friends. As close as brothers. Until the accident.

"I'm sorry for you, too, Jase." And for herself, and for what might have been.

They were both quiet. The silence of the apartment around them something neither was ready to break. But what more was there to say?

Good talk...

Phew, now that that's out of the way...

Glad to finally clear the air...

"Jase, I know I didn't want to talk about what happened," she began tentatively. "But what you said means everything to me. I needed to hear it, more than I realized. I needed to let it go." Hard to believe she hadn't seen that until just then.

"Do you think you can? Put it behind you?"

Swallowing past a lump of emotion, she managed the words she truly meant.

"I do."

Elbows resting on his spread knees, Jase let his head fall forward and shoved his fingers through his hair. His eyes slanted to her, the relief in them matching his next words. "That's good, Em. That's really good."

Nodding, she stood, pulling the comforter securely around her. "I really do have to go, Jase. I need to get over to the office for a couple of hours, and there are a few errands I offered to help out with for the wedding."

He stood, and the sheet wrapped at his waist slipped slightly lower. He rubbed a hand over the hard planks of his abdomen. "Can I give you a ride over tonight?"

She walked backward toward the bedroom to change, an amorphous sort of anxiety churning her stomach. "What? Oh, that's nice. Thank you. But I'm riding with the girls."

Closing the bedroom door behind her, she tossed the comforter back on the bed and pulled on her bra and then dress in record time.

She'd meant what she said about putting the past aside, but it was like there'd been this seemingly insurmountable boulder between them, and after so long, it had quietly become a part of their foundation. Without it, everything suddenly seemed less stable. Uncertain.

A little dangerous.

From the other side of the door, close enough Jase had to be standing right there, he called, "But not with Mitchel, right?"

She opened the door to see the corner of Jase's mouth kicked up in that way that made her a little weak. Managing a laugh, she shook her head. "No, not with Mitchel."

"Okay then." Bigger grin. Of the *sorry, not sorry* variety. "See you tonight, Em."

———

Jase swung his strawberry-blond dance partner around the dance floor in the center of the reception banquet hall. The little beauty was six years old, done up in a miniature version of the bride's gown for her flower girl duties, cute as a button, and determined as hell. And so light that he could barely feel her tiny feet perched on the tops of his shoes.

The wedding, in Jase's estimation, was what all weddings should aspire to: short and sweet. Delphine was a knockout, and Marcos had that smacked look on his face Jase liked to see on all his grooms. The guy even choked up during the vows. Add to that the little ring bearer with the big, brown eyes and full mop of dark curls who'd cut his trip down the aisle short at about the two-thirds mark before going to hide behind his dad in the pew.

Good stuff.

The one fly in the ointment—Emily.

She was off.

"So Elsa is my *favorite*," came the vehement assertion from his dance partner. One she made bouncing on her toes for emphasis. "She's the best of the princesses, and I have them all."

"I have them all too," he assured her, straight-faced. Because if there was one thing Jase had learned over the years of dancing with flower girls, it was that the hierarchy of princesses was no laughing matter. "Elsa is the best."

Satisfied, she went on to elaborate all the ways in which Elsa qualified as best. Jase scanned the crowd, his eyes landing on the strawberry blond he hadn't been able to score more than five minutes of conversation with since they'd arrived at the church.

Dressed in a shimmering, ice-blue gown that matched his tie, she was standing by the gifts table, her eyes lost in some middle space.

It had been a mistake to dredge up their past before the wedding, but something had clicked last night, and when he'd woken up this morning, hell, he hadn't been able to let another minute pass without giving Emily the apology she should have had years ago.

He needed to talk to her.

A tug on his hand brought his eyes back to his flower-girl dance passenger.

"You aren't dancing."

A new song was already playing, that Shania Twain wedding favorite "Forever and For Always," which always made him cringe a little on the inside, because… well, look at the blindside she'd had.

Before he had to try to let the six-year-old down easy, her dad stepped up and offered to cut in. Saved.

One of the other bridesmaids was already heading in his direction, but again that sense of urgency gripped him, and he cut through the crowd, offering a few nods and smiles along the way, until… Shit.

Where was she?

Twenty feet off, leaning in for a powwow with the photographer, a list in hand.

Right. Because Emily was the super attendant, verifying that the photographer knew which guests to make sure he got pictures of throughout the night.

Two songs later, Brody was holding up the wall across from the bar with Jase, pointing out some girl who'd caught his eye. Jase gave a subtle nod toward the brunette with the sequins.

"No, man, she's got the honey-blond hair and"— Brody swallowed and adjusted his jacket like it was suddenly too tight—"and that dress that ties behind her neck."

Jase started scanning the area, but got distracted when he saw Emily making the rounds of the tables.

Collecting the full disposable cameras and dropping new ones.

Smiling and talking with everyone.

"That guy she's sitting with is her date, but look at 'em. She's chattering away and he's on his phone, totally detached. I don't think they're *together* together."

"I don't know. Maybe." He didn't know because he was still watching Emily. But then he'd had enough watching. "Good luck, Brod."

Catching up to Emily back at the gifts table, Jase

shoved his hands into his pockets and turned so he was facing her and the crowd. So maybe it didn't look like he was watching her as closely as he was. "Having fun?"

She emptied her bag of disposable cameras into the oversize glass bowl.

A nod and smile. One that almost looked like the real thing.

"Very much. And you?"

"Oh yeah." Great. And now the woman who'd never had a shortage of words for him was suddenly giving him the kind of stunted small talk usually reserved for awkward encounters with out-of-town cousins who only made the lineup by birthright.

"You've been running around since we got here. How about a dance, or maybe you want to sit down and take a break? I'll get you a drink."

Her answer was in her eyes. *And it wasn't the one he was hoping for.*

"I'm good. Really. I just offered to take care of this stuff. You know me," she said with a less-than-convincing shrug. "I like to stay busy. And actually, I've got a couple of—" She broke off and looked at her hands. After a breath, she met his eyes. "It's not you, Jase. It's just… Today was kind of a lot."

He was such an ass. "I feel like crap about it, Em. I shouldn't have—"

"No," she said clearly, firmly. "I'm glad you did. But still, closure is kind of a big deal," she said with a quiet laugh that made that spot in the center of his chest ache. "I think maybe I just need a minute with it, you know?"

Space. What she needed was some space, not some full-court press.

Not yet.

"I can give you space." He leaned in and pressed a brief kiss to her temple. "Anything you need."

———∿∿∿———

"That's it?" Lena all but choked from where she'd been leaning over their end of the communal-style lunch table at Star of Siam, her glass of chardonnay suspended a few inches from her mouth. "We're leaving this with him giving you space?"

Emily smiled at the way Lena nearly spat the word, a bite of som tum carelessly dangling from her chopsticks as though she wasn't worried about it dropping onto her neat white suit. Emily would be terrified. With good reason.

"I think so, yeah. I mean, I know he was saying he wanted more, but after we talked… Lena, I think maybe it was more about closure. About putting the past behind us and moving forward as…" Okay, this was where she wasn't entirely sure. Because Jase hadn't said anything about them being friends. In fact, he'd been pretty clear that he'd never actually seen her as a friend. Even though he'd wished maybe he had. But now?

"Moving forward without all the baggage."

Lena sat back, careful not to bump the woman sharing the bench seating behind her, and stuck out her deep-burgundy bottom lip. "But he was trying to get you back into bed. To *sleep* sleep with him."

Yeah, and as tempting as that was coming from a guy like Jase, it also made her nervous. Because it smacked of the "next step" business Emily preferred to avoid.

And when she'd initially given in to that pull between

them, a part of her had only been able to do it because Jase wasn't a "next step" kind of guy.

He'd seemed so safe.

"I know you're all deep in your honeymoon phase and ready to start recruiting. But believe me when I tell you that Jase and I aren't quality happily-ever-after candidates."

Lena shook her head. "Obviously, I don't know the guy like you do…or I'd have some serious explaining to do." She snickered with a flash of mischief in her eyes. "But I've seen him with some of his other girlfriends when everyone meets up for a show or dinner or something. And the way Dean tells it, Jase isn't the kind of guy who has trouble letting women out of his bed the next morning. That is, if he even let them in it. Isn't he one of those 'your place, not mine' guys?"

Emily didn't know.

"All I'm saying is, he sounds *different* with you."

"I think you just want him to be different. But even if he was… Lena, *I'm not interested*. What we had was fun and satisfying. But I'm not looking for forever any more than he is."

"Right now," Lena added, taking a bite of her salad and then dumping the extra side of peanut sauce she'd ordered over the whole thing. "You aren't interested in forever *right now*, but you will be some day."

This time, it was Emily taking the deep swallow of wine, followed by another bigger bite of spicy, green shredded papaya. Which she chewed thoroughly.

From across the table, one neatly sculpted black eyebrow pushed toward the ceiling.

"Emily, don't you want to get married?"

As close as Lena and Emily were, this was one of those subjects about which Emily had always managed to be a better listener than a contributor. And having started their careers together working for Lena's dad, Paul, it wasn't like they didn't have a million *other* things to get caught up in conversation over.

Emily usually managed to worm her way out of this particular conversation with everyone. Even when her mother had cornered her last Thanksgiving, she'd found an out.

But the way Lena was watching her, there was no use hiding. The jig was up.

"I used to," Emily answered honestly. "I used to think I wanted a husband. A family. Three little kids and a dog. But as I've gotten older—"

"Twenty-seven. Gasp. You're as old as the hills. A downright elder in the community. Do they tell folktales about you? Do the young-uns come seeking your wisdom?"

This was why Emily loved Lena. The woman could always be counted on to make her laugh.

Setting down her chopsticks, she shook her head and looked at her friend affectionately. "Yes, actually. They do come to me for wisdom."

An eye roll was Lena's reply, quickly followed by one of those waving hands, not so politely requesting more information.

"I just don't feel the same way about marriage and family as I used to. I mean, I see you and Dean, and I couldn't be happier for you both. Same with Sally. I love *love*. But I love it more for you guys than for me. In my own life…" She broke off, letting her eyes roam over nothing and everything as she tried to think how best to explain. "Lena, I didn't get over what happened with Eddie the way you got over what happened with… he-who-must-not-be-named. You were so strong and so determined, and I'm so glad you found Dean.

"But when I think about getting serious, it's like I can't breathe. Like I want to run away. And the thing is, I'm not sad about it. I don't feel like I'm missing some critical piece of something. I just… I think I'm happier being my own. I like that I don't have to answer to anyone about my schedule. I like having my own place. I like knowing that I can do anything I want, any time I want."

"That sounds more like you aren't ready to settle down, though."

"Maybe," Emily said, picking up her chopsticks again, hoping to resume lunch and move on to a more comfortable topic.

Lena looked like she was debating whether to press, but in the end she just sighed. "So you didn't leave it any particular way with Jase."

"No."

"So really he might—"

"I don't think so, Lena. I think if anything we'd go forward as…"

Again, she couldn't quite make herself say *friends*, but the way he'd looked at her had been with real caring. She didn't know. "Whatever happens with us, I think it's going to be a lot easier than it has been in the past."

Chapter 16

March

HOW IN THE HELL HAD SHE THOUGHT THIS WAS going to be *easier*? Nothing was ever easy when it came to Jase Foster.

"Friends? I thought we already had this conversation," Jase said, pitching his voice to be heard over the crowded bar where Romeo was playing bass guitar with his band. "I don't think of you as a friend."

"I remember. You never have. But I guess I thought maybe after our talk and how it's been between us lately, I thought you might now."

Jase let out a short laugh, then did that laser-tracking thing with his eyes where she couldn't quite force herself to look away. "How it's been between us *lately* should have told you exactly why friends isn't where we're headed."

The words probably should have stung, but with the way Jase was looking at her with that small curve at the corner of his mouth… No, she wasn't taking it hard.

"Okay, so you don't want to be friends. What do you want?"

The question slipped past her lips before she had a chance to think how ridiculous it was. Because what Jase wanted was obvious.

An unoccupied storage closet in close proximity.

A car with enough legroom for two individuals of above-average height to be able to get up to no good.

A quick hookup—or not so quick, if he was in the mood to push his luck—in any semi-private space he could find.

Jase wanted sex.

Which she'd been great with before, but now, sex suddenly felt…complicated. Which was making her nervous.

"What I want," Jase said, leaning down into her space and then brushing her hair back so that when he spoke quietly into her ear, his lips grazed the outer shell, sending tingles shooting down her arms, "is to take you on a proper date."

She blinked, momentarily mesmerized by his sexy smell and the deep rumble of his voice. She blinked again.

"Wait, what?" she asked, pulling out of smelling range to shake off the crazy effect he had on her.

Jase held her eyes, that cocky grin firmly in place. "A date. You've heard of them, I assume. You know, where I take you out for a meal and a bottle of wine…before I take you back to my place and spend the rest of the night making you beg and moan and gasp my name in that way you know drives me wild."

Wow, and the goose bumps were rolling across her skin like a wave rushing to shore.

Okay, that sounded good. Very good, actually. Except for the part about it being a very bad idea.

"I'm sorry, Jase. But I think that would be a mistake."

"Really?" he asked, that smile not giving an inch. "Why?"

"Jase, neither of us is interested in a relationship. And honestly, I'm a little concerned that if we keep on the way we have been, someone's emotions are going to end up getting involved."

He nodded, those bright blue eyes tracking around the crowded bar before landing back on hers. "If I ask you a question, can you promise you'll be honest with me when you answer?"

She owed him at least that much. "Of course."

"That dress," he started, jutting the square of his chin toward the deep vee at the neck of her chocolate wrap. "Were you thinking of me when you picked it out?"

Had she actually been idiot enough to tell Jase she'd answer him with honesty?

Blowing out a long breath, she womaned up. Sort of. "I've been thinking about you a lot lately. So much has happened, you know?"

The corner of Jase's mouth twitched, but he didn't call her out on the sidestepping cheat. Instead, he nodded like he absolutely agreed. And then, "How about what's underneath? Were you thinking I'd like what you've got on beneath that damn-near-impossible-not-to-touch velvety plaything?"

She swallowed and felt her pulse speed and a slow-spreading heat move through her center.

Because while she hadn't actually been planning for Jase to see them when she selected the set in soft cream—cut sparse in all the places that mattered—there had been that single fleeting moment where she envisioned Jase's big hands reversing her progress and pulling them free. Pressing his mouth where the silk had been and—

"Yeah, that's what I thought," Jase growled, that too-confident, too-sexy smile gone and something predatory in its place. And then his arm was wrapped around her shoulders, holding her close to him as they cut through the crowd toward the back of the bar.

This was nuts. She shouldn't be going with him. She shouldn't be eagerly matching his stride as Jase sought out someplace barely private to investigate exactly what kind of sexy the bra and panties she was wearing had going on. Because by ending things, there would be no risk. No worry of anyone getting in too deep. No messy emotions going off the chain when all she wanted was the security of emotions that were well contained.

But here they were again.

And now that she'd accepted she was going to take this one last night with him and then never think of him while selecting panties again, she wasn't even waiting for him to lead the way. She was cutting ahead of the crowd, catching his fingers with hers to lead to the back of the bar. Her heartbeat coming heavier than the bass pumping through the sound system, her skin beginning to tingle in anticipation of a touch she'd told herself she couldn't have again.

They turned into the back hall. There was a line of women waiting for the ladies' room, and no way she was going into the men's.

Jase pressed up against her, wrapping his long arms around her middle and pulling her in close so her back was tucked tight against the solid wall of his chest. Tighter still as he ducked his head to her ear.

"Where are you taking me, Emily?"

God, his breath on her neck. His words like a deep rumble moving inside her.

"I thought maybe there was someplace quiet back here, but—"

"Keep walking. Almost there."

Her fingers slid between Jase's as they continued to advance down the hall. Until they got to the back exit.

She glanced at him from over her shoulder. "Through here?" she asked, anticipation ramping up with every second that passed. Because…the *alley*? Because never had anyone even thought for a second to take her to the places Jase did.

They stepped out into the brisk night air, and Emily shivered. Hooking her fingers through the buttons of Jase's shirt front, she pulled him closer. "It's freezing. We're going to have to be quick."

His brow quirked, and another, even sexier smile presented itself as he shrugged out of one shoulder of his jacket and then the other, swinging it around to cover her.

"Put your arms in the sleeves, Em. It'll keep you warmer."

She did and then she was stepping back into Jase, going to her toes because she could and tipping back to take his kiss. She opened beneath the press of his lips, moaned around the stroke of his tongue, and shifted closer.

The air was cold, but well above freezing. And as Jase kissed her, and kissed her and kissed her, she slowly stopped feeling the cold at all. In fact, quite the opposite. She was beginning to burn for him.

But his arms, while still wrapped tightly around her, hadn't made any headway toward the lower quadrant of her dress. Or her sexy, silky panties. Or even her bra.

Restless, she shifted her hips into him, getting even hotter as she encountered the hard length of his erection. He groaned against her mouth, his fists balling at the sides of her hips.

"Let me buy you dinner tomorrow."

Emily stilled, all that achy tension begging for release. "What?"

"A date, Emily. And then"—the hands that had been

at her hips splayed over her waist and coasted upward until his thumbs were brushing the bottom swells of her breasts—"I take you back to my place and—"

"Blackmail?" she gasped, a nervous laugh following on its heels, because no way. Even Jase wouldn't stoop so low. And *please*, like she was so desperate for a few moans that she'd agree to a date she wasn't interested in?

"Persuasion," Jase corrected with a low laugh. Brushing his thumbs once more, barely grazing her nipples and then slowly withdrawing. "I want a date, Emily, not your Swiss bank account."

Oh and *how dare he* with that barely there contact that had her insides standing up to beg.

"I love how wholesome you make it sound," she snapped.

This time, the laugh was deeper, fuller. Doing something totally different to her.

Then he was looking into her eyes again, cupping her cheek in his palm. "There's nothing wholesome about the way I want you, Em. But the way I want you isn't just about sex."

A part of her was clamoring to let go. Give in and just say yes. Lean in to Jase's kiss and let him take her out for a movie or fro-yo—and do all the things he'd promised after. But the greater part of her couldn't ignore the uncomfortable tension in her back or the increase in her pulse that wasn't exactly fun. The tightening of her chest.

"You date, Emily. I've seen you out. And there's something between us, so why not me?"

She could barely breathe. Why wouldn't he just let it go?

Those precious few hookups between them had been off-the-charts hot. Satisfying to the nth degree.

And they'd both walked away smiling. So why push it?

Jase's brows pulled together, his eyes darkening as he searched her face. "Emily—"

"Because *I don't trust you*. That's why, Jase," she whispered, the air feeling thin in her lungs.

Jase didn't move. She could feel his eyes on her, but she wouldn't look back, staring at the patches of broken concrete around her feet instead.

"It's too cold to be standing out here," she muttered, retreating a step and then another. "Especially if I'm not going to get warmed up the way that kiss promised I would."

"Em."

Slipping out of Jase's jacket, she checked the door they'd just come through and, finding it locked, kept walking toward the mouth of the alley. She'd go around front and pay the cover again if she had to. Anything but stand there with Jase Foster staring into her eyes like he wanted the one thing she thought would never be an issue with a guy like him.

"Emily, damn it," Jase bit out, catching her arm and coming to stop in front of her. "What just happened?"

She looked down at where Jase's fingers were wrapped in a loose hold around her arm and felt the phantom pain of another hand there. A hold too tight. One that would leave bruises she'd have to cover for a week. Reflexively, she jerked away, rubbing at the spot as Jase's expression morphed from startled shock to dawning understanding to a potent, jaw-grinding, barely banked rage.

"Eddie?" he demanded, stepping toward her, his eyes

more intense than she'd ever seen them. But then, just as quickly, he stepped back, holding his hands out to the sides so she could see he wasn't about to put them on her.

So he wouldn't scare her.

Something inside her died in that moment.

Because with Jase, no matter how they'd fought, no matter what insults were thrown, they'd always been on level ground. A part of her reveled in going head-to-head with him, because every time she was reminded that this man saw her as a worthy adversary. This man knew she was strong enough to take him on.

And until that very moment, she hadn't realized how important it was to her.

"Tell me. Was this fucking *Eddie*?" he asked, his voice little more than a low threat.

She wasn't going to talk to him about this. Not now. Not with those stupid tears pushing at her lids.

"Emily, wait."

But she shook her head. Then, shoulders back, she stepped around Jase, giving him a wide berth, though she'd known he wouldn't touch her again.

"I'm going inside, Jase. Don't stop me."

He let her go.

It wasn't until she was standing back at the booth where Sally had camped out for the night that she realized she was still clutching Jase's jacket tight. Holding it against her chest, like she didn't know how to let it go.

———

"What happened to you last night?" Brody asked, shouldering his broad frame—made all the broader by the addition of an insulated food tote and four overflowing handle bags—into Jase's place. "Thought you were going to stop in at Belfast when Santos finished his gig."

Jase checked down the hall for any of the guys or Molly coming off the elevator, since he'd found another brick propping the "security" door that morning.

"Sorry, man. Emily was there with Sally, and—"

The insulated tote swung in front of his face like it was warding off a coming too-much-information moment. "Not like that, so don't get your man panties in a bunch."

"Ahh, what then?" Brody asked, walking past him into the kitchen.

"I fucked up with her," Jase said, the weight of those words hanging over him.

Hefting his bags onto the counter, Brody clucked his tongue. Christ, the guy could be such an old lady.

"Come on, man, leave the poor girl alone, will you?" Brody answered without turning around. "Joe here yet? I brought him something special."

Brody loved Jase's dad and was always bringing him beer from the farthest reaches to try out. "He's not coming. Some buddy in town or something. And as to Emily, I don't think I can. But what happened with Eddie... It's worse than I thought." Jase leaned back against the counter, Emily's face when she'd jerked away from him—that fear and pain etched sharp into every soft line—burned into the forefront of his mind. He didn't think he could ever forget it. "I should have been there for her. I mean, I *really* should have been there for her."

Brody turned, that menacing look you almost never saw from him there in his eyes.

"*Worse*, like we need to pay for gas with cash when we drive out to Upstate New York so there's no paper trail when we drop in to 'visit' Eddie—that kind of worse?"

"No. Not for you, man." But in truth, that's about where Jase's head had been the night before. Seeing the way Emily had reacted to his hand on her arm, it had taken everything he had not to hop in his car, punch the gas, and drive until he had Eddie up against a wall and the answers he needed, obtained in whatever manner worked. But somehow he'd managed.

And then he'd followed the pull in his chest back into the bar, where he found Emily at the table with their friends, laughing like she didn't have a care in the world. Like she hadn't just been white as a sheet, flinching from his touch as she blinked back her tears.

She hadn't gone to hide in some corner.

She hadn't sought out comfort from a friend.

She'd just put on a face no one would ever suspect wasn't as genuinely happy, confident, and unencumbered as it looked, and she'd gone back to her night. And that was the worst of it. How good she was at covering up. How practiced.

Just the thought of her honing that particular skill made him sick. But he hadn't turned away.

He'd waited until Emily left with Sally and Romeo, watching her from across the bar until then, keeping his distance because the way her eyes skimmed over him without stopping for even a beat suggested that was what she wanted. And yet, she hadn't let go of his jacket once. He'd watched her walk out of the bar with it clutched in her hands.

And then he'd gone home and thrown up.

Because he could have stopped it. Whatever Eddie did to her, if he'd just opened his eyes for one damn minute, he could have ended it. He could have stopped it before it began.

He'd never forgive himself.

"I don't know what he did *exactly*. I don't know how bad it was, except to say it was bad enough that Emily's still got the emotional scars. She hides them really well, but last night"—his stomach wrenched again—"I saw."

"She wouldn't talk to you?" Brody asked, shrugging out of his North Face jacket and then tossing it across to the chair in the corner.

"I tried, but she wasn't having any part of it." Shoving his fingers back through his hair, Jase laced them behind his head. "Not that I blame her. She tried to talk to me a hundred times when all this shit was going on. When it mattered and I might have been able to do something about it. But I shut her down at every turn, and now it's ten years too late and—*the look on her face*, man."

"So, yeah," Brody planted his hands on the counter, leaning into the space above it. "You fucked up, big."

That was the thing about Brody. The guy could always be counted on to tell you what you needed to hear. The truth.

"Here's the way I see it, Jase," he said. Digging into the cabinets beneath the island, he pulled out a heavy sauté pan, then eyed it with blatant disapproval, but Jase was long past trying to keep his buddy satisfied in the kitchen. Besides, he knew Brody wasn't done.

"It sounds like Emily got a raw deal, and to some extent, you played a part in it. What's done is done, and while there's no going back to change the past, you can learn from it for the future, yeah?"

"Right."

"So figure out how you let her down and make up for it."

How he let her down? Easy. He wasn't her friend when he'd let her believe he would be.

Brody thumbed the blade of Jase's kitchen knife and scowled at him. "I sharpened this the last time I was here. What, have you been cutting through tin cans or something?"

He might have used it to break into the plastic clamshell his new running earbuds had come in.

Jase took Brody's coat to the front hall closet and hung it up, standing there a minute after thinking about what Brody had said.

Friends.

With Emily.

Before last night, he hadn't wanted to be her friend. He'd wanted her back in his bed. He'd wanted her to be his standing date from Saturday night through early Sunday afternoon. He'd wanted to take her to the next wedding instead of running into her there, and as much fun as all that hot, burning *will they, won't they* anticipation could be, he'd wanted to *know* that after the band shut down, she'd be going home with him.

But now, more than all that, what he wanted, *the only thing that mattered*, was making sure he never had to see that look on her face again. If he had any hope of being able to look himself in the mirror, for once he *needed* to do the right thing by her.

Pulling the phone from his jeans pocket, he headed

into his office and sat down at his desk. It didn't feel right, so he moved to the couch. Stretched out, but then stood again before coming to grips with the fact that it wasn't the seat making him squirm.

Screw it, he'd get comfortable with this later on.

"Hey, Em, I know it's late notice, but I've got some people coming over to watch the Blackhawks play at two thirty and thought, if you didn't have anything going on, you'd like to come. You know…as friends."

Chapter 17

FRIENDS.

If any other guy had thrown her a line like that, Emily would have laughed in his face. Okay, she wouldn't do that because even guys with bad lines had feelings. But she'd have been thinking "Ha!" in her head as she nodded politely and then found a considerate way to say no…in no uncertain terms.

But this wasn't any other guy. This was Jase. The man who'd told *her* in no uncertain terms that she wasn't friendship material. And now he was asking her for a chance to try again. To show her that he could be the friend he should have been in high school. To prove to her that she could trust him…with more than just her body.

Talk about the stuff of nightmares.

Intentionally making herself vulnerable to the guy whose shabby treatment of her in the past had devastated her? She'd have to be crazy.

He knew it too. Which was probably why, when she'd been too stunned to even answer, he'd filled the silence with the simple statement, "Just think about it. I hope you'll come."

She wished she could say that simple curiosity had kept her from dismissing the offer out of hand. A need to discover for herself what friendship, Jase-style, encompassed. If there was a benefits package. How quickly she'd be eligible.

Only deep down she knew it was more than that.

Which made the fact that she was standing outside his door—with bags of pretzels, Bloody Mary mix, an arsenal of drink fixings, and vodka in one hand, and a Pyrex dish of her favorite fatty, cheese-based dip topped with sweet-pepper relish in the other—absolutely insane.

It wasn't too late. She could still leave. He'd never have to know she'd been there.

Yeah, that's what she'd do. She'd take the dip, go home, and eat the whole damn thing herself.

She hadn't taken a step when the door opened. But Jase hadn't seen her yet. He was turned into the apartment, telling someone behind him that Molly was on her way up. She knew enough about Jase and his group of besties to know that Molly was Molly Brandt, Max's sister. The only double X chromosome in their group and, from the few brief encounters they'd had, a crazy lot of fun. She could do this.

Just then, Jase turned and the instant his eyes landed on her, that easy smile he'd been wearing was wiped from his mouth, replaced by a look of clear shock.

Emily shifted uneasily, her eyes darting down the hall for Molly, or anyone, before she looked back at Jase and, with a resigned sigh, handed him his jacket. "I didn't... Um... Thanks for this last night."

Then clearing her throat, she nodded down to what she was carrying. "So I didn't know how much to bring."

Suddenly, that smile he'd been wearing was back, only brighter and more devastating in every way.

"You brought yourself. That's all I was hoping for," he said, stepping back to let her into the apartment instead of pulling her into his arms. Which made sense under the framework of friendship, she figured. And her hands were full. Then he was taking her bags and leading her back to the kitchen she knew in the biblical sense—where Brody O'Donnel was wearing a half apron tied around his waist, his jaw-length russet hair tied back from his face while sautéing something that smelled unbelievable.

"Hey, Emily, good to see you," he offered, then held up a wooden spoon. "Try this, and tell me if it needs more heat."

Jase was setting her bags down on the impressively sturdy breakfast table she'd been introduced to before when he turned back. "You still like spicy, right, Em?"

She nodded and accepted the taste, moaning in a way that only Jase had ever made her moan before.

Maybe he recognized the sound, because suddenly he'd stopped what he was doing and turned to her with a raised brow.

Heat rushed into her cheeks and she lifted her hands, laughing. "It was *that* good."

"Better have been out of this damn world to earn that sound from you," Jase teased, standing just close enough to keep it between them. Then—in the name of friendship, she supposed—he stepped back again. "She brought Bloody Marys."

"Can I make you one?" she asked.

"Hell, yes," Brody boomed with a smile suggesting she'd offered him a first-class upgrade on his international flight rather than a drink, and she found herself laughing for no real reason, except that the guy just had a way of making her feel good.

She started on the drinks, happy to have something

to do rather than stand around ogling Brody's cooking or, worse yet, Jase in his jeans, sexy bare feet, and Blackhawks jersey.

"Hey, boys," a singsong voice called from where Jase had left the front door open. Then Molly was breezing in, a shock of fuchsia mixing with her flyaway white-blond hair. She stopped, her mouth dropping open. "Emily, so cool you're here. And with drinks too!"

Molly piled her load with the rest, unloading a couple of bags of chips, a tub of french onion dip, and three beers. "Max is running late, but he'll be here in about thirty, and Sean will be up anytime. He was stuck on his phone out front, doing that thing where he pinches his temples with one hand and looks like he's talking to his shoes. I'm guessing it's his dad."

Molly ripped open a bag of her chips and stuffed one in her mouth, chewing with an indulgent smirk. "Tasty."

"How you doing, Molly?" Jase asked, walking over to take her coat and grab a chip of his own.

"Better now that I'm here."

Jase popped the chip into his mouth, coughed, and grabbed the bag, his face a mask of horror.

"Dill pickle? Jesus, if I were less of a man, I'd be spitting that shit in the sink."

Molly laughed and called him a pussy. Which of course had Emily laughing too.

Then Molly was leaning against the wall beside the counter where Emily was assembling skewers of cheese squares, pickles, and a cooked shrimp for the Bloody Marys. "Those look awesome. I would've brought more beer, but that douche drank most of the twelve-pack I picked up yesterday."

Brody's head shot up, and his pan clanked against the burner. "Are you fucking kidding me? What did I tell you about him?"

For a moment Emily struggled to remember Molly's relationship status, but thinking back, she couldn't recall ever seeing her at a wedding without one of these guys. And at parties or when they ended up at the same club, well, Molly had always seemed part of the crowd rather than *with* anyone in particular.

"Yeah, yeah. He needs to go," she agreed, accepting a drink from Emily with a wide smile. "And he will, just as soon as I find someone else to cover his rent."

Jase and Brody spoke up together: "I'll cover it."

Which had Emily's brows pushing high.

The guys exchanged a look and shrugged.

"Aww, you two. Thanks, but pass. I'll handle my roommate myself." And in case either of them had any ideas about pushing the topic, Molly gave them a look eerily reminiscent of one of her brother's and added, "End of discussion."

Wow. Molly had always struck her as pretty cool, but now Emily was really looking forward to getting to know her better.

The rest of the guys eventually straggled in, all of them far too polished in the art of wingmanship to show even a hint of surprise at Jase having invited her to join what she'd heard was a fairly closed group. They were welcoming, and the conversation and laughter never stopped.

"Any updates on Janice?" Max asked, returning with what had to be his sixth plate of food from the kitchen.

Holy cow, the guy could eat, but he didn't have an ounce of fat on him.

Jase's head rocked back, and he covered his stomach with his hand like he was suddenly sick. Emily sat up a little straighter.

"Nothing. I talked to her this morning—"

Molly held her skewer up, now down to only the cheese cube. "Wait, you made your secretary, who's thirteen months pregnant, talk to you on a Sunday morning? There's a special place in hell for you, mister."

But then Jase was waving her off, giving her an annoyed, but not really, look before going on. "Okay, first, she called *me*," he said, defending himself.

At which point, Emily cocked her head. "Your pregnant secretary calls *you* on Sunday mornings?"

Jase's head snapped around to her and he put up a staying hand, warding off whatever unholy thought she'd had about this Janice.

"It's not like that. We've been working together for years, and I care about her a lot. She's thirty-five, this is her first baby, and she's just—"

"She's scary," Molly cut in matter-of-factly. "I mean, I love her. But—"

"But she's already six days past her due date, and I'm concerned for her. Like any boss would be."

Emily felt something deep in her chest warm at the thought of Jase worrying over a pregnant woman.

This time, Max piped up. "I don't know, man. I'm not sure just any boss would be quite as involved as you. How big is the binder these days?"

Jase flushed, and Emily sat straighter still. "Binder?"

Brody laughed and slapped Jase on the shoulder.

"With all the safety reports Jase started printing out for her when he found out she was prego."

Sean—who was apparently the grown-up of the group, the most reserved and polite by far—turned to her, a pitying look in his eyes. "He researched breast pumps."

And that was when everyone in the room, Emily especially, fell apart.

—∿∿—

The game was a nail-biter, going into overtime before the Hawks brought home the win. Emily had had a great time, never once feeling left out. The guys made it a point to include her, going to the trouble to give her the backstory whenever an insider joke came up—and there were dozens.

They grilled her about Jase in high school, and despite their past, she had more than enough cherished memories from those early days to share with the group. It was funny to think that these people had known Jase almost as long as she had. They'd all lived in the same dorm freshman year—except Molly, who was three years younger and hadn't gone to college except to visit her brother at his. Apparently, she'd spent enough time there the school had been ready to start charging her rent. And while technically, Emily had known Jase longer, these friends knew him in a way she didn't. They knew the guy he'd been *and* everything that had happened along the way to make him the man he'd become today.

They were lucky.

"Have fun?" Jase asked, coming up beside her as she loaded the remains of her cocktail bar back into her bag.

She smiled. "I did. Thank you for inviting me. You sure I can't help clean up?"

"Nah." He met her eyes, but then looked down to the floor and stuffed his hands in the pockets of his jeans. "But maybe we could all hang out like this again sometime? We play darts at Belfast on Wednesdays. And before you get all nervous that I'm trying to trick you into a date and planning to show up with flowers and a box of candy, Wednesday is friends' night. We used to call it guys' night, but then Molly got all pissy because she'd been tagging along since the start—and anyway, it's not gender exclusive. Wednesday is for friends. Been that way since college."

"And no way would you break that code."

His mouth slanted into the smile that left Emily thinking thoughts that weren't exclusively friendly.

"These guys would never let me live it down. Meet us there?"

As appealing as it was to believe that somehow she and Jase could become friends, especially after the afternoon she'd spent as part of that inner circle, the truth was it didn't seem possible.

This time, she was the one to look away. "Maybe."

⌁⌁⌁

When Jase walked back into the apartment, cleanup was in full swing. Brody was scrubbing out the sauté pan, Molly was on drying duty, and Sean was bagging up the garbage. Meanwhile, Max was reorganizing Jase's refrigerator. Again.

"Thanks for waiting until she was gone," Jase said, returning the platter Molly had just dried to the cabinet over the fridge. Yes, he was interested in more time with Emily, but he'd been worried about what would happen if she stayed. If somehow she'd ended up being the last one there. If they were alone, and the part of him still hungry for Emily in his bed got in the way of the part of him working to become her friend.

Based on what had happened at the club, Emily might not have minded. But once the sex was over, they'd be right back to her walking out of his place, thanking him for a good time—and PS, don't bother calling.

That wasn't what Jase wanted. Not anymore. And now that he'd admitted it to himself... Well, drastic measures were needed until all parts of him got in line.

"So Emily, huh?" Sean asked, propping a hip against the counter. "Molly said there was something going on with you two, but after Skolnic's wedding, I thought she was full of shit."

And with the audience gone, Sean had let his hair down.

"I told you so," Molly sang quietly, the small smile playing at her lips making her look a hell of a lot sweeter than she actually was.

Jase grabbed the stack of plates next. "I know. And sorry for springing her on you. It's just that she and I go back pretty far. And there's some stuff I need to make up to her before I can—"

"Do her," Max suggested, that too-serious face of his split into a mischievous grin.

Molly shook her head, muttering something about Max being the funniest guy she knew, earning a snort from Sean.

"Bite it, Max. It's not like that... I mean, yeah, I'm into her." What fool wouldn't be? "But with all the crap we've been through, my first priority is proving to her that she can trust me. Showing her that we can be friends."

Max closed the fridge and crossed his arms, the grin gone.

"So you're trying to convince her she's your friend, so she'll trust you enough to let you nail her?"

Molly whistled out a breath and, eyeing Jase like he was a festering boil, mouthed "Douche bag."

"Jesus, do you seriously think I'm trying to scam her into the sack? I want something with her. Something real."

"You talking more *real* than what you had with Tiffany or Camila?" Brody asked, the look on his face no less disapproving than the others. "Because *real* usually implies lasting, Jase. Which isn't exactly your MO. And Emily's had enough of your shit."

Jase got it. Tiffany and Camila were the last two women he'd dated, Tiffany before Skolnic's wedding and Camila about three months before that. He'd had to work on Camila to go out with him. Something about his reputation preceding him, if memory served. He'd convinced her, but not by promising something he had no intention of delivering. He'd convinced her that what he was offering—all he'd been offering—was something she wouldn't want to miss.

And when they'd broken it off—amicably, he might add—she'd told him he'd been right.

Tiffany? Well, he could still remember that slap landing across his cheek, but he'd known she was drama going in. He hadn't offered her anything more than he had Camila, but somewhere along the way, Tiffany had gotten it into her head that he should have. Their parting hadn't been quite so amicable. It happened.

Both were fairly representative of his relationships in general, but neither of them could be compared to what was happening with Emily. Nothing could.

He didn't know why things were so different with her.

Why she pulled at the places other women couldn't touch. But when he was with her, it wasn't just about want. It was about *need*.

And whatever that pull was, it had already taken him beyond the limits he'd set for every other relationship he'd gone into. He was now in uncharted territory. He didn't know where it was going to lead, but he knew he didn't want to be there alone.

"She's different." That was all he could say. His only defense. Well, that and… "I invited her to Belfast on Wednesday."

Silence.

The weird kind.

And then Molly clutched her hands together, her lips pinched between her teeth. Sean grunted, grabbed the sack of trash, and walked out to dump it. Max reopened the fridge and resumed his grumbling over the jelly being hidden behind the milk and what they were doing on the same shelf. And Brody… Brody stepped in close so the others couldn't hear.

"No more fuckups with this one, Jase. She doesn't need it."

Okay, so they were good.

Wednesday night took its sweet time rolling around. The week was rough. Jase was worried about Janice, who still hadn't had her baby and to his consternation had continued marching into the office each morning like she wasn't walking around with a stomach so big and round it looked ready to pop. Only these days, that belly didn't always look so round. This morning it had been disconcertingly off-center. A little oblong. And damn, was it hard.

He wanted her at home with her feet up and a nurse standing at the ready. A phone in her hand with Labor and Delivery set on speed dial.

But no. That wasn't Janice.

So he'd spent the better part of his workweek hovering around his assistant, trying to come up with quality, on-the-spot lies to cover his actions. Because the hovering? She didn't appreciate it. Just like she hadn't appreciated the arugula salad he'd tried to get her to eat when he read it helped start labor. And she didn't like the yoga ball he'd replaced her chair with for the same reason.

She'd disliked it so much that she'd all but shoved him into his office that afternoon, closed the door behind her, and then done the unthinkable.

"You brought this on yourself, Foster," she'd hissed, pulling up her stretchy maternity shirt to just above her belly button. And that straining, mottled orb... Holy hell, there were some things a guy just couldn't unsee.

No more yoga balls. Check.

The only thing that had gotten him through the day had been the idea of confessing his arugula sins to the one woman whose laugh might make the trauma go away.

But here he was at Belfast at quarter to ten, surrounded by friends who'd officially transitioned from upbeat assurances she'd be there to sympathetic looks mirroring what he already knew. She wouldn't.

The only question now was what was he going to do about it?

Chapter 18

"RAFE, YOU KNOW I LOVE WHAT YOU DID HERE. IT'S genius, like everything you touch," Emily assured him, stroking an ego that was already on the brink of going supernova. "But for Basker Bourbon, we're looking to work an edge in with the old-school feel. I think if we—"

"Emily?"

She turned to find Avi, her new intern, blushing at the threshold of the art director's office, trying to keep her eyes from roving over the admittedly attractive man. She was failing. Miserably.

"What's up?"

"Um, sorry to interrupt, but there's a Jason Foster for you in the lobby."

Emily bumped her knee on the edge of Rafe's drafting table, then turned a heel navigating through the cluster of sleek, red club chairs.

"I'm coming," she croaked, bending to rub her ankle. "Just have him wait in my office. I'll be right there."

Turning back to Rafe, she apologized for the interruption, finished her thought, and after some more heavy petting regarding his unparalleled talent, she started back through the maze of thirty-second-floor hallways toward certain…friction.

She should have called. Texted.

Something to let Jase know she wouldn't be there last night. But she hadn't really known herself until the back-and-forth indecision that had been eating her up since Sunday—and had her vacillating between standing at the door with her coat on and stalking back into her bedroom—eventually ate up all the hours of the evening. Doing nothing had made the decision for her. Because the night was over and she hadn't gone.

It was for the best. Right?

Probably not, if Jase was sitting in her office.

Outside her door, she stopped and smoothed her skirt. Her hair. She took a breath and pressed a hand against the spot in her belly where the butterflies had started to build.

Shoot. That never ended well.

Pushing through the door with a confident smile, she braced for whatever was coming. Then froze when she found Jase kicked back in the chair across from her desk, a spread of sandwiches, chips, and sodas laid out in front of him.

"Thought you might be hungry," he said by way of greeting with no indication of any feelings, hard or not, about the night before. "You free for a few?"

She looked over the spread and felt her stomach grumble.

Jase waved her to her desk. "Sit. Relax. It's only from the deli around the corner from my building, not takeout from Spiaggia. Eat."

"Friend food?" she asked quietly, her guilt over ignoring Jase's offer of amity the night before making her squirm.

"*Celebration* food," he corrected, then held up a couple of cookies she hadn't seen as if they clarified things. "Janice had her baby at 3:01 this morning. Little monster's a boy. Seven pounds, five ounces. Nineteen inches long."

Emily rocked back in her chair, delight washing through her.

"Jase, you must be so proud," she teased, warming at the smile she'd earned.

"Actually, I am." And then he proceeded to tell her about the arugula salad he thought might have cost him his manhood yesterday, and then the text from Wayne, Janice's husband, informing him that she'd actually brought it home with her and eaten it for dinner. Two hours later, they were in business.

Emily laughed until she was wiping tears from the corners of her eyes with her deli napkin. And Jase was sitting back in his chair wearing that sexy, satisfied grin on his face.

They talked a while more, and then Jase gathered the trash from their lunch before heading for the door. No last lingering look, no kiss good-bye, just a devastating grin, and as he walked out, a simple "See you around, Em."

From behind her desk, she smiled and answered quietly, "That would be nice."

Saturday morning, bleary-eyed and confused, Emily buzzed Jase up to her apartment, where he handed her a bottle of Gatorade and told her to get dressed. They were going for a run.

She wanted to take offense. To tell him where he could stick his electrolytes and demand to know where he got off showing up at her door like that. But they were looking at one of those freak sixty-five-degree March days, and a run sounded good. Almost as good as Jase looked in black-and-gray Under Armour that fit in a way that had her eyes going wide, despite the fact that she'd woken up approximately thirty-seven seconds before.

Plus, hard to scrounge up much outrage when she'd done almost the same thing to Lena the week before. Of course she'd had the good sense to bring doughnut holes instead of Gatorade, but still.

Ten minutes later, they were pounding down the lakefront path past Belmont Harbor, Jase bemoaning the shortcomings of his temporary assistant. By the time they reached North Avenue Beach, Emily had told him about the band she'd seen the night before and the girl-friend who'd been suspiciously absent for about thirty minutes following the show, only to return with a hickey the size of a quarter on her neck and a new appreciation for drummers' rhythm.

Once they reached Navy Pier, the endorphins must have kicked in because she was feeling pretty good and couldn't help asking the question that had been plaguing her since Jase Foster started making nuptial headlines with his less-than-exemplary record of getting grooms to the church without incident.

"Okay, here's the deal with the Wallace wedding"—Jase's eyes cut to hers—"and I'm trusting this stays between us."

Emily nodded, wiping the sweat from her brow.

"We didn't run out of gas," he said, his words following the cadence of his steps. "I'd never make that kind of mistake with a wedding at stake. But Neil was freaking out. He didn't know if he could go through with it. I took him out to talk, figuring the best bet was to work through it with him and risk being late, rather than risk him not showing up at all. Hell, there's only so much a girl is willing to forgive, right?

"Neil got it together, and we made up the part about the gas in the boat so Maryanne could blame me instead of him. She never needed to know that on the most special day of her life, the guy she was pledging her heart to had almost bailed."

Emily was stunned. It wasn't exactly how she would have handled things, but like the Jase she'd thought she'd known back in high school, this man took care of the people he loved.

"The eye patch on Jim?" she asked.

"That was my bad. Finger football seemed harmless at the time. Live and learn."

Okay, that was all well and good, but she wasn't sure the antibiotics were going to be so easy to explain away.

"Trey? Oh, man, I told that guy it was a mistake to accept free tacos from a lunch truck. I said there had to be a catch, but did he listen?"

It went on like that a while, the two of them trading truths. Telling stories, pointing out their favorite spots along the path, and laughing.

God, being with Jase was fun.

And then the laughter eased as they stopped in front of Buckingham Fountain. Their eyes met and Emily could feel the moment tugging at her, asking her if this was what she wanted, because if she did, it was right there, ready to take.

But like the night he'd invited her to Belfast, she couldn't make herself reach for it.

Jase was amazing, but she couldn't quiet the little

voice whispering in the back of her head, reminding her that was what she'd thought before. Maybe it was just too soon, and all she needed was a little time before she'd be ready to give Jase her trust. But a part of her wondered if any amount of time would be enough.

"You ready to head back?" she asked.

Jase searched her eyes a moment longer, and Emily thought she might have seen recognition in them. Understanding. But then he wiped his big hand over his face and gave her a smile. "Yeah, whatever you want, Em."

Tuesday night, Jase still couldn't get it out of his head. Emily and that look in her eyes when they'd been standing in front of the fountain. That look he'd tried to dismiss but couldn't ignore.

She wasn't going to let him in.

He thought maybe she wanted to. Hell, he was pretty sure of it. But something in that look had told him that she just *couldn't*.

And the worst of it was that he couldn't blame her. Not a bit.

But even knowing he deserved what he had coming didn't make it any easier to take. So he'd hopped in the car after work, ready to do battle with the Eisenhower. It had been three weeks since Jase had been out to the house, which never happened. And yeah, his dad had made the drive into the city one night for dinner, so it wasn't like he hadn't seen the guy—but it wasn't the same as going home and sitting in the space that had been theirs, and theirs alone, for twenty years. Shooting the shit a while and throwing around a few good-natured jabs just to say they cared.

Maybe scoring a slice of banana bread if Jase was lucky.

Catching a game. He wondered if Emily would be watching a game.

Damn it, why couldn't he stop thinking about her? Why hadn't he been able to pull his head out of his ass for five minutes back in high school and listen to her? Look at her? Look at what the friend he'd been trying to protect was becoming and see who really needed protecting?

Slamming his hands against the wheel, he cursed. Why hadn't he fought for her when there'd still been a chance for any of them to win?

Jase cut the engine. If there wasn't any banana bread, he'd get his dad to show him how to make it.

At the front stoop, he heard the TV coming from inside and pushed through the door the way he'd been doing since he was old enough to reach the knob.

The first thing that reached him was the sound of laughter. Deep and booming, mixed with something…lighter. More melodic. He swallowed. Familiar in a way he shouldn't be thinking about because there was no way—

"Jase," his dad said, jumping up from the couch at the sound of the keys hitting the floor.

His father lifted a hand in Jase's direction, one of those let's-everyone-just-stay-calm moves, but the nervous way his old man's eyes were shifting between Jase and the brunette who'd also risen from the couch but had yet to meet Jase's eyes said Joe Foster was anything but calm. Welcome to the club.

"Is this a joke?" Jase demanded, looking at his father because it was easier than looking at *her*.

"Jase, I'm sorry. I didn't want you to find out like this. I know it must be a shock. Your mom and I, we were just waiting for the right time."

—⁂—

Jase couldn't remember the last time he'd felt like this. The last time he'd had this kind of hollow feeling inside. Or maybe he could, because that day twenty years ago had never really left him.

How could his dad—?

How was it possible that after all this time his mom—? *How?*

He spent the next hour in traffic with that one word ricocheting around his brain as he kept his eyes on the road and paid attention to his speed and the cars around him. Basically making it his mission to live until he could get back to Lakeview where he would safely park his car and then go get blind fucking drunk. Because if ever there was a call for a bender, busting his parents on the couch after not seeing one of them for twenty years seemed like it.

But as he drove east on Belmont, instead of turning on Sheffield for Belfast, he kept going, past the turnoff to his place, toward the lake until he hit Sheridan. Where Emily lived. Was it even possible she'd be home at eight on a Tuesday night instead of neck-deep in whatever activity she'd committed to with whichever of her six hundred best friends she was making time for just then? Probably not. Just like she probably wasn't the right person for him to be going to anyway. But he couldn't make himself turn around.

He just wanted to see her. He wanted someone—soft.

He wanted someone warm. He wanted someone he could count on.

He wanted her. Just to talk. Just for a little while.

He found a spot two blocks up and then walked to her place, feeling the cold leaching into that empty spot inside him despite not being able to feel it anywhere else. It was unsettling in a distant way. Within the lobby, he buzzed her apartment and waited. The seconds turned to minutes, and that cold empty space inside him grew.

She would have answered if she'd been there. Just as well.

Probably better for him to be alone.

He turned to go just as the security door swung open, and there she was. Her hair was pulled up in a messy bun, and she had on a charcoal peacoat with some kind of lumpy, bright-colored scarf wound around her neck a few times.

Christ, she was pretty.

And clearly surprised to see him. "Jase, what are you doing here?"

"Sorry, I should have called. I was just… I thought I'd try my luck. But you're heading out, so I'll catch you another time."

Feeling like an ass, he pushed a hand back through his hair and realized it must have been drizzling outside because his hair was wet.

Emily stepped closer. "I was going out for a beer with… Hey, are you okay?"

Then more urgently, "Jase, what happened?"

Emily had never met his mother. She'd moved to town years after his mom left. But she'd been close enough in high school for a while there to have gathered the broad strokes. Or to have heard the rumors. Hearing that Clara Foster was back, Emily pulled out her phone and told whomever she was meeting that she wouldn't make it.

And that hollow space inside felt just that much smaller.

Up in her apartment, Emily opened a couple of Heinekens and pointed him toward her couch.

"So when did you find out?" she asked, all that softness he'd been looking for right there in her eyes.

"About an hour and a half ago. I hadn't seen as much of my dad as I usually do and thought I'd drive out. I couldn't believe it was really her. It was like a flashback, Em. I mean, they were laughing. They were just sitting there laughing together like the last twenty years hadn't happened. Like she hadn't blown out of town with some douche while we stood there watching the exhaust fade, my dad's heart broken in half. Like she hadn't been the shittiest wife on the books even before that." Jase looked up at the ceiling. "And I'll be damned if my dad didn't look happier tonight than I'd seen him since the day she left."

"So is it a done thing—they're reconciling?" she asked, her voice quiet, like she wasn't sure if she should say the words aloud.

"They moved her things back in Sunday. I guess they were waiting to tell me, to make sure it was right first. Which feels a little strange, seeing as how I'm almost thirty. But here I am having a meltdown, so I guess I haven't outgrown all my childhood issues the way I thought."

Emily rested her hand over the center of his chest. "It's okay to be freaked out about this. The way things were around your mother leaving, I don't know how anyone would be okay with her showing back up."

Jase shook his head, not knowing what to say. What to feel. Except that somehow, being there with Emily, it was better.

He covered her hand with his own, stroking his thumb over her knuckles. "Honestly, I don't know how I am, Em. I mean, it's not my marriage. I get that—but God, I stood there in the house that used to belong to the three of us, and I talked about her like she wasn't even there. I was so pissed and shocked that I basically demanded to know what my dad was thinking, letting the woman who ruined his damned life back into it. How he could even let her past the front door after everything she'd done—screwing around on him, abandoning him. Fucking wrecking him."

"What did he say?" Emily asked gently.

Jase was embarrassed to even think about it. "He wasn't nuts about what I had to say. Told me to put a lid on it."

Actually, his dad had gotten in his face, telling him in no uncertain terms that that was enough.

It had been a blow to the gut, when Jase was the one who'd stayed. The one who had loved Joe even after the months it had taken him to become a functioning parent again.

But then Jase had realized his old man was right.

He shouldn't have said those things about his mother while she was right there. Even if they were true.

Because what he had to say was *family business*, and she wasn't family. If he didn't agree with what his dad was doing, then he should have spoken to him privately about it.

"And your mom?"

He looked up then, not sure what Emily was asking.

"What did she say? Did she apologize or try to hug you or say she missed you or anything?"

Jase shook his head, trying to remember. "I think she said hello. But everything happened pretty quick. It was mostly my dad and me, going back and forth until he asked me to take off. Cool down. Said we'd talk tomorrow. He's coming down here."

When Emily just stared at him, looking confused, Jase shrugged, figuring she didn't get the way it was with his mother. Who would?

"Em, my mom and I were never really close, so I guess it doesn't surprise me that she wasn't all over me at her first opportunity. I know that's not how it's supposed to work with moms, but even before she left, she hadn't really been one to me. Sometimes, though, she'd still been a wife to my dad. So when she left, it was bad. He loved her."

Quietly, Emily asked, "But you didn't?"

The question took him so off guard that all Jase could do was stare at her. Then, finally, he just told her the truth.

"I don't know."

⁓

They'd stayed on the couch a long while after they'd stopped talking. Emily had shifted so her head and hand were resting on his chest, her legs tucked up on the couch, with his arm wrapped around her shoulders.

And at some point they must have fallen asleep. Because now Emily was brushing a few loose strands of strawberry-blond from her sleepy brown eyes. It was a sight Jase could definitely get used to—all that soft, so very close. But he wouldn't have the chance.

The way he'd treated her in the past had consequences in the present. And he couldn't blame her for not being able to trust him.

"I didn't mean to stay so late," he said, reluctantly letting her go.

He took her hand and pulled her up with him, caught her chin with the crook of his finger and met her eyes. "Thank you."

A small furrow dug between her brows as she seemed to search his eyes.

"Em, you okay?"

She shook her head. "I don't want you to go."

Time slowed and his heart thumped hard.

This wasn't what he thought it was. It couldn't be. "Why?"

Lifting one shoulder almost helplessly, she whispered, "Because we're friends, Jase. And I think maybe you could use one a little longer."

"I don't get it. *Friends?*" Lena sneered, like it was some dirty four-letter word. Then, riding her treadmill to the end, she hopped off. "What is that? This is the guy with the proven track record of ruination. And you spent the night together, but *didn't* have sex? It's already seven twelve, and you're standing in my bedroom in some college-era throwback sweat suit and not a lick of makeup. Don't you have a meeting in, like, thirty minutes?"

"Postponed it." Emily's hands were clutched in front of her, her breath coming in a rush like she'd been the one tearing up the miles on Lena's machine instead of just pacing back and forth in front of it while her friend worked out in her bedroom. "Yes. And it was good, Lena. Really, *really* good. He *held me* the whole night."

And God, waking up this morning to that one barely there kiss as Jase leaned over her to say good-bye before he left. *Chills.*

"What does that even mean? I get that at first you were just hooking up. You weren't friends. The well of caring between you was maybe a little shallow. But then you two seemed to find a deeper connection, *while* you were still getting the *goods and services*," Lena added with a meaningful nod, as if Emily had any question about what goods and services were being implied. "And now?"

"Now it means I trust him." Emily hadn't thought she could, but then he'd shown up at her door, hurting like she never wanted to see him hurt. And the biggest, strongest man she knew had trusted her with this piece of himself. A piece that was broken and fragile, and somehow powerful enough to knock down those last walls she'd built against him.

"And whatever happens in the goods-and-services department from here forward, there's going to be friendship at the heart of it."

Lena pulled the elastic from her ponytail and shook out her dark hair. "Okay, that sounds pretty good."

Emily checked her phone and saw a message from Jase.

Belfast tonight for darts?

She smiled, that flutter in her belly going full tilt as she texted back: See you there.

Chapter 19

April

BELFAST WAS EMILY'S NEW FAVORITE BAR.

And not just because she'd gone there that first night with the high of Jase's friendship still fresh on her lips. Or because being on a welcome-hug basis with both Brody and Molly meant she couldn't get within a swallow of the last sip of her drink before some attentive server would swoop in with the offer of another. Or even because her favorite local band, Westher, had been playing when she'd walked in the door and seen Jase grinning at her from over the crowd.

But because Belfast had totally lived up to the hype.

For years, it had been the one watering hole in Chicagoland that she'd avoided like the plague, no matter how many friends raved about it. That's because it was Brody O'Donnel's bar. And everyone knew that Brody and Jase were BFFs of the highest order. If she pretty much wanted to guarantee that she would run into Jase, Belfast was where she would have gone. And until this last week, interacting with Jase hadn't made her to-do list.

But everything was different now.

After darts on Wednesday, she'd found her way back Saturday night with a couple of girlfriends who'd been pushing her to go for months. She'd known Jase had other plans that night—he was seeing a play written by one of his friends—which meant she hadn't felt quite so conspicuous showing up there. She didn't have to worry about seeming like maybe she was hoping for the chance to take things a little further than they'd gone Wednesday night—which hadn't been anywhere. Jase had been deep in the friend zone, barely working a baby toe out to sling his arm around the back of her chair for a minute and a half while she waited for her turn to throw.

Fine by her. It was still the best time she'd had in as long as she could remember.

Tonight was her third straight Wednesday joining the guys for darts and a most momentous occasion, because she and Molly had just soundly beaten Jase and Sean. After that, Sean went to grab another round, and then Molly left on a quest to find out what—or rather who— the holdup might be.

Elbows propped on the tabletop, Jase took a swallow of the Newcastle he was nursing. Then holding the bottle by the neck, he swirled the foamy beer around the bottom.

"Sorry about bailing on our run Sunday," he offered, shooting a quick glance over his shoulder before going on. "Dad called and wanted to grab lunch."

Brows arched, Emily angled herself to face him. Jase and his father hadn't resolved much since the night Jase found his parents together, and she knew the estrangement was eating at him. "How'd it go? Are they still together?"

He took a deep breath and set the bottle down. "Didn't go as well as I'd hoped it would. I mean, I thought by now he'd have seen reason. But she's still there and he says she's staying."

"He loves her?" Emily asked, though the answer was obvious.

"He never stopped." The blue eyes that met hers were filled with frustration. "I just don't get how it's possible. The stuff she did to him before she left was brutal. She slept around on him, took off for days at a time. It wasn't even like she was discreet. Everyone knew. Everyone talked. Everyone pitied him. And that was just the stuff from before she left. After… *Hell.* The mind games, Em. My dad never got over it. He barely got through it. If it hadn't been for—"

Jase cut off, but Emily knew what he'd been about to say.

"Bob Gainer," she supplied, because Eddie had told her the part his father had played in helping the Fosters through that time. How Bob had all but moved Jase into their house while he and the guys had taken shifts getting Joe Foster to pull himself together. Whatever her past with Eddie, nothing could diminish what his family had done for Jase's. She wouldn't want it to.

Jase nodded. "Bob and Ray, Mick and Bear. They were the kind of constant my mom should have been. They got us through."

She leaned a shoulder into Jase's. Supportive. Friendly.

"How did you leave things with your dad?"

A humorless laugh. "Awkward. I mean, he told me I was welcome in the house any time. Which was fucking weird to have him say. And weirder still was the tagged-on caveat that I have to treat Clara with respect."

Emily straightened. "Will you go?"

"I don't know."

"It's okay to need some time, Jase. It's a lot to get used to. Just don't let it keep you from your dad."

"No way. And he wouldn't let that happen. He's going to come out to my place every other Sunday." Jase pinched the bridge of his nose, closing his eyes so those long, dark lashes fanned across his heavy cheekbones. "Like shared custody or something."

She couldn't imagine how difficult it was for him, considering how close he was to his father. She and Jase talked some more, lightening the mood by joking about which sporting events constituted holidays he should fight for with his dad. Super Bowls and Stanley Cup Playoffs were the obvious picks, but Emily thought Jase ought to also get a couple weeks every other year for the Olympics.

In the end they were both laughing so hard that they were wiping tears from their eyes. Slowly their laughter ebbed until they were smiling at each other as they found their breath.

"I needed that," Jase confessed, running his hand over the scarred tabletop before giving it a single knock. "Kinda feelin' like an ass here after all my years of dodging the friends thing, Em. Turns out you make a pretty good one."

Their eyes met and her heart started getting that over-full feeling exclusive to Jase.

"Told you," she said quietly.

He wasn't breaking away. Just giving her that deep-blue, searching look that had the butterflies stirring within her. "I guess you did."

His voice was so deep.

He was sitting so close.

If he leaned in—

Jase leaned back, stretching his arms out to the sides as he scanned the bar. His grin going wider, he jutted his chin toward the bar. "About time, Wyse. What, did you have to go pick the hops yourself?"

Emily turned around in time to catch Sean with his fisted hand giving the air in front of his fly a few crude tugs. *Sean?* Mr. Clean-Cut, all manners, boring…Sean?

Or maybe not.

Sean's eyes cut to hers and she'd swear he blanched, but then the polished facade was back in place—his hand going quickly to the back of his neck.

"Emily, how are your parents?" he asked, going all polite and flashing that politician's smile.

Too late. She'd seen the *Van Wilder* gleam in his eyes.

This guy was no gentleman at all. Which was *awesome*.

"Not a chance, Sean," she said, crossing her arms over her chest Officer Brandt–style, as Molly, who'd been right behind him, crowed "Busted" for the table to hear.

It was almost enough to distract Emily from the sinking feeling in her belly and the question that had come to her the moment before. Had Jase actually thought she'd meant *friends* friends? Or worse…was that what *he'd* meant?

"I don't know what you guys are talking about," Sean stated, confidence coming off him in waves.

"Give it up, man." Jase shook his head. "I swear I don't know why you even try—"

"Because I'm the guy in line to take over Wyse hotels…" Sean leaned in to Jase, his voice low, but not low enough for Emily to miss the grumbled "douche biscuit" before he straightened to finish, "and appearances matter."

Molly was giving him crap about the air jerk and going blind if he kept that up, and Sean was mumbling something about Belfast being his "safe place" while Jase seemed to be watching Emily.

Their eyes met again, and she ached a little at the thought that friendship and sex might be mutually exclusive in Jase's mind. His eyes narrowed, and she looked away, because suddenly the truth she hadn't been ready to accept was impossible to ignore.

She didn't want just sex.

She wasn't imagining being buddies with benefits.

She wanted the whole, real, messy, emotional, cuddly, sexy, affectionate, snuggle-with-me-while-we-watch-a-movie *relationship*.

And Jase was looking at her with the same fond, friendly, platonic smile he had for Sean, who was suggesting that Jase kiss his "beanbag."

Molly threw an arm around Emily's shoulders and gave her a rattling shake. "Emily, meet Sean. Hope you like dick jokes."

As it happened, Emily did like dick jokes, almost as much as she liked the significantly loosened-up version of Sean. She liked laughing with Molly and teasing Jase and not feeling like she needed to guard her words quite so carefully around Sean.

She liked everything until the night wrapped up and they all pulled on their coats and said good-bye like friends do. But without the full-body embrace that was just long enough for the heat from one person to find its way into another. Without the threading of fingers and lingering last contact.

Without the tongue.

Back at her apartment, she'd closed the door, thinking about that night at the hotel with Jase. The feel of his big, bare chest against her back. His arms warm around her. His low rumbling laughter teasing at her ear.

The floor in front of her blurred, and she blinked. Brought her fingers to the corners of her eyes and found them wet.

Tears?

She shouldn't be—

Her phone rang and she straightened, clearing her throat. It could be a client.

Pulling the phone from her pocket, she stalled at seeing the name on the screen.

Jase Foster.

"Jase, what's up? Did I forget something at the bar?" She sounded normal. Totally.

"No, nothing like that. I've got this wedding on Saturday for a buddy's little brother I got into our IT department at the bank. Think I can convince you to go with me?"

Her heart tripped, clumsy and uncertain, because he'd taken Molly to lots of weddings. It could be the same sort of friendly gesture.

"Sure, that's what friends are for, right?" she replied, fishing just a little as she cut through her apartment toward her closet.

Either way, she needed a dress. One that would challenge the most platonic of intentions.

Jase's laugh was low.

"Yeah, but I'm not asking you to go as my friend." His voice deepened, taking on a persuasive rumble. "There'll be dancing."

She stopped, turning away from her closet and crossing her room to her lingerie drawer instead. The smile on her face spread like the warmth through her chest. "Only if you promise not to drop me on my ass if I accidentally step on your foot."

"Your *sweet* ass, Emily. I promise," he said with another low laugh she could almost feel. "It's a *date* then. Pick you up at three."

A date. Heat swirled through her belly as she closed the drawer.

A date required something new and drop-dead spectacular.

She needed to go shopping.

"So this is a date with Jase Foster." Emily sighed, leaning against the door to her place, her heart seeming to skip every other beat as she glanced down at the bouquet of oriental lilies, spray roses, and snapdragons. "Definitely different."

Jase chuckled, looking down at himself and then around him. "I just walked in."

Yeah, he had, and looking painfully good too. He'd dressed in a gorgeous blue suit with a sapphire tie to match his eyes, his neatly mussed hair so perfect it would give Henry Cavill envy. One look at him and it was as if a giant digital clock had appeared above his head, counting down to when she could get him back here. To when she'd be able to get her fingers into those thick, dark waves and make them not so neatly mussed.

"But you're picking me up, instead of meeting me at the church. You brought me *flowers*."

"Wow, if only I'd known how low the bar was set."

Not at all. Not even close.

But after all the waiting, the wondering, and—God help her—the hoping, she was experiencing every little detail on the grandest scale. Like the compliment he'd paid her when she opened the door. The one that had turned her knees to mush, not so much because of the words themselves but the way he'd said them. Rubbing that big hand of his across his mouth as he slowly looked her over from head to toe, and then murmured that it wasn't good manners to show up the bride on her wedding day. *Without* backing her up against the wall with his hand beneath her skirt.

Okay, that she wasn't entirely sure was a good thing. But it was sweet. And different. And she had to believe that if she played her cards right, there'd be some quality wall time in her near future.

"That dress is something else, Em." He looked like he might be about to run his hands over the flowy skirt she'd fallen in love with on sight but resisted. Leaning in, Jase dropped a kiss on her cheek. "You look beautiful."

She turned into him, her mouth less than an inch from his, her breath thin as she met his eyes.

He could have had her then. That very second if he wanted her. Backed her into the living room and had her on the couch, or just taken her right there against the coat closet door. Messed up the hair and makeup she'd taken nearly an hour to get right. And the only thing she'd have to say about it would be *yes*.

Instead, Jase cupped her cheek and, with a pained look in his eyes, brushed it once with his thumb before stepping back.

"I'm trying to be good here, Em. I swore I'd give you at least one real date before carrying you back to that bed and doing all the things I want to do to you."

"Why?" she asked, alarmed at his sudden bout of crazy. "That's nice, but unnecessary. *Really*." Then stepping into the space Jase had just stepped out of, she walked her fingers up his chest. "Ooh, loophole. We could forget the bed altogether, and you could do all those things right here."

She tapped the floor with her bare foot. "This spot looks comfy."

"*Emily.*"

Her eyes trailed over him in a way she could only hope didn't make him feel too cheap, but she just couldn't help it. "Maybe you could just tell me all the things."

"Behave," he groaned, looking like he was really suffering.

"Fine, I'll finish getting ready. There's a vase under the sink. How about you take care of my flowers?"

She excused herself to take care of the last touches, adding a pavé link bracelet that was just the right amount of chunky and a pair of four-inch, strappy gold heels that contrasted nicely with the aquamarine color of her dress—and did things for her legs that even she had to admire.

A dab of perfume at her wrists…and another behind her knees, because with a date like Jase, a girl could only be counted on to behave for so long.

When they were ready to leave, Jase helped her with her coat, standing too close behind her so she could feel the heat of his body against her back, all that hard muscle tempting her to press into him and see how his restraint held up when truly tested. He scattered her plans by ducking in to press his lips against the side of her throat.

Once.

For about a second.

"Let's go, gorgeous."

Damn him.

They'd driven up to Rogers Park at the far north end of the city, and Emily was ashamed to admit how seeing a house of God with Jase in such close proximity affected her.

He took her hand and kissed her softly between her knuckles, something in his eyes telling her he knew exactly where her express-freight-to-hell thoughts were headed.

"Ready?"

Mustering a shred of that old spite, she narrowed her eyes on him. *You did this to me.*

He winked. "Don't you forget it."

The wedding was lovely. There was no chance of Tyra being overshadowed, and Bill's smile was filled with such love that though Emily hadn't met either of them before, she found herself dabbing a tear or two when they finally kissed.

Curious whether Jase had been as affected as she was, she turned to see a look in his eyes that she didn't recognize but felt to the deepest part of her.

"Beautiful wedding," she said, suddenly feeling shy.

Jase opened his mouth to say something, but then took her hand instead and nodded, looking up to the happy couple.

Outside the church, Jase's hand slid down to wrap possessively around her hip, tucking her body close to his as they walked back to the car.

She'd never been able to walk with anyone this way. Her height made it damn near impossible, but not with Jase. With Jase, for the first time, Emily felt like she'd found her perfect fit.

———

Jase knew what Emily did to his restraint and that he'd been playing with fire from the second he walked into her place instead of having her meet him downstairs. But he hadn't been able to resist building the anticipation. Teasing her with the light touches he knew got to her almost as much as seeing the evidence of their effects got to him—the trailing goose bumps, the parted lips, and puffs of breath. The way his name sometimes slipped past her lips in that needy way. He'd wanted her thinking about him, *ready* for him, *aching* for him the way he'd been aching for her for—hell, too damn long.

And now he had what he'd been dying for.

Emily giving him that soft smile and sexy laugh, those little looks that made him feel like he was the luckiest fucking guy on the planet—because *how*? After everything, how had he gotten this girl?

They were dancing. The party was winding down, the music was slow, and he had Emily pulled close as they swayed to Ella Fitzgerald's timeless "Unforgettable."

Her fingers threaded into his hair where her hands met behind his neck.

"So how long does a girl have to behave on a date with you, Jase?" she asked, her smile turning just a little wicked.

"You're killing me, Emily." But damned if he wanted her to stop.

Her hips turned within his hold, moving in time with the music. Following his lead. Making him think about his hands on her hips when there weren't any clothes in the way, and how hot it was when she moved over him.

"Am I?" she asked, knowing full well she was.

Forcing his fingers to relax where he'd started working up a satisfying grip, he pulled her in closer. Close enough so their bodies barely brushed with each step and sway of the dance.

She noticed.

Then leaning in to her ear, he started talking. "I've been telling myself I can't keep risking getting caught with you. But then I see that room at the back of the hall, where everyone dropped off the gifts at the beginning of the reception, but no one's been in for the past hour, and I think about slowly dancing you to the edge of the floor, winding our way through those round tables, and slipping into that room."

Emily had fallen out of sync with the music, her movements slowing as he spoke.

"I keep thinking about getting my hand under all this flowy business and finding out how wet I can get you."

"*Jase*." Her fingers had tightened in his hair, pulling in the way that drove him nuts.

"I keep wondering how many different ways I can get you to say my name before someone walks in and sees me *taking* what I *couldn't wait for*."

She shuddered, and when he straightened, her eyes were hazy with need.

She turned, looking at the door to that little fantasy, and heat rushed into her cheeks as Tyra's mom and great-aunt walked out.

Laughter punched out of Jase's lungs, and Emily grabbed the lapels of his jacket and buried her face in his chest, giving in to the humor of the moment before peeking up at him.

"Well, we know the room's empty now."

Damn, this woman.

Chapter 20

IT WAS AFTER TEN WHEN JASE ADMITTED DEFEAT. THE reception was still going strong, and from what his buddy had told him, the hall was booked until two. No way was he going to make it that long. Though Femily seemed to have embraced this prolonged torture with open arms. That wicked, wonderful mind of hers was finding new and creative ways to short-circuit his brain every five minutes or so.

She had a gift.

The last notes of the pop ballad faded, and Jase caught Emily's hand. Backing her through the crowd, he led her from the dance floor to the coatroom. Where he did not pull her in, despite Emily's sly grin as she asked him, "Is it later?"

So tempting, but what he wanted from Emily tonight, *for* Emily tonight, was more than that. What he wanted would take time and—if they didn't want the cops showing up—walls and a locked door too. "Soon."

Jase used the last of his restraint on the drive home, keeping his eyes on the road instead of the way Emily was shifting her legs in the seat beside him. And it paid off, because now Emily was unlocking her apartment, her fingers wrapped lightly around the lapel of his coat.

Like she thought he might make a move to leave if she let go.

Not likely.

Her door was open, her apartment lit only by the overhead hall light she'd left on.

She turned to him, those big brown eyes drifting to his mouth. "Jase," she murmured.

"I know."

His hand curved around the back of her neck, pulling her toward him as he lowered his mouth to hers, sinking slowly into the kiss he'd been dreaming of. So sweet, and that soft sigh was sweeter still.

He hadn't kissed her like this before. Like they had all the time in the world. Like it was about the journey, not the destination. Like he wanted more than her body. And more than anything, he wanted it to last.

There'd always been too many other things driving them. But not tonight.

Tonight was about something new. Something pure. Something right.

Her lips parted as they met in that soft back-and-forth glide.

He tasted her then, a slow stroke of his tongue against the lush pad of her bottom lip.

She trembled, her hands fisting against the fabric of his shirt, an urgency rising within them both.

Angling to deepen the kiss, he groaned as she opened wider beneath him, offering what he needed to take. Pressing closer. Clutching tighter.

Yes.

He reached past her, catching the side of the door toward the top, and pushing it closed behind them. And then they were alone. Eyes locked with his, Emily backed down the hall, those killer heels clicking against the hardwood with each step. Mesmerized by the sight of her, he watched as she lifted one beckoning arm to him. Jerking his tie free and yanking his belt loose, he followed, leaving just enough distance to tease them both.

He started on the buttons next and she stopped where she was, her lips parting on a gasp, her eyes glazing with lust. Christ, her desire was so damned sexy.

She leaned against the wall halfway to her bedroom, knee cocked so one sexy heel rested flat against the wall behind her, while her hands worked a slow roam over that flowy fabric at her thighs.

Her eyes flicked to his before returning to where he was half through with his shirt. "Don't stop on my account. I'll just hang out here and enjoy the show."

"You want to watch, Emily?" he asked, taking his time with the next button.

She licked her lip and nodded.

"What about me?" he asked, jutting his chin toward the dress she hadn't made nearly enough progress in taking off.

"What about you, Jase?" she replied, a sensual challenge in her tone that flipped every switch he had.

He swallowed hard, wondering how he'd ever thought *she'd* be the one to end up ruined for all others. "Yeah, I'm good."

He tugged the tails of his shirt from his pants and freed the last few buttons, completely caught up in the way Emily responded to his shrugging out of one shoulder and then the other.

She was hot as hell, and she wasn't really doing anything at all. It was just the look on her face. The need.

His shirt hit the floor, and those perfect white teeth pressed into her soft bottom lip. So pretty.

"God, you have the best body. Not that your ego needs any more stroking, but from the first time I saw you, you took my breath away."

High school. That's what she was talking about. "Yeah?"

"I liked how tall you were. But it was more than that. I think even if you'd been an inch shorter than me, I'd have been drooling over those shoulders and how broad your chest was. Is. You're just so solid, but in a way that's the perfect mix of genes and athleticism. I had so much trouble concentrating in classes around you."

Jase undid the top button of his pants. "Believe me, I was worse off. I dropped a half grade in every class we had together. You nearly cost me my 4.0."

"Liar," she said, skimming her hands up her belly and teasing him by stopping just beneath the swell of her breasts.

He growled, wanting her to touch them.

Maybe she read his mind. Because now her palms were cupping her breasts, and his fly was unzipping by the power of his hard-on alone. He wanted her to take that dress off and to see her play with those petal-pink nipples until there wasn't anything soft about them. And he wanted to watch her do it while she watched him.

"I thought you were beautiful. You know I did."

A shadow passed behind her eyes, but then it was gone.

Releasing the catch behind her neck, she eased the straps of her dress down her shoulders and arms. "And now?"

He finished with the zipper and slid his thumbs into

the straining waistband of his boxer briefs. Pulled them over the top of his cock and pushed them low so Emily could see him. How much he wanted her. What she did to him.

Expelling a harsh breath, she sought out his eyes, asking him with a look for what she wanted.

He stroked a hand up and down his length, doing it again when she slowly peeled the top of her dress down far enough for him to see the tight pink tips of her nipples.

"Beautiful."

"Do it again," she whispered, nodding to where his hand still held his cock.

Oh fuck.

"What, baby, this?" he asked, knowing damn well.

A slow heat had been burning up her neck and settled into her cheeks, hinting at that shy girl thing she'd had going back when he first met her. The one that pushed all his buttons.

But add to that this sexy-as-hell bit of kink.

God, she was perfect.

He stroked again, slowly. Setting a rhythm that wouldn't leave him embarrassing himself within the next thirty seconds. If he focused really hard on banking regulations. Maybe.

But then her hands were on the move again, her fingers playing with her nipples. Rubbing back and forth as he watched. As he stroked. As his breath went ragged and she planted both heels on the floor, her knees looking like they wouldn't hold her much longer.

"*Jase.*" And if the needy quality of his name alone wasn't enough, the next words she said sure as hell were. "I can't wait anymore."

He closed the distance between them in a flash. His hands gathered all that sexy skirt while Emily wrapped her smooth hand around him, stroking once herself before letting go when he caught her behind the knee and pulled her against his hip.

Tugging her soaked panties to the side, he groaned, making contact with her wet heat.

"I'm going to make you come like this, Em," he told her, sweeping a single finger through all that slippery moisture. Spreading it around her swollen sex. Circling back to that throbbing point that had her eyes locking with his and her breath fracturing across his lips.

Around and around, slow and soft.

Her body was tensing, her grip on his shoulder and side tightening.

"Yes."

"And after I make you come with my hands"—he stroked back to her opening and dipped inside, felt her clench around him, as she gasped his name—"I'm going to make you do it again with my mouth."

Another shallow thrust of his finger and he took her mouth with his kiss. With his tongue.

He sank deep, then deeper. Stroking in and out. Kissing her like he was touching her, *like she was his*.

Just the thought had his cock pulsing between them.

He added a second finger and her hips were rocking into his thrusts. Her pleas falling against his lips. "Please…like that… Yes, *yes!*"

Enough. He needed his mouth on her.

"Come for me, baby," he growled against her ear, pressing his thumb to the spot where she needed him most.

"Jase!"

Liquid heat spilled down his fingers as Emily spasmed around him, her inner walls hugging him rhythmically.

So damn hot.

And then he had her in his arms as he strode the short distance to her bedroom.

Emily's eyes were wide, hazed with the kind of satisfaction that got a guy off just from looking at it. "That was—"

"Just the beginning, Em."

He was sucking his fingers.

Emily had never seen anything sexier in her entire life as the powerhouse of a man in front of her, his shirt hanging open over that hard, sculpted torso, the fly of his suit pants undone—though he must have tucked himself back inside his boxer briefs—as he slowly licked her pleasure from his hand.

She gulped.

But then Jase went to his knees in front of her, that urgent, intense look in his eyes, and told her to take off her dress.

Not asked. Not suggested.

Told.

While he was on his knees!

Legs backed up to her bed, heart racing, she reached behind her and, with trembling hands, eased the partially open zipper down the rest of the way. Then shifting her hips slowly back and forth, she let the dress pool around her feet. Which left her in a pair of itty-bitty, bronze silk panties trimmed with lace, her gold heels, linked bracelet, and the chandelier earrings she'd hoped weren't too much.

Jase shook his head, almost like he couldn't believe what he was seeing.

Her skin was hot, her sex and breasts achy as Jase smoothed his palms over her hips and thighs, and then, hooking his fingers into the string-cut sides of her panties, slid them down her legs.

"Sit."

Another shockingly hot not-suggestion, accompanied by his hands settling firmly at her hips and guiding her to the edge of the bed.

Just as well. Her knees wouldn't have lasted another second the way he'd been looking at her.

"Jesus, Em," he said, letting his hands coast down the length of her thighs. "I can't wait."

He opened her, spreading her knees with his hands and then the bulk of his shoulders. His mouth working hot, wet kisses from her knee up, up, up…until he was *there*.

She cried out at the first brush of his mouth. Even seeing it coming hadn't been enough to prepare her. And then he was kissing her like he'd kissed her mouth. Softly, gently, thoroughly. The pressure building with her need until he'd found her center…

"So damned sweet, Em."

…and licked.

Another cry, and she fell back on her elbows as her body clenched with a need Jase was both satisfying and exploiting with every lick, nibble, and swirl.

She'd come less than five minutes ago, but already that delicious tension was lacing through her center again. Tightening the places that had gone lax.

Her knees were opened wide, Jase's hands cupping her bottom as he held her to his mouth. So good.

Swirling the point of his tongue, he made her pant and grasp at his hair.

Then he was running that firm point back down to where—

"Jase!"

—he speared inside. Wet and slick and hard, he thrust in and out of her until she was mindless, her head beginning to thrash.

"Do you need more, baby?" he asked, again rubbing his mouth against the tender spread of her sex. Making her writhe. Because he knew.

"Yes," she panted, tipping her hips into his kiss. "More. Please."

And then he was kissing that straining, aching little bud, closing his lips around it as—oh God, yes—he filled her with his fingers. That subtle stretch was just what she needed, the slow pumping motion taking her higher, faster. His fingers flexed inside her, twisting slowly, stroking over that hidden spot.

She was close…so close…

Teeth sinking into her bottom lip, she watched as Jase looked up to meet her eyes while he pleasured her.

That look…that connection…Jase…

He sucked, drawing hard against her. And the world came apart.

She screamed, tumbling through sensation like she'd never known, pleasure like she'd never imagined.

But still it wasn't enough. Barely reaching the other side of the climax of the century, Emily tugged desperately at Jase's hair, her legs squirming in an effort to get him where she needed him to be.

"Please, Jase. All of you."

She wanted him inside her, his body hot and hard above hers. The crazy, intense eye contact doing things that made this more than sex.

She needed it.

Jase's hair stood on end in utter disarray, and sweat beaded his forehead as he shucked the last of his clothes and climbed up her waiting body.

Her knees coasted up the outside of his hips, her gold heels at the backs of his thighs urging him as she met his kiss, tasted herself on his lips and tongue. She was shaking with need, her body begging.

Jase's touch had gone rough as he pulled her to him, like he'd spent the last of his restraint. Or maybe not.

"Condom," he ground out through gritted teeth, already beginning to reverse his path. "One second, Em."

Her heel at Jase's ass stopped him from retreating any farther.

"You know I'm on the pill. And I've always been safe." Smoothing her fingertips over the heavily muscled terrain of Jase's chest, she asked, "Is there any reason we can't—"

His mouth crashed down on hers, a savage sort of growl emanating from deep in his chest as one powerful arm wrapped beneath her, pulling her up and into him. Holding her close.

Then against her lips, he answered, "I always use protection. *Always.* But with you, Em, *Christ.* I want to feel you around me. With you"—his brows furrowed as he searched her eyes—"I want *everything.*"

She could barely breathe. The weight of that single word resting over the center of her chest was almost too much to bear. With any other man, at any other time, she would have frozen up under a statement like that. Shoved it off her and started backing away. It would have been the end. But now, looking up into the deep blue of Jase's eyes, that weight was a welcome one. And instead of the end, it felt like the beginning of something she hadn't let herself think about in ten years.

Reaching for his face, she kissed him. Slowly. Tenderly. She whispered, "Then take it."

"*Emily.*"

Oh God, he was pushing inside her, sinking in steadily with one velvety soft, steely hard thrust that cost her the air in her lungs. No barriers. Nothing to mute the sensation. Nothing to dull the pleasure's edge of Jase filling her with as much as she could take.

"Wait," she begged, pressing her forehead against his shoulder, as she wound her fingers into his hair. "I can't… It's too much…too good…too soon."

It was so right it terrified her.

But then Jase was smoothing his palm over her cheek, gently tipping her head back.

"Look at me, Em. That's right, sweetheart." He brushed the pad of his thumb across her bottom lip. "I've got you."

She believed him. Trusted him. And then she gave herself to him.

Cupping the side of her face, he kissed her, slipped his tongue between her lips softly, slowly. His hips started to move, pulling back, dragging his thick shaft over a million too-sensitive nerves, making her moan and gasp before he sank deep, rocking his hips so for one fleeting second she felt him *everywhere*.

"Yes," she gasped when he did it again, and then

again after that, falling into a rhythm where every pass upped the sensation, ramped the pleasure, destroyed the last of her defenses.

"I missed you, Em," he admitted on a harsh breath. Her lashes fluttered as she worked to meet his eyes. "I missed the way it feels when we're together like this. I missed being able to touch you."

Still moving inside her, he braced on one arm and pressed his palm to her cheek. "I missed you looking at me like you are right now."

She wanted to ask him what he was seeing in her eyes. If he knew the last of her secrets. That she was falling. If he knew how terrifying it was to give in and just let go. But then he canted forward, shifting just enough so on every deep thrust, his groin kissed the open spread of her sex. That spot that made her mindless.

"Jase!"

He was driving into her now. Faster. Harder.

Over and over and—

"I missed watching you come for me, Em."

—over again.

"Come, baby."

Her body seized, clenching hard around him as she cried out his name and moaned into his mouth when he gave her his kiss, pushing her orgasm even further by adding the deep thrust of his tongue.

And then finally, when she'd ridden the wave as far as it would take her, Jase drove deep once more. His big body tensed above hers. The muscles along his neck and shoulders flexed as he spilled inside her.

It had never been like this.

And she never wanted it to stop.

The sun had been up for hours by the time Emily and Jase found their way out of bed. Now, beneath the spray of the shower, Jase held her with one arm around her middle, her back to his front.

"I'm pretty sure we're clean." Emily sighed contentedly as he made another sudsy pass around her breasts with the bath sponge.

"If it was *clean* I was after, we'd have been dried off thirty minutes ago."

Emily laughed, her head falling back against his shoulder. "So what you're after is something *dirty*, then?"

She could feel the curve of his lips against her neck. "Usually."

But not right then.

She got it. This wasn't about sex. Or rather it wasn't just about sex. It was about *being together*.

"I meant what I said last night, Em." He hung the sponge on its hook, loosening his hold on her just enough so she could turn to face him and wrap her arms around his neck. "I missed you."

Her heart was doing that slow, almost painful thudding. The kind that might make a cautious person worry just a little, even if they didn't want it to stop.

"I've been right here. We've hung out a few times every week."

He nodded, sending a drop of water running from the damp Superman curl falling over his brow. "And being friends with you... It means a lot to me. I could have been happy with it if that's all you wanted. But sweetheart, *this* is different."

Pushing to her toes, she pressed a lingering kiss to his lips. "Different good."

Catching one of her hands, he gave it a kiss. "Definitely good."

The corner of his mouth hitched in that sexy way of his as he examined her fingers. "You're turning into a prune. Let's get out of here."

They dried off together, and Emily again amended her previous assertion about the sexiest thing she'd ever seen. Because Jase standing there with her Blue Lagoon towel wrapped low around his hips while he used a hand towel to dry the damp mess of his hair... She swallowed. Definitely a contender.

Heck, she could see the muscled indent at the side of his ass.

Propping a hip against the sink, she settled in to enjoy the view.

Snapping twice in rapid succession, Jase veed his index and middle fingers in the universally recognized *Eyes up here, perv* flag.

"What?" she asked, only bothering to meet his eyes for a second before letting them drop again. This time getting distracted by the muscles banding across his abdomen and the trim line of dark hair bisecting them.

Hawt.

"Get dressed," Jase instructed with a warm laugh. "I'm taking you to Ann Sather for breakfast."

Emily's belly perked up, and she straightened, glancing around the still-steamy room. She grabbed a hair elastic, stuck her toothbrush in her mouth, and skipped out of the bathroom.

Jase's body was mouthwatering…but Ann Sather's cinnamon rolls were nothing short of a miracle.

Brushing her teeth with one hand, she wrestled herself into panties and a suitably stretchy pair of yoga pants. She passed Jase pulling on his suit from the night before as she ducked back in to spit.

"I'll agree to stopping by your place for a change of clothes before we go, but you better promise to be fast." She rinsed and then turned back to him, ready to elaborate on what exactly constituted fast when she stopped short at the accusing eyes locked on her.

"I *knew* it," he stated, his voice thick with censure and…satisfaction?

Something told her she was in trouble, sort of, maybe…

"What?" Maybe that sounded a little defensive. Coupled with her crossed arms and the step back she'd taken, possibly a lot.

Jase was shaking his head at her, reaching into the bathroom, and then towing her back out. Pulling her to him and pinning her there as he grinned down into her face.

"You are the most competitive woman I've ever met."

Yeah. But it wasn't like that was something new, so what…?

Following Jase's outstretched arm to her open closet door and the *dartboard* she'd mounted against it two weeks earlier, she cringed. Just a little.

"Oh, that."

"I asked you how you upped your game so fast. And what did you say? Natural talent or some such BS?"

Cocking a brow, she corrected him. "It might have been 'I'm just that good.'"

He bit his lip and looked her over. "You can't stand to lose."

A puff of laughter escaped her. "Like you can?"

"How many hours of practice did it take?" he asked, his sexy, stubbled jaw so close she just wanted to lean into him and bite it.

"Not as many as you *wished* it took." Okay, probably twice that many. But he was right; she'd *really* wanted to win. *And she had.*

His focus dropped to her mouth before returning to her eyes. "That so?"

Her breath was coming faster. "In your face, Foster."

Catching her by the backs of the thighs, he hoisted her, squealing, over his shoulder.

"Jase!" Her hands were on his ass, his thighs. Her laughter spilling free like she was sixteen again. "Let me go!"

He tossed her onto the bed and crawled over her, using his body to cage her in. Turning her insides molten with one hot look. "Not for all the cinnamon rolls in Ann Sather, baby."

Chapter 21

May

BELFAST DID A PRETTY SOLID WEEKDAY BUSINESS, BUT with the steady drizzle they'd had over the past two days, Jase wasn't entirely surprised to find only two of the four pool tables in use and a handful of available seats at the typically standing-room-only bar.

Catching Jill's eye from where she was waiting on an order at the end of the bar, he motioned for a beer.

"Newcastle?" she mouthed, because even with the reduced crowd, there was too much noise to hear.

He nodded and then glanced down at the phone that had started to vibrate in his hand.

Emily.

Signaling that he'd be back, he pointed to the table where Max, Sean, and Molly were already gathered. Jill nodded. And he stepped back out to the sidewalk so he'd be able to hear.

"Hey, gorgeous, meeting get out early?" *Early* being a relative term since it was already after seven.

"It did, but now I've got another one coming up in a half hour. It'll probably be close to nine before I get over there."

Jase frowned. Not because of the timing. That was how it went with Emily's job. She was a drop-of-the-hat, any-hour, get-it-done-and-done-right woman when it came to work—or anything she cared about. Anyone.

It was the sound of her voice, the drawn-out quality to her breath, that gave him pause.

"Em, what's going on?"

She sighed through the line and he felt it wrap around his chest and pull. She was upset.

"It's this account. We busted ass landing it, and everything was going great until one of our junior associates came up with an idea they 'accidentally' copied the client on. They thought Charlie Teller would hit our mark as a celebrity spokesman."

"Yeah, I know the name." He'd seen *Forest for the Trees* like every other guy in America, and it had been hard to miss the media feeding frenzy when, after taking home a best supporting actor award at the Oscars, Teller announced he'd had it with the Hollywood bullshit.

"Everybody does. He'd be perfect. Only I've been trying to score a meeting with this guy for two years and can't get anywhere near him. But because our client saw his name, now he's all they want. And they're talking about jumping ship if we can't get him."

"If you can't get him, no one else is going to be able to either," Jase said, certain beyond a shadow of a doubt that he was right. "And screw this client. If they're shortsighted enough to miss what they have with you, then you don't want them. There are hundreds of brands or companies or industries or empires out there just waiting for you to land them. Dump these losers. You've got—"

Emily's soft laughter cut him off where he was. The sound hit him hard, but in all the right places.

"That's what I needed," she said quietly, the smile back in her voice. "*That's* why I called."

Jase kicked at a crumbling section of curb. "For my stellar advice?"

Another laugh, even better than the first. "Not really. I just knew you'd make me feel better. And you did."

Simple words. Ones he'd heard from different women at different times over the years. But they'd never mattered to him like they did in that moment.

"I've gotta run," she said, the sounds of her gathering up her things in the background. "Save a beer for me. I'm going to need it. Actually, some food too. I haven't eaten anything but that granola bar you stuck in my bag this morning."

"Text me when you're leaving, and I'll have a beer and a burger waiting for you. The Stampede with the bacon done extra crispy the way you like and extra barbecue sauce on the side for your fries."

"My hero," she purred, teasing him.

But he'd take it because, damn, she made him want to be just that.

"You know it, baby."

"Bye, Jase."

Jase pocketed his phone and followed a couple of women huddled under an umbrella back into Belfast. Stepping past them, he headed to the table where Molly, Sean, and Max were finishing what he'd guess had been a couple of burgers and a basket of fish and chips for Moll.

"Sorry I'm late," he said, snagging one of Sean's fries before hanging his overcoat on a hook on the wall.

Max dropped a crumpled napkin on his plate. "What'd you do, swim over?"

Jase pushed his hair back from his brow, his hand

coming away wet. "Guess I didn't realize how hard it was coming down."

Or how long he'd been standing in it.

"Emily's held up with another meeting," he said, grabbing the empty chair next to Molly. "But she'll be over in an hour or so."

Sean slumped back in his chair, hand over his chest. "Thank *God*, man. I was worried."

Molly flicked his ear, earning herself a hissed "demon woman" from Sean, though Jase was pretty sure half the shit the guy pulled was to get a rise out of her. The other half being for Max.

"Ahh, bite me," Jase suggested, reaching for the beer Jill had waiting for him. Then nodding across to Sean, he added, "Saw your ugly mug in the paper on Sunday."

Sean shifted in his chair.

"Yeah, hospital benefit. It wasn't too bad."

"You and Valerie looked pretty comfortable." At least from the snap they'd caught with her hand on his lapel and Sean looking down into her face, his smile at least close to the real thing. Or at least the real thing when he was with the guys.

The other smile, the polite one he reserved for dates and public appearances… Hell, with all the play it got, that one might have been real too.

Sean wagged his head. "She's a good girl. Smart, stylish. Nice. And I mean not just faking-it-for-the-boyfriend nice. But really nice."

What Sean didn't have to say was that she also met the other criteria, making her eligible as a maybe Mrs. Wyse. She'd gone to the right schools. Knew the right people. Came preapproved and hand-selected by the parental units.

"That's great, man. Hey, Emily has tickets to the symphony in two weeks. She suggested you guys join us."

Molly's beer hit the table with a thud, bringing all eyes to her. "Sorry, it slipped." Then she hopped up from her seat and started stacking the plates and silverware from their meals. She wasn't working, but she probably wanted to check in with Brody anyway. "Want anything while I'm up?" she asked.

They were good, so she headed back to the kitchen.

Sean rubbed a hand over his mouth, seeming to weigh the idea of joining them for the symphony. "I wasn't planning on seeing her again quite that soon, but that'd be cool. She'd like it. Text me the date and time, and I'll have her check her calendar."

Jase nodded, used to the way Sean handled his dates.

Sean wanted to get married. He wanted a life like the one his parents had. He wanted to be his dad, and he was well on his way. He'd gone to his father's school, now worked as an executive in his father's company, and lived in the apartment below his parents in his father's hotel. The only hitch seemed to be the girl. He hadn't found just the right partner yet.

Jase had a few ideas as to why that was, but he'd given up trying to talk relationship sense into the guy back in college. Besides, until Emily, their relationship management techniques hadn't been much different.

He laughed to himself thinking about his date-night rules and how he'd all but blown them to hell within the first week of Emily granting him more-than-friends status. Now they spent the night together at one of their places more often than they spent the night apart.

He checked his watch. Man, he hoped Emily's second

meeting was going better than the first. He kept thinking about the sound of her voice at the beginning of that call.

Max was giving Sean shit about the picture from the paper looking like love, and asking whether Sean's parents were already picking out invitations, when Molly came back with the darts.

"Okay, ladies," she crooned. "Ready for your weekly shaming?"

Apparently not, because Jase and Max beat the snot out of Molly and Sean.

"It's the trash talk, Moll. Just keep it coming," Jase urged, getting ready to start the next game. "Fires me up every time."

Bull's-eye.

"Aww, shit," Molly moaned, as Sean started dancing around on the balls of his feet, shaking out his head and shoulders like a fighter getting ready for a big match.

Handing over the darts, Jase stepped back, checking the message that had just come through on his phone.

> Mtg over but haven't got it in me to hit the bar.
> Going home to collapse in a heap and eat left-
> over Thai from Mon.

He stared at the message, hating that Emily was feeling so beaten down.

In the past, if a woman he'd been dating had had a rough day, he'd have been grateful for the out. It wasn't that he didn't have any feelings or that the women didn't matter. Of course they did. But those relationships hadn't been about support and friendship. They'd been about fun. End of story.

Tonight, though, he didn't want to wait until Emily was in better spirits to see her. He just wanted to be with her. But only if that was what she wanted too.

Am I still coming over? he texted back.

After a second: Yes pls.

Then a few seconds later, Have fun. See you later.

Why did that feel like he'd just scored a slam-dunk?

"Dude, you going to hang on your phone all night, mooning over your *special friend*?" Sean asked, holding the darts out for Jase to take.

Pocketing the device, he shook his head.

"Nope. No more calls."

Max's brows pulled together and then went wide as he barked out a laugh. "No way, man."

Way.

Slumped against the back wall of the elevator, Emily was pretty sure the ride up from the lobby to her floor was going to kill her. She'd never make it. Not with gravity getting in on the beat-down this day had already given her.

That meeting. She'd known it was going to be bad, but…

Pressing her palms into her eyes, she tried to ease the throbbing behind them. Telling herself it wasn't her fault.

The elevator dinged and she heard the doors open. Knew she was only a few steps from home. From food. Wine. And eventually Jase.

Which meant that unless she wanted him to find her riding this car up and down like it was her eternal penance, she needed to drag her butt out of it.

With a heavy sigh, she dropped her hands and opened her eyes.

"Shit!" she shrieked, her heart slamming against her ribs.

Arms crossed, one shoulder propped against the open elevator door, Jase stood smiling in at her. "Think you're ready to make the trek down to your place, or should I carry you?"

She smiled. Something she hadn't been expecting to happen for another few hours. "What are you doing here?"

Jase pushed off the door and reached in to take Emily's computer bag as she stepped out.

"That Thai food can't be good anymore. Figured after the day you'd had, you might want something better."

That's when she smelled it. Grilled meat, hot grease, and enough fat and carbs to merit an EMT standing by. *The Stampede.*

Sure enough, down by her door she spotted the two white paper bags—geez, how much food had he brought?—a bottle of wine, and a movie.

This was going to be super embarrassing if she started to cry, but her chest was already pushing past that too-full place, because the whole way home, all she'd been thinking was how much she wanted to see him, how badly she wanted to feel his arms around her, and now *Jase was here*.

"Thank you," she managed a little brokenly, hating what a mess she must be.

"Hey, come here." And then he gave her exactly what she needed. Right there in the seventh-floor hall, he wrapped his arms around her and just held her.

She tried to fight it, but her shoulders quaked.

"That bad?" he asked against the top of her head, his hand smoothing down her back.

"They made me fire him," she sniffed, thinking of how the kid had tried to hold it together. How he'd asked her what he was supposed to do.

"The junior associate who sent the email?"

She nodded, knowing the tears had her beat.

"Ahh, Em, I'm sorry."

An hour later, they'd talked out Emily's day and Jase was refilling their glasses in the kitchen. Tucked into the corner of the couch with her arms folded over the back, she asked what had happened at Belfast.

"Did everyone take off early?"

"Nah, they'll probably be there another hour at least." Jase stuck the cork in the bottle and then headed back into the living room to join her.

"Jase, I feel guilty about messing up your night." When she'd come home, all she'd been able to think was how glad she was to see him there. How much better it made her feel. But now it felt a little like they were painting outside the lines. Again. And she just hoped he wouldn't resent her for it.

"It's one night." He stopped beside her, waiting as she shifted over to make room for him in the corner. "I see those guys all the time."

He'd been seeing her all the time lately too. Spending more time with her than she ever spent with the guys she was dating. More time than she'd ever wanted to. But with Jase, she wasn't thinking about whether he was getting too close. Too invested. Too intense.

She was just thinking about how good it felt to be with him.

She trusted him.

And no matter whether she'd woken in his arms that

morning or just crawled out of his bed, the minute they said good-bye, she couldn't wait to see him again.

Jase sat back in the corner of the couch she'd been keeping warm for him, carefully holding her wine out of the way for her as she snuggled back under his arm. She got the couch for her legs; he had the coffee table. When they were just right, she felt the muscled strength behind her give. Her own body seemed to melt into his.

Setting his wineglass on the end table, he picked up the remote.

"Besides, babe, our movie's been burning a hole in my pocket since I picked it up at lunch." He hit Start and the opening credits to *Guardians of the Galaxy* began to play. "I'd have ended up dragging you out of there early either way."

This man. If she wasn't careful, she was going to lose her heart to him completely.

And for the first time, she wondered if that would be such a bad thing after all.

Chapter 22

June

"Okay, okay. Fine, I admit it." Emily laughed, weaving through the maze of bodies lazing around Jase's living room. "In the blind taste-off, Brody's flourless chocolate cake was better than mine."

A round of cheers erupted from Team Brody, composed of Max and Sean. While Team Em—Jase and Molly—groused and grumbled, making her feel only marginally better about the humiliating loss.

She'd thought her recipe rocked and had talked so much trash about it over the past two weeks that Brody had finally called her out for a blind taste test. It had been a split decision, but she'd started to suspect Jase might have cheated when she saw him slip Molly a twenty.

Whatever. She'd had two spectacular slices of cake, definitely too much wine, and an absolutely awesome night playing Cards Against Humanity.

Now Jase caught her hand as she edged past, tugging her back so she tumbled into his lap, while he joked with Max about needing to stoke the competitive culinary fires between her and Brody to see what else they could score.

She leaned back against Jase's arm, loving the way he'd pause every now and then to look at her, give her a quick kiss, or just rub a bit of her hair between his fingers. Loving how easy everything was now that she'd stopped fighting it.

Loving this feeling of finding a perfect fit for the first time in her life.

Loving that she could finally let go, because she trusted that Jase would be there to catch her.

Jase turned to her. "What's that smile about?"

"Just that I think I might be able to take him with my bananas Foster."

This time, Jase, who'd pretty much become her number one cheerleader, gave her a pitying smile. "I'm not going to lie to you, sweetheart. Your chances will be far better if you steer clear of any recipe calling for booze. You know that's his thing."

She did. Like she knew so many things about all of them that she hadn't before. She knew Max was a player of the highest order, and the guy seemed to have a rule for everything—especially the women he'd take out. She knew that Sean wasn't even close to the gentleman she'd first thought he was, but she liked him a heck of a lot better now that she'd seen him for who he really was—dick jokes and all. She knew that once in a while Molly's eyes would linger on Sean just long enough that, despite Jase's assurances to the contrary, Emily had started to wonder if maybe there was something else to know there as well.

And she knew that as much as Jase loved his friends, in about fifteen minutes he was going to kick them out. And that once they were alone, she'd learn something new about the man who'd made her start to believe in all the things she'd thought she'd given up forever.

"Okay, kids," Jase announced, proving just how

much she knew indeed. "Bedtime. Grab your trash and get out of here."

Within minutes, the apartment was empty except for the two of them.

Jase threw the lock on the door behind him and gave her that crooked, sexy smile that did crazy things to her belly.

"Had to get them out of here before they finished everything off."

She raised a brow, giggling a little because, really? "You didn't want to share the cake?"

Jase gave her one of those "come on" looks, moving toward her with slow, predatory intent that had her heart skipping a beat. "The cake was spectacular. Yours in particular. But I'm talking about the *whipped cream* you made for on top."

She swallowed, taking a step back toward Jase's bedroom. And then another. "I didn't know you were a whipped-cream man." Her words were barely a whisper.

"Neither did I until you tested it, scooping up that little glob and then licking it as it started to slip down your finger. Jesus, Em… A man can only take so much."

She knew the feeling. When he shaved in the morning? God help her.

Standing there in his towel and nothing else, his body clean, his hair damp dry in those soft, tumbled waves, methodically revealing one strip of fresh, smooth skin after another? She'd snapped the first time she watched him, barely managing to get the razor out of Jase's hands before dropping to her knees and delivering the kind of good-morning kiss that cost them their bus.

"So the whipped cream is your limit?" she teased breathlessly.

Jase stopped where he was and looked at her as though he'd just realized something. "I think *you* are."

She swallowed, her heart thumping hard. Because that look. Those words. That very moment was when it happened. When she knew.

She loved him.

—◦◦◦—

Jase stared at the reports in front of him, ready to pull the hair from his head. He was on his third temporary assistant now, and based on what he was looking at, number four was right around the corner. It didn't make sense—had she even used the accounts he'd given her?

Rubbing at the back of his neck, he groaned as he pulled up everything he'd sent the day before.

And that's when he sensed it. That disapproving stare burning into him from the open door.

His head shot up, and—hell yes—he was out of his seat in the blink of an eye.

"Janice, oh love of my life, tell me you're back. Please. That you'll never leave me again."

"Don't get excited." Janice held up the little SnugRide car seat with tiny Jeremy mauling his baby fist inside. "We've got three more weeks."

"Just here to torment me with what I can't have then, huh?" Jase asked, only half joking. Because damn he missed her.

Reluctantly, Janice handed him the carrier, and he headed back to his desk, where Jeremy got parked on top of a pile of useless reports headed for the circular file. Unfastening the little buckles, Jase carefully scooped up the little boy he hadn't seen since he was a week old. He smiled. She'd dressed him in one of the tiny outfits Jase had picked up at Neiman Marcus.

Jase tucked the baby against his chest, keeping an eye on Mom to make sure he was doing everything right. "Geez, Janice, what are you feeding this guy? He's growing like a weed."

She raised a brow. "You really want to know?"

Jase winced and shook his head. "No. But he's definitely getting big. And he's kind of firm now too—"

"Mmm-hmm, he's cute, Jase. I built him. I know."

The impatient tone had him turning a wary eye toward Janice. But then he got it, recognized the look from too many conversations in this very office.

She wasn't even working, and someone had leaked her the news about his love life.

"You're right, I should have told you," he started, cradling Jeremy's little butt and head in his hands. But he'd really thought she wouldn't hear until she was back. And then he'd planned to tell her the whole sordid tale. Like a back-to-work present. "You already know it's Emily, right?"

"Of course I know it's Emily." Janice sat back in her chair and snapped her fingers for the baby, who was still trying to get his fist in his mouth.

One of these days, he was going to have to figure out who her informant was. Reluctantly, Jase handed Jeremy back. Then watched as Janice adjusted and cooed over her little boy, looking in that moment softer than he'd ever seen her.

If a woman as hard as Janice could look that soft with her son, what would Emily look like? He could almost see her leaning over a little body with tiny, kicking legs, whispering sweet nothings in her gentle voice.

And where the hell had that come from?

Janice was clearing her throat, obviously waiting for Jase to start dishing the dirt on all things Emily.

"So you remember we didn't exactly get along, right?"

"I had a baby, not a stroke, Jase."

Man, he couldn't wait for Janice to come back.

"Where's my girl?" Brody called as Jase cut through the high tops toward the table where Molly, Max, and Brody were already situated. He grinned, stupidly pleased to hear Brody claiming Emily as one of his own, but hell, he wanted them to like her. *Really* like her, so it meant a lot.

"Work. Or drinks for work, I guess. She's downtown, meeting with the head of some corporate account they're trying to score." Then nodding to the spot where Sean would normally sit, he asked, "And how about *my girl*?"

Molly rolled her eyes. "Hotel thing."

Max took a long swallow. "Think he took Valerie Lennox out again."

Jase slid into his seat, glancing back to see who was around to take his order since Molly wasn't working. "Yeah, nice woman. We went out with them a few weeks back. Easy to talk to. Very proper. Polite. A lot like Sean when he's… You know." Jase looked around the table, waving his hand in a sort of circle the rest of them seemed to follow, since they were all nodding in understanding.

"Didn't he see her last week for something too?

Valerie's going to start getting ideas pretty soon," Brody said, making eye contact with someone across the bar. A nod, and within three seconds, Jill was over taking Jase's order.

Max blew out a low whistle, a sorry look on his face. "I don't know. I'm starting to think Sean might be the next to fall. I give him six months before he cracks."

Molly made a scoffing noise. "Right. Um, have you seen the guy sitting next to you?"

Jase looked at Brody, who was on Max's other side. But then he realized all eyes were on *him*.

"What, me?" Great, and the way his voice just cracked... not cool at all. And not even close. "That's nuts."

"Okay." He didn't care for the way Brody was eye-balling him, or the blatant insinuation in that single-word reply.

Right, like he didn't know *exactly* what that meant.

Then Max was leaning forward, his arms folded in front of him on the table, a slanted smirk riding his mouth. "He did bail on hoops last week to go hang out at Emily's parents' house."

"For fuck's sake, they were out of town and the sump alarm went off. The basement had a foot of water in it."

"No need to get defensive," Molly clucked, the corners of her mouth twitching.

And then it was like some kind of feeding frenzy, with all of them—including Jill and one of the other girls from the bar—getting in on the fun by citing observations, incidents, and excuses backing up their assertion that he was done. All but ready to get down on one knee.

"And wasn't there a second toothbrush on her counter?"

"That whole thing where it's like he can't look away…"

"The 'let me check with Em first' business…"

"…like he's the luckiest fucking man on the planet…"

"…every time she walks in the room…"

"Can you even sleep if she's not there?"

They were just ribbing him, and considering the way he dished it, God knew he'd better be able to take it, but man… He pulled at his collar.

Because all of it was true.

Being with Emily was amazing. There wasn't any bullshit with her, like there had always been with the other women he'd dated. His fault, not theirs. But with Emily, nothing. The time he spent with her was because he wanted to. Needed to. It wasn't about some end goal or making sure he had a little company available, should he decide he wanted it. It was about making her smile and feeling like he'd done something with his day. It was about relaxing in a way he hadn't even known he could—just because she was with him.

She never pushed him for anything in their relationship. Hell, most of the time he was the one who couldn't resist nudging past the next commitment marker. Moving from that point where he asked when she was free again to assuming they'd see each other the next night unless someone said otherwise. All but skipping past the stage of occasionally sleeping over due to extreme sexual fatigue to asking whose place they were going to stay at that night so one of them knew to pack a bag.

And he liked it. He liked that after a couple of weeks of heavy social commitments they'd taken a Saturday off and spent the entire day watching TV in bed. Talking. Laughing. Making love.

It was *good*.

They were good.

But suddenly, he was wondering just how deep he had gotten himself.

"I don't know, man." Max grinned from across the table. "For a guy who swore he'd never get married, you have been giving off all the right signs."

Jase pushed up from the table, waving them all off with a laugh and a threatening "Yeah, yeah, bite it, fuckers" just to show there weren't any hard feelings.

Then he headed out front to the sidewalk. Because suddenly he desperately needed some air and a little space.

Something was up with Jase. Emily couldn't put her finger on it, but for the last couple of days things had been…*off*. He'd shown up after work on Tuesday and told her he was slammed at the office, that he'd probably be going in early and that it would be easier if they slept at their own apartments for a couple of days. No problem. If anyone understood about the need to put work ahead of fun once in a while, she did. Heck, her phone was glued to her side for that very reason. If something came up, she had to handle it *then*. Even if *then* happened to be in the middle of dinner with friends or at 2:00 a.m.

She didn't think twice about it. Until she saw him two nights later for dinner. He'd wrapped her in his arms the way he'd been doing every time he saw her for nearly the last three months, but instead of the usual lingering hold that always made her feel like he truly didn't want to let go, it was so brief that it almost felt like he *needed* to let go. Work, she figured. He was tense. No big thing.

Only now it was Saturday morning, and Jase was walking through her place with those deep lines cut between his brows as he picked up a hat, a pair of sunglasses, a copy of *Men's Health*.

The Under Armour shorts he wore in the morning before they figured out what they were going to do and he got dressed for real.

"I can't believe how much I leave around here. Em, you gotta tell me to clear my crap out when I go."

His toothbrush. A razor.

Leaning against the bathroom door, she caught his eyes in the mirror. "Jase, they're just a few things. I don't mind."

He laughed, but it wasn't the laugh she loved. This one sounded strained. This one made her nervous.

"Yeah, but it's not like we're living together, right?"

"Right. No, of course not." But then she had to ask. "Is everything okay? Are we okay?"

Pain flashed through his eyes. Muttering a curse, he pulled her into his arms, holding her the way she was used to. The way she loved.

"We're good, sweetheart. Of course we're good."

She wanted to believe him. But even in that perfect hold, she couldn't shake the sense that Jase wasn't just trying to reassure her; he was trying to reassure them both.

"Just settle down, man," Jase said, watching Romeo wear a hole in Jase's office carpet.

The guy had shown up twenty minutes earlier, sporting the kind of shell-shocked expression that had Jase clearing his calendar on the spot. He'd barely been able to breathe when he asked if something was wrong with little Gloria, the month-old baby girl who'd stolen everyone's heart. But nothing was.

"You're overreacting," Jase promised. "It can't be what you think, because Sally would never… She just wouldn't."

"She admitted it." Romeo covered his eyes. He sucked in a breath, his back quaking once before he fisted his hands against his brow. "Not at first. But then, yeah, she told me. It's true."

Jase was sick. Too stunned to speak, because… No. Just no. Sally couldn't. She loved Romeo. Jase had seen it. Felt it. Knew it.

He wasn't wrong about her. There was just no way.

Only the kind of twisted agony coming off the man breaking in front of him said that it was. Jesus, he'd seen this before. In his father's eyes… Fuck, in Eddie's eyes.

Though as soon as the thought crossed his mind, he felt a stab of guilt and shook his head. No, Eddie was different. What happened with Eddie was the kid's own doing.

Not like with Romeo and Sally.

Sally. He couldn't wrap his head around it. Yeah, they'd had some bumps, like any couple. And yeah, the engagement had come up pretty fast.

His stomach knotted.

Maybe he should have seen it. Maybe he'd let Romeo down by not pushing him to give the relationship more time.

Maybe that's what his friend had needed when he first came to talk to him about popping the question.

But the guy had been so sure. So certain. So…blindly in love, and once again Jase had just wanted to believe.

Damn it.

Twenty years ago, there was nothing Jase could have done to help his dad. Not the first time his wife cheated, or the second, or the third. Not when she left. And hell, as much as he might wish it were otherwise, not even now that she was back.

But Romeo… Hell, Jase didn't want his father's past to become Romeo's future. Romeo didn't deserve this.

"It's going to be okay," he said gently, knowing better than to try to touch the guy. "Let's sit down, and we'll talk this out."

<hr />

Emily was late meeting Jase. With the rain, it seemed every cab in the city had been snatched up, and when she'd finally caught one, traffic had been moving at a slow crawl, giving her too much time to worry. To think.

Maybe she should have canceled dinner and seen if he'd be up for staying in instead, but she hadn't wanted to risk him suggesting they take a rain check. Not with what she needed to talk to him about tonight.

Inside the restaurant, she found Jase at the bar, rubbing a weary hand over his face and looking almost as bad as she felt.

He leaned in to kiss the corner of her mouth. "Man, are you a sight for sore eyes."

Pretty much what she was thinking. And now she regretted not staying home even more, because one look at Jase and all she wanted was to curl up with him on the couch. Feel his arms around her and rest her head against his chest.

"Em, you look like you're about to cry."

She felt like it. But then Jase was holding her hand, and somehow that made things better.

"Have you talked to Romeo?"

Jase's face changed, his jaw tensing as he leaned back on his stool. "I was wondering if Sally would have the nerve to tell you."

Maybe it was his cool tone or the hard look in his eyes, but either way her shoulders tensed. "I spent the afternoon with her. She's a mess. Do you know Romeo is talking about moving out?"

Jase nodded and threw a couple of bills on the bar before grabbing his coat. "Yeah. I told him to."

Five minutes later, they were in the back of a cab, Jase in one corner, Emily in the other, the warmth and comfort she'd begun to associate with this man nowhere to be found.

"She slept with another man!" he roared, glaring at her from across the seat. "You bet your ass I'm going to get behind my guy when he finds out."

The wipers slapped across the windshield and a horn blared.

"Believe me, you getting behind your guy is not a surprise, Jase," she snapped back, too many old feelings she'd thought she put aside rushing to the surface. "But don't you think you *owe it to your guy* to consider that there's more to this than just—"

"You're damn right there is. Because it wasn't just some *random* she took home to screw. It was Aiden Mickey, her ex-fiancé, who Romeo fucking hates and has had the shit luck of working down the hall from for the last three years. The dickhead who's probably been laughing his ass off for the last year over what a chump Romeo is."

God, Sally's choice of rebound hookup couldn't have been worse. There was no denying that.

"Two weeks, Em," he went on. "Two weeks before she took Romeo's ring and put it on her finger, she let Aiden put his—"

"She thought they had broken up! She was devastated. Romeo hadn't spoken to her in five days, after telling her he 'wasn't doing this anymore' and walking out. He wasn't returning her calls or texts. From where she was sitting, she was well within her rights to do whatever she wanted with whomever she wanted."

Jase looked like she'd slapped him. "Jesus, Emily, how can you defend—"

He shook his head, then raised his hands in a calming gesture. For her or himself, she didn't know.

All she did know was her stomach felt like the floor had just dropped out from under her.

"The only reason Romeo didn't call her back was because he dropped his phone in a toilet in Mexico. Which he told her when he came back. Which he apologized for. Which was when she should have explained that she'd had sex with Aiden *the night before*, instead of hiding the truth and hoping Romeo never found out."

If Sally had come to Emily for advice, that was what she would have told her to do. But that wasn't how it had happened. Sally had been too afraid to tell anyone. So when the truth came out, it was thanks to an acquaintance's off-the-cuff comment leading to a whole lot of questions and one devastating confession.

"She didn't want to hurt him. And she didn't want to

risk losing him because of one night with a guy who just happened to be in the right place at the wrong time. She loves Romeo. They're married *with a month-old baby*! How could you tell him to leave her?" Emily demanded, on the brink of tears. "If you give them a chance and get out of Romeo's head with this talk about him moving, they can work it out."

Jase balked. "That's what I'm afraid of! Romeo already tried to end it with her once and ended up putting a ring on her finger instead. Emily, some guys just can't see straight where women are concerned. They get caught up in all that soft and sweet, and they don't even recognize what else is there." Shoving a hand through his hair, Jase blew out a long breath. "Romeo deserves better than a lifetime of waiting around for whatever betrayal his wife has lined up next. Wondering how many people already know. Asking himself what happened to the life he thought he was going to have."

Emily couldn't believe what she was hearing. "Jase, this is *Sally* we're talking about. You're making her out to be some praying mantis, just waiting to devour her mate."

"I know she's your friend, Emily, and you want to believe the best, but she screwed another guy. And while I believe she was hoping it would stay quiet, it didn't. People know. But even if they didn't, what does it say that she chose *the one guy that would hurt Romeo worse than any other on the planet*." He looked out the window. "She *broke* him, Em."

Her heart ached, thinking about what was happening to this new, fragile family.

Reaching for Jase, she squeezed his arm.

"He's hurt. It's terrible what they're going through. But they can get through this, Jase. Sally loves him. They love *each other*. They're a *family*."

Jase turned back to her with haunted eyes. "Eddie loved you. He was sure of it."

Her stomach churned, the breath leaking out of her in a rush.

"I can't go back and protect you from it, Em. I think about it every day, what I could have done. What I should have done." Gently, so gently, he brushed his thumb over the place on her wrist that Eddie had once bruised. "What I could have stopped."

"It's not the same," she whispered.

"I couldn't help my dad twenty years ago. Hell, I can't even help him now. But Romeo? I can help him through this. I can be on his side, Em. And if that means supporting him getting out now—while he's still got a chance to recover and little Gloria doesn't have to spend years watching some screwed-up dynamic tear her dad down to nothing—then I'm all for it."

She crumpled into her corner of the cab. "It was a mistake, Jase. *One* mistake Sally will regret for the rest of her life."

"It's never just one." Jase sounded exhausted. "It might be Sally's *first* mistake. But women like her... Cheaters cheat, Em. They don't just do it once."

Chapter 23

WOMEN LIKE HER.

Maybe it was something about the way Jase said it, but suddenly Emily was taken back to that horrible night so long ago. To Jase glaring down at her outside the emergency room, firing one accusation after another.

"You think you can play with people like dolls. Like the consequences don't matter."

The cuts on her hands and arms from trying to get to Eddie weren't bleeding anymore. The bigger one at her wrist had been stitched and bandaged, and a sort of numbness had replaced the pain and shock of what she'd just witnessed.

The crumpled metal, the broken glass. The blood. Eddie's blood. So much of it.

"What are you talking about?" she asked, the words sounding slow and slightly muffled. "I've spent the entire summer trying to be there for Eddie. Me. I called you again and again. I told you there was something going on with him. There was something wrong. You're the one who didn't—"

"Bullshit, Emily. This is on you. I know about the other guys. I know about the head games. I know the reason my best friend is in surgery right now, and it's you."

Everything he was saying was wrong. All of it.

She ought to defend herself, to say something. The sort of fog she'd been walking around in began to clear.

"You think I was messing around on Eddie?" she half whispered. "Did he tell you that?"

Of course he had. But how could Jase believe him? He knew her. How could he even think—

"How could you, Emily?" Jase shoved his hands back into his dark hair, fisting them at the sides of his head. "He loves you."

She took a step back, slowly straightening her shoulders, because she had nothing to be ashamed about.

She would never have betrayed Eddie that way. Yes, she wanted out of their relationship—but she wouldn't have used another guy to get there. She'd told Eddie it was over. That's why he drove into the divider, and that's why he was in surgery.

"I wasn't... Jase, I was trying to help him."

Pressing the heels of his hands into his eyes, Jase bowed his head. "I thought you were different, Em. Shit, I needed you to be different. Girls like you, you have no idea the damage you can do to a guy."

Emily stood there a moment, silent. There was nothing she could say. Jase wouldn't believe her, so why bother?

Slowly she turned back to the ER, squinting into the overhead light.

Her parents were inside with Eddie's, and hopefully the Gainers would be ready to hear what she'd been trying to tell them for months about their son. Hopefully, her parents would support her this time.

Hopefully, Eddie would get the help he needed.

The only thing she knew for certain was that it would

be without her. She wasn't what he needed. Tonight proved that.

She was finally going to be free. No matter how much everyone hated her for it.

Now, Emily rubbed at the faint scar on her wrist from that night and looked at Jase, the man she'd been quietly, helplessly falling in love with. "When you say 'women like her,' Jase, do you mean *women like me?*"

He didn't still believe it. He'd been upset that night, but he'd had years to think about it. And he'd told her that he'd realized a long time ago how unfair he'd been. He had to have meant about this too.

"This isn't about us."

The nonanswer tore at her, ripping open old wounds, the hurt she'd tried to put behind her.

"I don't know," she said quietly. "It seems like maybe it should be."

"Em, don't be like that."

She waited, breath held, for him to tell her he knew her better *now*. That he'd been wrong to think she would ever be unfaithful. That maybe, after all these years, he finally understood.

But instead, he turned to the window, cocking his jaw to one side as he stared out at the night. "Eddie did a number on you. I get that now. So whatever you did, I'm not judging."

She almost laughed, but the tears pushing at the backs of her eyes got in the way. "But you don't totally trust me either, do you?"

And then it hit her.

"Jase, is that what's been going on this last week? Did you suddenly realize things were progressing further than they should with *a woman like me*? Is that why you've been pulling back, putting a distance between us where there wasn't any before?"

"Don't do this," he warned, as though there was any stopping what had already begun. As though he hadn't just given her his answer.

An answer that knocked the wind out of her, it hit her so hard.

"Then why?" she asked when she finally found her breath. "I get those first few times. The sex. It was hot and intense and…" She closed her eyes against the memory of his lips at her ear, his body moving with hers, the words that had chipped at her defenses until they were nothing but rubble. "I get it. But you could have left it at that. Why ask for that first date?" she demanded. "Why push? Why spend weeks trying to sell me on something that *doesn't even exist*?"

"Don't say that," he shot back.

"Tell me why!"

"Because I couldn't fucking help myself! Is that what you want to hear?"

No, it most definitely wasn't what she wanted to hear.

Jase swore, his expression a mix of fury and agony, looking like he wanted to take the words back.

But it was too late. They'd already become a part of her.

"Emily, I couldn't walk away and then I didn't want to." He reached for her hand, leaning into what he was about to say next. "I don't know why we're even talking about this. Sally and Romeo are the ones with the problem. What you and I have is good. It works."

"How can you say that?" she whispered, wiping at a

tear. "If you don't really trust me, Jase—if you don't really know me, and you're putting up walls where I've just knocked mine down, then no. What we have is not good."

⁓

They'd broken up in a cab.

Riding the elevator up to her floor, Emily contemplated who to call. Which of the girlfriends she'd been there for so many times to ring up and invite over for a couple of bottles of wine and a shoulder to cry on. A hug. A rousing speech about independence and finding the right man.

But by the time she got to her floor, she knew she wasn't going to call anyone. Because the only person she wanted to talk to was the man who'd just broken her heart.

She couldn't believe what had happened. It didn't make sense. She'd wanted to talk to Jase about Sally because somehow over the past months she'd come to see him as the man capable of leaping tall buildings in a single bound. He could handle anything, cared about everyone—and saw things with the kind of clarity that had made him her go-to guy in sorting out complicated situations.

She'd been wrong.

But even knowing that, a part of her still wanted to run to his place so she could feel his arms around her and, for just a moment, lose herself in the security of that hold.

But that warm blanket of security she'd been snuggling up in wasn't any more real than the trust or the friendship, or any of the other fairy tales she'd been stupid enough to start believing in again.

God, how long would it take her to get over him this time?

Inside her apartment, she dropped her coat and bag by the door, too tired to put them in their place. She kicked off her heels and undid her hair. Unzipped her dress and left it in the wake of her despair. She wanted her pj's, but first things first.

Standing in her bra and panties, she opened the fridge and pulled out the stopper on the nice bottle of white she and Jase had opened two nights before. Without bothering with a glass, she took a long, forlorn swallow.

Let the pity party begin.

———

"Hey, man, wasn't expecting to see you here tonight," Brody said from behind the bar where he'd been talking with a buddy. Then being Brody, the observant one, his face turned serious as he gave Jase the once-over. "Okay, my office."

They walked to the back, a space Jase seldom visited because Brody usually preferred a table by the front window so he could keep an eye on both the inside and out. But Jase must have looked almost as bad as he felt.

"Jesus, you look like shit," Brody said, dropping into his office chair.

Suspicion confirmed.

Jase sank into the black leather couch and folded forward, holding his head above his spread knees. "Insider tip: I'm not the next one getting married."

Brody opened his desk drawer and pulled out a bottle with a handmade label and two thick, stubby glasses.

"I'm telling you, it's all part of the dysfunction running core deep within me." Emily stabbed her warm nacho chip, laden with sour cream and guacamole, toward Lena and watched a glob drip onto the vinyl table cover, adding, "It's textbook."

Two days into her breakup with Jase, and she was pretty sure it was, anyway. It had been a while since her Psych 101 class, and now that she thought about it, it had been a while since that cute waiter had promised to bring her a fresh margarita too.

Leaning back in her chair and looking way too entertained, Lena waved her hand in invitation for more. "Explain."

"I planned this from the start. Subconsciously sabotaging myself by picking the one guy to 'risk' getting serious with—who I know, deep down, isn't any more capable of committing than I am. Then I get to be all surprised and hurt and look-how-I-put-myself-out-there—which, handily enough, totally validates my future avoidance of all things relationship—because *he* let me down. I am the mastermind who got exactly what she wanted. Which is why there will be no boo-hooing out of me and we are here to celebrate."

Being the good friend that she was, Lena didn't point out Emily's still tear-swollen eyes or the blotchy redness around her nose that no amount of concealer had been able to conquer.

The waiter returned with their drinks, and Emily offered up her firstborn if he'd make sure she had another on the table before she made it down to the ice.

"So you're happy?" Lena asked, clinking their glasses with a gentle smile. "Relieved to be free?"

Emily nodded with a professional-grade smile. "I am. I really, really am."

Or at least she would be once she convinced herself she hadn't actually fallen in love with Jase. That she hadn't let herself believe in something she'd been denying for too many years to count.

The sympathy was there in her friend's eyes as she scooped up her own heaping chip. "Okay, then we'll celebrate."

—⁓—

"Bull's-eye." Jase crossed to the board and pulled out his darts, realizing only after that he hadn't bothered to check what he'd scored.

Sean would know. Even deep in conversation with Max and Brody back at their table, the guy was like Rain Man when it came to keeping tallies, counting anything really. One of the reasons they *never* played cards with him. A fact that had Emily screwing up her face when he'd told her. She'd laughed in disbelief, her eyes crinkling at the corner, her mouth…

Shit.

Handing the darts off to Brody, Jase stepped aside.

Three sets of eyes followed him and he grimaced. "What?"

Sean cleared his throat uncomfortably, that pitying look of his causing the muscles along Jase's spine to tighten. He was sick of that look. It was almost as bad as the one he'd been facing in the mirror every morning and night for six damn days now.

"Game's over, Jase," Sean said, then clarified. "Actually, Brody won before your toss."

Molly stopped by their table to clear a few empties, cutting Jase a no-nonsense look. "You talk to her yet?"

He had to give the girl credit. None of the guys had had the balls to ask what he was pretty sure was on all of their minds.

"No. There wasn't a whole lot of uncertainty about how we left things. And honestly, it was probably for the best."

It had taken a couple of days for him to get to that way of thinking. Days of trying to come up with a solid reason to call, and then cursing himself for having been such a thorough fuck in clearing his stuff out of her place toward the end. Wondering if he should just check in and make sure she was okay—only to remind himself that even if she wasn't, he wasn't the guy she was going to want to chat with about it.

Molly set her tray down.

"The best?" she coughed out, her arms crossing over her chest in a move that was eerily similar to her brother's and had Jase edging into the seat farthest from where she was standing. "Have you even seen yourself, Jase? You're a mess. Minus the hot."

Max gave a single-shoulder shrug beside him. "She's right. You look like hell."

"Week-old roadkill," Sean chimed in with a grin, stretching back in his chair.

"It's this business," Brody offered, sort of circling his hands around his head as a whole, before splaying his fingers wide and making explosion noises.

Molly scowled at the guys and then turned back to Jase. Snapped her fingers in his face. "Get your hands out of your hair, for crying out loud. It looks like you've been yanking on it for days."

Jase lowered his hands. "Guess I've been... stressed some."

She raised an accusing brow. "Janice texted that you showed up at work on Monday looking like some kind of Sasquatch."

Et tu, Janice?

"I was trying something new. Beards are in these days."

A sad, sorry, disgusted little huff of breath was his answer. Well, his first answer.

"Not for you, Jase. I thought I made this clear when you were in college. You're a clean-shaven kind of guy. When you feel like being a rebel, one day of stubble max. Anything more and—" She sighed. "If you ever want her back, you're going to need to pull your shit together and fix your hair."

If he wanted her back.

That was the thing.

Brody cleared his throat, leaning forward over his arms. "You do want her back though, right?"

Scrubbing his palm over his mouth, Jase shook his head. "A part of me feels like I'm dying without her." Like he could barely breathe every time he thought about those last words between them in that fucking cab.

The way she'd given up on wiping at the tears and just let them fall.

"I'm sorry, Jase."

"I'm sorry too."

How the sight of her walking away through the rain had left him gutted.

It had been bad, and it wasn't getting any better.

"So do something about it, man. Call her up. Send her flowers. Just go over there."

Brody the fixer.

"Grovel, Jase."

With his sidekick, Molly.

Jase shook his head. "That's the thing. As bad as this is, I don't think it was a mistake."

"The fuck?" Sean snapped, that laid-back posture going ramrod straight. "You're kidding me, right?"

"No, man. I'm not." And he'd stopped kidding himself too. Though it hadn't come easily. "This thing with Emily was never going to last. Hell, neither one of us was looking for a relationship to go the distance."

Molly's mouth had firmed into a thin line. "That's bull. You might not have been looking for it, but if you were willing to pull your head out of your ass for five minutes, I think you'd realize you could have had it."

Jase thought about his mom, back again after all these years. "Yeah, well, just because something can go the distance doesn't always mean it should."

He'd gotten in too deep with Emily. Lost sight of his own priorities.

"Sometimes a clean break is the best-case scenario."

The guys didn't look like they were buying it, but being guys, they shrugged. Molly, on the other hand, wasn't a guy, no matter how much she hung out with them.

Her eyes moved from Jase to Brody to Max and then Sean, her temper showing more with each stop. "You guys are such idiots."

Brody's hands came up in front of him. "What did I do?"

She shook her head and picked up her tray again, muttering "Nothing. Just forget it" as she turned back to the bar.

Sean stared after her a second, all humor wiped clean from his face.

"Moll seeing someone I didn't know about?" he asked, pushing up from his seat and looking like he was going to follow her until Max's hand landing on his shoulder set him back in his chair.

"I got this."

Sean brushed Max's arm free. "Screw that. You're a damned vault. No way I'm letting you go find out what bee's in her bonnet alone."

Max rolled his eyes, but then they both got up and headed toward the servers' station.

Jase slumped back against his chair, tired. Worn out.

Brody picked up his pint and took a long swallow. Closed his eyes, savoring the dark stout. Emily had liked that shit too, joking it was like eating a sandwich.

His stomach churned, and he did what he'd sworn he wouldn't.

"She been in here at all?"

Brody shook his head. "Only been a few days. Give you a month before beating your ass for costing me a customer."

A month.

The thought was like something unpleasant rising up in his throat.

Forcing a smile, Jase smacked the table and stood. "Heading up to the bar. You want anything?"

"I'm good."

Cutting through the tables, Jase nodded to the faces

he knew. Kept his feet moving until he was standing at the polished bar.

"Hiya, Jase. What can I get you?" Dillon asked while filling someone's Blue Moon order.

A whiskey sounded good. Or maybe three would do what his beer hadn't. Numb him up just enough to stop thinking about Emily and actually fall asleep.

"Just a water, thanks." He wasn't going to spiral out like his father had. Not over some woman he didn't even—

The thought ground to a halt before he could even get the rest of the lie formed in his mind.

Because that's what it would be. A lie.

Well, there it was.

He loved her. He'd gone and fallen in love with Emily…which didn't change anything except his projected estimate on how long it would take him to get over this feeling of being gutted every time he thought about her.

And he pretty much thought about her all the time.

Two heavy hands landed on his shoulders, giving him a rough squeeze. Max, apparently through with Molly.

"What do you say to another game?"

Jase didn't want to. Hell, he didn't want to do anything. But he pushed off the bar and, bringing his water with him, headed back to the dartboard.

"One last game."

Emily had moved around a lot growing up. Her father's work took them to a new city and state every couple of years until they landed in Oak Park for good when she was sixteen. She'd seen her share of the country, and of all the places she'd lived and visited, Chicago's summertime lakefront was her favorite. Or it had been.

These last three weeks, the winding paths and vast, blue-green expanse of moody water were more of an escape.

A place to turn off her mind, at least for a little while.

Because if she ran long enough and hard enough, eventually that's what happened.

Except today, it seemed.

She'd set out early like she always did, taking advantage of the cooler temperatures, the muted light, and the quiet while she had them. She'd run past Belmont Harbor and North Avenue Beach, down past Oak Street. Mile after mile. And still her head wouldn't stop taking her to all the places she didn't want to go.

So she pushed her pace, pushed it some more, and—

"Ahh!"

—stumbled to a limping stop, where she bent over and rubbed at her throbbing calf.

"That doesn't look good."

Emily startled at the familiar voice. Pushing a few escapee ponytail hairs back from her eyes, she straightened.

"Max, I didn't see you," she gasped, still catching her breath as she tried a few steps to see if she could walk it off.

Max was crossing a grassy area between the sidewalk and path, a cup of coffee in one hand and an actual newspaper in the other. Old school. Typical Max.

"Guess not," he said with that stern almost-smile of his. "Looked like you were running for your life there."

That obvious? Ugh.

"You know, angry mob of zombies," she joked, not really knowing what else to say. "Think I lost them, though."

"Good thing, the way you're hobbling around there, Em." Then, more seriously, he asked, "Feel like you tore something?"

She leaned down again, gingerly testing the muscle. Stretching it out a bit. "Just a strain, probably."

But there wouldn't be any more running today. Which meant she was going to have to count on work to distract her. And good luck with that, after seeing one of Jase's best friends.

If she was smart, she'd limp away as fast as her good leg would take her. But seeing Max was just…nice. She'd missed hanging out with the gang, but as close as she'd gotten with them over the time she and Jase had been together, calling them up or stopping by just seemed wrong.

This accidental encounter though?

Why not.

"How've you been? I was wondering whether you got that fishing trip set up with the guys from the precinct."

Max nodded, taking a sip of his coffee, the movement stretching his T-shirt around his bicep. The man was seriously buff.

"Yeah, Richy and me and a couple of other guys are goin' end of August. Thanks again for tippin' us off to those island campgrounds."

She grinned, happy it was working out for them. They talked a bit more about the spot. About Molly giving him the hard-core sulk when she found out it was cops only and she couldn't come. And Brody giving him a lecture, more than he ever wanted to know, on healthy versus unhealthy fish.

But nothing about Jase.

Which was probably for the best. Even if the ache in her heart was growing with every second that passed.

"It was great seeing you, Max. I've got to head back if I'm going to make it in to the office by eight. Enjoy your coffee and paper."

She turned to go and winced.

"No way, Em. You can barely walk on that. Jase would kill me if I left you like this."

There it was. The *J* word. And more than that, the suggestion that he was still emotionally invested in her well-being.

For a moment her heart soared, but just as quickly she tumbled back to earth. To the reality that it didn't matter if he still cared. Or that she did.

Max cleared his throat beside her. "Hey, I was sorry to hear about you guys."

She tried to smile, but it broke a little as she answered, "Me too."

"Aww hell, Emily," Max groaned, the big guy looking like he was ready to bolt. "Don't cry. I can't take the tears."

She'd heard that from Jase. She loved that such a hard man had such a soft weakness.

Swiping at her eyes, she shook her head. "Not crying. Just some pollen or sand or something. I promise."

"If you say so. Look, I don't want you to be late for work. My car's just across the road."

A minute later, he'd pulled up to the curb and she was carefully climbing into the black Charger.

They made small talk about plans and friends. The reverse commute. Max getting a haircut later that afternoon.

"Belmont exit?" he asked when they were getting closer.

"Yeah, and thanks for this. But, um, do you think maybe we could keep the *sand* that got in my eyes between us?"

"Yeah, we can do that." Max snickered. "And, Emily, I don't know if it helps any to hear it, but Jase isn't any better off than you are."

Scrunching down in her seat, she turned to the passenger window.

At the stoplight a block from her place, Max let out a tight breath and handed her a tissue. "For the sand."

Chapter 24

July

Jase had known it was coming.

Hell, he'd planned for it. Waited nearly a whole damned week for it after Molly spilled the news that Brody had seen Emily riding in Max's car on Tuesday morning, and he'd spent the next thirteen hours working Max for intel until he hit the jackpot. Emily was going to be at some mutual friends' party that weekend.

A party he'd had a swift change of heart about attending.

So he'd known he was going to see her.

He'd told himself it would be good. The closure he needed.

But seeing Emily step out onto Shannon and Mike's rooftop hit him like a sucker punch and left him barely able to catch his breath.

Jesus, she looked good. Different from the last time he'd seen her. Even beneath the strung lanterns and burnt-orange evening light, he could see the sun showing across her cheeks and nose. Her shoulders too.

And that dress—black with some kind of big flower pattern, it tied behind her neck, fit around her waist, and then swung loose just to her knees—gorgeous.

He swallowed, his throat suddenly dry.

"Ahh shit, Jase," Brody said, his arm thrown around

a pretty blond he hadn't come with, their fingers tangled at her shoulder. "At least it looks like she's alone."

"Yeah." That was a ledge he'd been talking himself off for nearly a month now. Because the idea of her not being alone—he couldn't go there. Not yet.

Still standing by the exit door, Emily laughed at something Shannon said, that smile of hers making him ache in a way that actually felt better than the empty pit that had been growing in his gut these last weeks.

He loved that smile. He loved the way it made everything brighter.

And then it happened. Emily's head turned as she was speaking. Their eyes met and her words stopped. And that smile he couldn't get enough of slipped from her lips.

It was like the lights went out in the city.

Like someone pulled the plug in his chest, and everything warm and good that had been filling it up drained out.

"Got a plan?"

Jase glanced back and realized Brody's blond was gone. How long had he been staring?

"I mean, we're here. And you've seen her." Brody scratched at what had to be at least three-day-old stubble and then shoved that wild mane back from his face. "You gonna try to get her back?"

Jase's jaw hardened, and Brody nodded his head for Jase to follow. At the far end of the roof, a couple of metal washtubs were filled with melting ice, assorted beers, and other hard drinks. Jase grabbed a couple of bottles of Fat Tire and handed one to Brody, who pulled an opener from his back pocket and pried both caps off.

"So, what? You thinking about trying the friends thing again?"

Kicking at the gravel roof with his foot, Jase shook his head. "Tried that already."

Brody's mouth pulled into a frown. "Sort of a slippery slope there, huh?"

"That it is. I mean, okay, so lots of people become friends after they'd been something else first, but for me and Em"—he thought about the way she'd looked at him in the cab, the hurt and betrayal in her eyes as she told him he didn't know her at all—"attraction was never the problem."

Jase looked over the crowd and found her in an instant when the wind kicked up and that strawberry-blond tempest gave her away. It stirred up memories he ought to have put behind him but that instead were slamming against his mind to get out.

She wasn't supposed to get to him like this.

Not anymore. But then he thought about his dad, and those calls that had come every year or two when his mother would move. It had never gone away for Joe. And even knowing how truly toxic Clara Foster had been to his life, the man had still welcomed her back with open arms.

Or at least that was the way it looked from Jase's rather uninformed perspective. He'd been seeing his dad every week, but never at the house, and they avoided the subject of women completely.

But even with that glaring example front and center, he couldn't ignore the pull. He couldn't do the smart thing.

"I just need to talk to her," he said, more to himself than to Brody.

If he knew she was okay, that she was good—he'd be good too. He'd be able to move on. Let go.

She'd moved over by the folding table set up with the wine at the east wall and was talking with a couple of girls whose names he should have been able to place.

Emily glanced up and their eyes met. Locked.

Connection.

Excusing herself from the other girls, she started toward him. That's when he saw it.

The uneven gait and the beige wrap around her calf.

"Jesus, you're hurt," he blurted out, closing the distance between them. "Is this still from Tuesday?"

Emily looked down at where his hands were on her arm and side. He pulled them back.

Right. No touching.

More comfortable, she gave him a small smile and brushed her hair back from her eyes. "It's a strain. Not a big deal, Jase."

"It's been five days," he pressed. Then, scanning the roof, he found the hibiscus Mike had told him Shannon made him carry up, along with half their living room furniture, for the party. Jackpot. "Come on, they've got some chairs set up and I'm pretty sure I see one of those Papasan chairs too."

Glancing past the makeshift wall of potted trees, Emily bit her lip and then, looking back at him, shook her head. "Honestly, I'm good. Really."

Some reluctant part of his brain made a checkmark beside the box labeled *She's good.*

He frowned and she shifted uncomfortably.

"Jase, I know why you're over here. I'm sorry for how I reacted when I first came in. I wasn't expecting to see you tonight, and my emotions just got away from me."

The kind of emotions that said he'd broken something inside her, and it had cost him her smile.

"No, don't worry about it," he assured her. "I get it. I knew you'd be here and it still rocked me to see you. But I mean, we've got a lot of friends in common, so—"

"It won't be a problem, Jase. We're good."

There it was again. Another check mark. *They* were good.

He had what he'd been looking for. What he needed to hear. Time to kiss her cheek, tell her it was nice seeing her, and move on.

It's what she was waiting for. He could see it in those big, soft eyes of hers.

He swallowed. "Have you seen a doctor yet?"

Emily blinked, looking almost hurt by the question. "My friend Gail looked at it."

"Wait, Gail with the red hair? She's an RN, not a doctor." He had his phone out then, and was scrolling through his contacts. "I don't think you've met Dex Oldman, but he's a specialist in sports injuries." He could take her over to his place tonight.

"I don't need a specialist." Her arms were crossed over her chest, and he knew it was time to back off—past time.

"Getting groceries can't be easy like that, though. I was going to hit the store tomorrow." *Pull out, man.* "Why don't you shoot me a list and I'll bring everything by?"

She wasn't even looking at him now. "Really, I'm fine."

"They're just groceries, Em. We're fri—"

"No," she snapped, her hands coming up between them. "Just stop. I don't need you to take me to the doctor, Jase. I don't want you helping me out or stopping by or checking on me. I don't want anything from you."

His heart was starting to race, and he could feel that pretense of control slipping away. "You could use a hand and I've got one. It doesn't have to mean anything other than I care about you, Em."

She let out a heartbreaking laugh. "Then leave me alone, Jase."

"Why?" he shot back, knowing he was doing everything wrong but unable to stop.

She sighed, shaking her head like it hurt that he even had to ask.

"Because, Jase, when I look at you now," she said, the tears in her eyes knocking him back a step, "all I see is the lie I fell in love with. And the truth just hurts too much."

The lie.

He let her go.

Barely tamping down the need to stop her with his hands and beg her to wait, to listen, to talk, Jase watched Emily turn away from him and walk out the door she'd walked in less than thirty minutes before.

His breath left him in a slow leak.

He couldn't have blown it more if he'd tried.

He'd taken this night Emily had planned to spend with her friends from her. Ruined whatever chance they'd had of things being even remotely easy between them at the next wedding. And killed what he'd just that minute recognized as the last shred of hope he'd been unwittingly holding on to about maybe, just maybe them working things out.

Lurching to the rail, he stared down the six stories to the sidewalk below, waiting for her to emerge. Because for the first time in a month, he was seeing things clearly.

Brody came up beside him, folding his burly arms over the rail to look down with Jase.

There she was. Head bowed, her shoulders slumped.

He'd done this.

When she'd stepped into a cab, Brody's eyes cut to him.

"Let me guess. You fucked up, again."

Jase pushed back from the rail, his stomach in knots, self-loathing clawing at him from the inside out. "Don't worry, man. I'll leave her alone."

The cab was nearly at her apartment when Emily leaned forward and gave the driver a new address. After some indignant huffing, the guy agreed, circling back toward the neighborhood they'd just come from. Only instead of dropping her at Shannon and Mike's again so her heart could break into even tinier pieces, he cut over a few blocks east. To Sally's.

Not Sally and Romeo's. Not anymore.

No need to check if she'd be there. Despite her parents' insistence that she and Gloria move back into the Willson home, Sally wasn't going anywhere. Or anywhere other than the market or the doctor's office.

Romeo came by most days for an hour or so, but Sally said it was always right after work or in the mornings on the weekends, so Emily knew she wouldn't

risk interrupting them. Not that there would be much
to interrupt. From what Sally had said, if she tried to
apologize or talk to Romeo, he'd just kiss Gloria good-
bye and then leave. But if she just sat there, watching
her husband love and play with their baby, he would
stay and she could almost pretend for a little while that
things were normal.

So that's what she'd been doing.

Emily paid the driver and then walked up to the big
greystone's entry. She waited for Sally to buzz her in
and then met her friend at her door.

Sally was too thin, her eyes rimmed red, but the
smile she had for Emily as she ushered her in was warm
and full.

"What are you doing here?" she asked in a new
mother's hushed tones.

Emily peeked past her into the classic Ralph Lauren–
styled apartment and to the one mismatched piece of
furniture in the place. The frilly, white ruffled bassinet
with a tiny head of dark curls visible within. Gloria
Santos was such perfection.

"It suddenly occurred to me that I'm a season behind
on *Scandal*. And I thought that maybe if I played my
cards right, I could score a little baby snuggle time and
give you a rest."

Sally's hands clutched together as she bounced in
place. "A sleepover? Puh-leeease tell me you'll sleep
over. I have ice cream. Really good ice cream purchased
in bulk."

Emily nodded, happy for the company as much as
Sally was to have it.

"Promise I'll be out before Romeo gets here."

"Deal." Sally skirted around the rich mahogany occasional table and grabbed an open bag of pretzels from the overstuffed chair. "I'll put these in a bowl!"

"I'll get the ice cream."

This was what she'd needed. The impossible-to-ignore reminder of why she couldn't let Jase bring her groceries, no matter what seeing him at Shannon's had done to her heart. No matter how he'd looked at her.

No matter how much she missed him.

Jase was a man who would never trust. Not entirely. And that lack of trust colored everything he saw. It warped his judgment. Blinded him and made him unforgiving. It made him dangerous to a woman like her. A woman who'd barely begun to learn to trust again herself.

Jase shoved a hand through his hair, rubbing the back of his scalp hard. The week since Shannon and Mike's party had been rough, to put it mildly. No one could stand to be around him. Janice had stopped picking on him altogether. The guys and Molly were there for him like they always were, but now when he walked into the room, the conversation would suddenly come to a halt.

Because they'd been talking about him.

Which might have bothered him if he could focus on anything other than how epically he'd annihilated what he was pretty certain had been a real shot at happiness with Emily. But it was there when he poured his cup of coffee in the morning, when he sat down at his desk, when he heard a funny joke, when he bought a sandwich for lunch. It was there at every instant he thought he might pick up his phone and call her.

But he couldn't call her, because she deserved a hell of a lot more than a man who couldn't see past his own emotional garbage long enough to realize that he'd allowed his fear to sabotage the only thing that mattered. He'd broken her heart because he'd been too chickenshit to allow himself to be truly vulnerable with her.

And now she was gone, and he couldn't seem to shake that roiling sense of being adrift. Of knowing something vital was missing from the very heart of him.

He didn't like it. And not just because… Shit… Well, who would like that feeling? But because it reminded him of something he'd sworn would never become a part of his life. It reminded him of his dad. Of the heart-break he'd nearly drowned in. Of the only weakness Jase had ever seen in the man who had been his best friend, his hero, and his role model in every way except those of the heart.

That's what he was doing out in Oak Park. Sitting three-quarters of a block down the street from his father's house, lurking like some kind of stalker. Watching the front windows and trying to gauge who was home. He hadn't been back since he'd found his mother there. Instead, he'd met his dad at restaurants, or that one time at Home Depot where they'd spent an hour and a half sorting through lumber before going their separate ways.

Man, that had sucked.

And no matter how adult he tried to be about it, it just wasn't fucking fair. For twenty years it had been the two of them. Jase and Joe taking care of each other. The Foster men against the world. And for twenty years, if

Jase had ever needed anyone to talk to, he knew down to the depths of his soul that his old man would be there to listen. Just the way Jase would listen when Joe needed someone to talk to.

They weren't just father and son; they were friends.

Or that's how it had been until *she* came back.

Now Clara was ruining everything. Straining every conversation and getting in the way of the things that had always come so easily between them.

And more than ever, Jase needed his dad. He needed to talk to someone who knew him better than anyone else on the planet. He needed a man with experience and perspective. He just needed to talk, damn it, and he didn't want to have to set it up through email so that they could meet in some neutral location.

He wanted to clean the gutters while he told his dad about the woman who was making him lose sleep. He wanted to help fix the dry rot on the garage door. And then he wanted to go inside and have a beer, or maybe some banana bread, and sit in the living room that had been theirs and theirs alone for so long *it mattered*. He wanted the comfort, the familiarity. He wanted—

Two quick knocks had him jolting in his seat, jerking around to look to the passenger window where his mom was peering in, her lips pressed into a firm line.

He rolled down the window, refusing to feel like a kid who'd just been busted stealing. "I was thinking I might see Dad outside. Catch him to talk for a few minutes."

"Your dad's not home. He's over at Bear's house, installing a new stove."

"Got it. I'll catch him another time."

"Jase, turn the car off and come inside. It's time we talk."

He didn't know what made him do it. Why he hadn't offered a simple "pass," peeled out of his spot, and driven home. But for whatever reason, he did what she told him. Turned off the car and walked up to the house and waited. At any other time in his life, he would've let himself right in. But now that she was back—this stranger who had a hold greater than his own on his father—it suddenly felt like the house wasn't his.

His mom opened the door…at which point Jase let out a string of obscenities, the potency of which surprised even him.

But what the fuck?

This was not his house.

Gone were the feather-duster paint job and the botanical wallpaper border in the living room. The floral-patterned couch and coffee table with the beveled-glass insert too. Along with every brass accent item he'd been grimacing at since they'd gone out of style God only knew how many years ago. The figurines had been cleared away, along with the clustered knickknacks that had haunted their shelves and tables for as long as he could remember.

"What did you do?" Jase demanded, his outrage building by the second.

His father had loved all that crap. And now it was all gone.

"Jase, sit, will you?" she said, waving a hand toward the new dining room chairs.

When Jase just stood there, she sighed and sat down herself.

"I know you're upset. You have every right to be. But this"—she gestured to the freshly decorated space around her—"it's not what you think, Jase."

He was fuming. "Then what is it?"

"It's me trying to help your dad. When I got back here and saw the way he preserved everything from before I left, it broke my heart. In two decades, he hadn't changed a thing. He'd been living in a house surrounded by painful memories."

"And so you come back and the first thing you do is to tell him it's not good enough? God, you're some piece of work."

His mother stared up at the ceiling and shook her head. "It wasn't anything like that. Jase, do you really think your father's first pick for color themes would have been fuchsia and teal?"

Jase crossed his arms. Because he knew where she was going with this.

His father had been trapped in a house he refused to change so that if his wife ever came back, it would be just the way she left it.

"Does he think you're staying?" Jase asked, knowing the answer but needing to hear it just the same. Waiting for her reply so he could rip into it and show her how wrong she was. For everything.

Only then he saw the look in his mother's eyes. It wasn't calculating or entitled. It wasn't even cold. She looked vulnerable. Sad.

She looked like someone he couldn't bully.

And when she replied, it wasn't with what he'd been expecting.

"Jase, do you know how old I am?"

The question threw him off guard. And even more than that, he realized he didn't know. But rather than clarify that he'd spent most of his youth trying to forget her, he answered instead with a simple no.

When he'd shown up and first found her there, he'd barely been able to look at her. And this afternoon, he'd been too surprised when she knocked on his car window to pay much attention to her face. Hell, he hadn't really looked at her since she'd been back. But he was now.

She looked tired maybe, with a sort of weathered softness to her face and sadness in her eyes that made him want to look away.

But her hair was still the same chestnut brown he remembered, with only a few grays streaking her temples. She was fit, her back straight, her shoulders and arms toned. Her blue eyes still bright.

She actually didn't look that old at all.

"I'm forty-six, Jase."

Some of the air left his lungs as the math presented information he didn't quite know what to do with. He pulled a chair from the table and sank into it. His mom had been eighteen when he was born.

"It's not an excuse," she went on. "I made decisions I'm not proud of, choices I wish I could take back."

Jase's head snapped up, but she shook her head.

"Probably the only thing I wouldn't change if I had it to do again was leaving you and your father."

Her words shouldn't have been able to touch him. So why did he feel like he was standing a hundred yards away from the woman who'd given him life, watching her throw her last bag in the back of a pickup with barely a backward glance? He cleared his throat. "It doesn't matter."

"It matters to me, Jase. Knowing that I did that one thing right matters. I wasn't a mother to you. Even when I managed to be a wife to your father, I didn't have it in me to take care of my son the way I should have. I couldn't even take care of myself. And I'm sorry for it."

"Eighteen," he groaned, because, *Jesus.*

"Seventeen when I got pregnant. Not that your father knew." Her eyes went distant. "I thought I was so mature. So grown up. I looked it, and of course I liked the attention I got from the older guys. So I snuck out, got into bars with a fake ID, and let guys like Joe buy me drinks and tell me jokes and make me feel like I was really something. Your dad thought I was twenty-two when we met. He had a good job working as an electrician, money, charm, and all those good looks. The way he treated me…" Something softened in her face.

His dad had been good to her. Of course he had.

"I wasn't used to being treated like that, and I fell for him hard. We were together for six months before I found out I was pregnant with you."

"But he still didn't know how old you were?" Jase asked, unable to imagine his dad—the guy who'd busted him at fifteen for having friends over when he wasn't supposed to because the carpet had been *too clean*—not catching on to something like that. "He hadn't met your family or friends?"

"No. I was careful about who he met. And my family… He knew we weren't close."

And it was always easy to believe what you wanted to be true.

No matter how farfetched it might be.

Jase closed his eyes, his thoughts circling back to

Emily for what might have been the hundredth time that day, the guilt that never quite went away spiking hard.

He'd wanted to believe the worst about Emily, while letting her believe the best about him. What kind of a man did that?

He looked back at his mother. What kind of a woman did what she'd done?

"Joe had already been talking about marrying me, but I was terrified that once he knew the truth, that I'd been lying to him and I was only seventeen, he wouldn't want me anymore. But that's not how it went. Sure, he was mad I'd deceived him, and he beat himself up pretty bad about my age. But he said he loved me, and if I loved him, we'd get married."

Jase couldn't imagine. But suddenly he had a new insight into his father's sense of responsibility toward the woman in front of him.

"Did you love him?" He didn't know why he'd asked. She could say anything, but as they sat across from each other, he had the feeling this woman had put her lies behind her.

"I thought I did. I thought I was getting everything I wanted. And then I had you. I'd turned eighteen two weeks before, and while most of my friends were going off to college, reveling in boyfriend drama, and trying to decide which party to go to, I was trying to figure out why this baby cried so much. Why he wouldn't sleep. Why he wouldn't let me sleep."

She was looking at him, studying his face, and Jase imagined she was searching for traces of the child she was telling him about.

"My parents weren't any kind of help. Your dad,

though, he was amazing. He'd work as many hours as he could, since we needed money, and then the minute he walked through the door he'd take you in his arms and suddenly everything would be okay. He'd tell me all the things I needed to hear but could only believe while he was saying them. That I was doing a terrific job. That he was the luckiest man alive. That everything was going to be great."

It hurt Jase's heart to hear that his mother had actually cared about his dad. That things might have been good between them, even for a short time. Because it had been so much easier to see her as a villain from the start.

"I wasn't ready to be a wife or a mother, Jase. No matter how good your father was to me, it couldn't change that fact. And pretty soon I started acting out. I'm not proud of the things I did, or the way I treated your father. How I disrespected him and the vows we took. And I'm not proud of the fact that I couldn't be a real mother to you. But I wasn't ready for the life I'd signed on for. You were small and helpless and so dependent on me. I should have cherished and nurtured that bond." Her head bowed and she looked away. "Instead, I resented you. I'm so sorry, Jase. You deserved better. Your father deserved better than what I did to him. And when I left, I thought—I hoped—you both might find it."

This was the part of the story he knew. The part that had shaped the man he'd become.

"We didn't. You broke him when you left. It took almost a year before he was able to pull himself back together. And then every time you called, it would be the same thing all over again. Weeks of heartbreak."

"I'm sorry about that. I didn't want to hurt him. I wanted to hear that he was okay, that you were."

Jase let out a humorless laugh. "Right. Look, I can buy into the fact that you were young, and you made some mistakes. But don't try to convince me you cared how I was doing. At best I registered as an afterthought, even when you were living here. But in twenty years, in all the times you called Dad, never once did you ask to speak to me, send me a card, or come back to visit. You couldn't even bother to say good-bye that last day when you left."

Jesus, he hadn't wanted to say any of that. Hadn't wanted her to know her actions had made any kind of impact on him.

His mother stared across the table at him, tears filling her eyes. "I didn't say good-bye because I was afraid if I did, I wouldn't be able to go. And I needed to. I didn't know how to be the things you needed. And every time I looked into your eyes, I saw the same pleading that was there in your father's, begging me for something I didn't have within me to give."

She shook her head and looked away. Wiped her eyes before turning back to him. "I loved you, Jase."

He should have laughed. Told her what a lot of good her love had done him. Only he couldn't toss the words back at her. He couldn't let them go at all.

They sat in silence a moment before Jase braved his next question. "What made you come back?"

"Your father asked me to. Though I think you know it wasn't the first time."

He knew. He remembered the aftermath of every call.

"You always said no."

"It was hard. I knew what I was missing. I'd look at the families around me. The moms scooping up their little boys for hugs, haggling with their teens about haircuts, stepping into their husbands' arms." She shook her head. "But I was afraid I wasn't ready. And by the time I was, you were eighteen, going off to school, starting a whole new phase of your life. There was a part of me that didn't want to disrupt that. I thought it wouldn't be fair to show up after I missed all of the years that mattered for you. And I was scared. The mistakes I'd made in the past had been so terrible that I didn't believe I had the right to ask for or deserved another chance with the family I threw away."

The air hissed out of his lungs as his hands fisted against his thighs.

Ten years.

His chest hurt thinking about *all that time*. Thinking about the melancholy in his dad's eyes when he didn't know Jase was looking. About the sound of his father's laugh when he'd walked in on them a few months back. About the time wasted.

She might have been back ten years ago, if only she'd been brave enough to ask for the chance.

"What changed?" He needed to know. To understand.

"About a year ago, I'd moved to a new city in Ohio and called your father. I don't really know what happened, but the conversation just…got away from us. It was good. And when we were getting off the phone, I didn't want it to end. I asked if I could call him again, and we started talking more regularly. He wanted to hear about my life. I wanted to hear about both of yours. We would talk about my work and his. We would talk about you."

Jase's throat was tight, his heart pounding. "You became friends."

She nodded. "And then one day he asked me if I had ever found what I was looking for. He wanted to know if I was happy. I told him that I'd found peace with my choices and that I'd built a life I could respect. I told him I had friends and I kept busy. And I almost left it at that… But after all the years of missing what I'd given up, I just couldn't do it. I had to take the risk and trust Joe with the truth—that a part of me had been empty since the day I left."

Now Jase was grinning. "And?"

"And he asked me if I would let him take me out on a date." A light began to shine in her eyes, and for the first time in more than twenty years, Jase saw her smile. And he got it, just a little bit. This hold she had on his father. "Maybe give it one more shot now that we're both older and wiser. I was living in Ohio, so the next Saturday we each hopped in our cars and drove to Indiana, where we had coffee. We met that way six more times before your father asked me if I would like to come up for a weekend."

Jase hadn't had a clue. "And the rest is history."

"Well, we took our time, but I guess you could say that." She paused and turned toward the front door as though looking for his father. "We were going to tell you, Jase. It's just that this thing was so new, and we were both so nervous. Neither one of us wanted to bring you into it until we felt confident about going forward."

Jase pinched the bridge of his nose. "So are you guys talking about getting married again?"

His mother laughed, the sound of it sweet and warm as

she reached across to pat his hand. "Your dad told me that for a kid who never wanted to get married, you sure spend a lot of time at weddings. Haven't you had enough?"

Jase shrugged, not sure he knew the answer to that himself.

A moment passed and Clara's smile faded, her eyes going somber.

"I know it's too late for me to be your mom. I know I gave up that privilege twenty years ago. But please know that I love you. I always asked your father about you. I always wanted to know. I just thought it would be easier for you if I..." She shrugged. "I did what I thought was best. And if it's something you can't forgive me for, then I'll respect that. But I hope in time you'll give me a chance to get to know the man you've turned out to be. I hear you're pretty great."

Chapter 25

THINGS WERE FINALLY BEGINNING TO COME AROUND. Two days after their *Scandal* binge sleepover, Sally called bubbling over with the kind of gushing enthusiasm Emily hadn't heard since her friend had first met Romeo. He'd asked if he could stay for dinner that night. She'd said it had been awkward, the conversation stilted and the silences filled with all the things they weren't ready to talk about—but *he'd been there*.

And that was the start Sally had been praying for.

The next night Romeo had asked if they could try to talk about what happened, and Wednesday morning Sally had called to report that their fight had been a blowout lasting until after midnight—but *they'd been talking*, and before he left, he'd told her he loved her.

For a few hours after that, Emily had been able to forget about her own problems and just be happy for her friend.

But soon enough she was back to thinking about Jase. Wondering about all the things that could have been different and how they might have found their way to an ending happier than this one. Work helped, but only as long as she kept going. Which was why at 2:11 a.m. on a Thursday—no, now Friday morning—Emily was drafting a pitch her team wouldn't even meet on until next week.

Busy was good. But as her finger strokes slowed on the keyboard, her mind drifted back to Jase and the sound of his gruff laugh at her ear, the feel of his arms tightening around her waist as he pulled her against him—she was reminded that busy wasn't always enough.

Of course that might have had something to do with finding out that afternoon her friend Kasie was engaged, and Emily was about ninety percent sure that Jase qualified as groomsman material for Vince.

She pushed up from her sofa and walked over to the windows where she tried to stretch out her shoulders and back. The streets below were quiet, with only a smattering of pedestrians and traffic at a minimum.

Had Jase found out about the engagement today too? Did he remember that she and Kasie were close? What would happen when they were paired up and she found out that Jase had already moved on to his next girlfriend?

Emily wrapped her arms across her belly, holding herself tight as she fought the nausea that rose at the mere thought of Jase with another woman. Kissing her. Holding her. Making her laugh and feel like maybe, just maybe... *This one*.

That was it. She was driving herself crazy, and the work wasn't helping. Stalking over to her closet, she was reaching for a parka when she caught sight of her button-down pink plaid pajamas in the mirror. Not exactly gym wear, and a hard workout that didn't include running was maybe the only thing left with the potential to clear her mind and wear her out enough to facilitate sleep. About to go change, she stopped at the ping of her phone.

A text message.

Her heart skipped a beat as she rushed back to the coffee table where she'd left her phone, way too enthusiastic about the prospect of some work emergency she would legitimately have to throw herself into. Only the text wasn't from any of her team reports. It wasn't from a client, and it wasn't from her boss.

Jase.

Coffee?

So that would be a yes on Jase already knowing about the engagement.

She'd told him she didn't want him stopping by. That it hurt too much. But she didn't think anything could feel worse than walking away from him on Saturday had. And if they were going to have to see each other again anyway…

She texted back: Now?

Two and a half seconds later, Jase was calling. She answered on the first ring.

"I didn't think you'd be awake," he said by way of greeting, the deep rumble of his voice both soothing and disconcerting. But mostly just good to hear. "I was hoping we could talk."

It was probably a good idea. She could keep it brief. Limit it to the wedding.

"What are you doing awake?" she asked instead, circling around to her sofa and dropping into the corner that hadn't felt nearly so comfortable ten minutes before. "You sound tired."

"I could ask you the same thing, only I don't really care why you're up—just that you are. That you answered." A pause. "Look, Em, I know you asked me to stay away, but I'd really like to talk to you sometime. Which sounds like bullshit even as I say it, because you don't owe me anything. But I just—"

The sound of a horn filtered through the line and Emily sat up straighter.

"Are you *out*?" Then she sat straighter still, her stomach pitching. "Jase, have you been drinking?"

Her answer was the sound of Jase's laughter rumbling through the line. God, she'd missed it.

"No. I just couldn't sleep and went out for a walk. I found myself in your neighborhood and… I don't know. I guess I thought a text wouldn't be too intrusive. Especially if you got it in the morning when you woke up." He chuckled again. "My mistake."

He was making light, turning something awkward into a joke, but she could hear the serious undertones beneath the words. Sense a regret that matched her own.

"I could make a pot of coffee."

She hated how they'd left things, and maybe what they needed was just a chance to talk. To say good-bye in a way that wasn't quite so heartbreaking, so when they saw each other again at the next party or wedding or bumped into each other on the street, neither would feel like they had to run the other way.

So she wouldn't feel like bursting into tears.

"Yeah, I'd like that."

She was standing at the door, holding it open, when Jase stepped off the elevator, and she was grateful for those panels of solid wood to support her, because when she saw him… Wow, he looked good. So good that she regretted not having thought to lose the ratty bun, because this business with the sneakers, long-sleeved white T-shirt, and pair of worn jeans that rode the perfect level of low on his hips… No one was supposed to look like that.

And when she'd finally braved up enough, she forced her eyes back to his face, taking in the rough stubble covering his jaw and throat, and the lines that looked just a little deeper around his eyes and mouth.

This was definitely a mistake. But being this close, right and wrong faded to the background and all that mattered was how badly she needed to see this man.

Jase stepped up to her, his big hand settling at her waist only long enough for him to drop a kiss at her temple and walk past into her apartment.

Emily shut the door behind her.

"So I started thinking that if neither of us can sleep already, maybe coffee isn't the best option. I can make it, but I do still have that bottle of Bulleit, if bourbon sounds better. Up to you," she added, feeling nervous about having Jase back in her space. About being this close to him after—well, after everything.

"Actually, a drink sounds great."

"You know where it is. Grab a glass for me too?"

"Got it," he replied, the exchange painfully familiar.

Emily had already cleared her makeshift office from the couch, but she felt at loose ends, not knowing what to do with herself now that Jase was there. Now that they were going to sit down for a friendly chat—at two a.m. while she was wrapped up in her pj's and bulky robe. So for the sake of looking busy, she moved everything again from the secretary table by the window over to the dining room.

Jase stepped out of the kitchen, two glasses in hand.

She expected him to take the couch opposite hers, but instead, he moved to sit beside her.

It wasn't weird.

She was being weird.

Because even with at least eighteen inches between them, she could still feel the air crackling in that empty space.

Jase handed her a glass and she took a hearty swallow, having forgotten that while she enjoyed a bourbon from time to time, she wasn't built for gulping it. Coughing into her hand, she tried to wave Jase off when he rubbed at her back and let out another low laugh.

"Slow down, slugger. It's not Gatorade."

She shook her head. "I know. Nervous, I guess."

The hand at her back stilled, and then it was gone and Jase was putting another couple of inches between them. "Maybe this was a mistake. Em, I can go."

"No, you're here," she assured him. "Stay."

It was better to get this out of the way.

Jase seemed to be trying to read her face, but then he nodded. "I'm sorry about the other night at the party. I haven't really been myself since we split up. It's no excuse. I shouldn't have been all over you like that."

"I might have overreacted. I just wasn't expecting to see you there."

"I should have warned you, done something so you would be prepared. I shouldn't have been so pushy... If you can believe it, I actually started out with closure in mind."

"Closure?" She laughed. "Wow, that's quite a wrong turn."

Jase smiled. "Tell me about it. And then it was just this eruption of words. The stench of desperation." He rubbed

a palm across his jaw, the amusement leaving his eyes.
"The acute awareness that letting you go was killing me."

Not trusting her own emotions, she closed her
eyes. "Jase."

"I know. I did this. We're where we are because of
me. Because I wasn't man enough to take the risk that
mattered most. And worse than that, I couldn't even see
what I was doing or what it was going to cost me. I was
wrong." She looked back to him then, the pain in his
eyes making her ache almost as much as the words themselves. "But what you said, Em, you were wrong too."

Wrong to let herself get in too deep? "To fall in love
with you?"

It had never been part of the plan.

And knowing what she did about Jase, it had been a
reckless gamble she never should have taken.

"No. Christ, not that. *Never* that."

"Then what?"

"I'm talking about what you said the other night—
about falling in love with a lie," he answered gruffly. "I
swear to you, what we had wasn't a lie. We were real.
So right that I didn't know how to handle it. The only lie
was the one I told myself."

Breath held, she waited for him to explain.

No more risks. No more exposing her hopes and
vulnerabilities.

"I let myself hold on to the idea that you'd been
unfaithful because it meant I didn't have to trust you
completely. Because it gave me an *excuse* to hold back
just that much. So if in the end, somehow, you turned
out to be like my mom, I could pretend it wouldn't be
the world-shattering devastation it most definitely would

be. So I could say I'd known what I was getting into and maybe not feel like such a fool."

There was her answer.

Heartbreaking as it was, now she understood.

Only what good did it do her—or either of them—now? There wasn't any solace in knowing she'd never had a chance. That the woman who'd created this amazing man had damaged him in such a significant way, he was incapable of trust.

Emily sat back. Maybe she wanted that drink after all.

After another sip, one that didn't leave her breathing fire, and then another after that, she closed her eyes, wishing so much that things could have been different between them. At any stage along the way.

"That's…very sad, Jase," she whispered.

"It's going to change. I'm through letting a bunch of twenty-year-old bullshit dictate my life." He turned so he was facing her, one knee on the floor as he took her hands in his. He looked up at her, determination burning in his eyes. "I love you, Emily. And I'm going to fight for you. I'm going to fight for *us*."

She shook her head, tears filling her eyes.

Because she knew better. She was through with destructive relationships.

"It's too late, Jase."

The muscle in his jaw flexed but he didn't look away.

"It might be," he answered, the words sounding pained. "I'm the one who keeps screwing up. I'm the one who keeps making mistakes, and the worst of them was making you feel like there wasn't any room for you to make a few along the way. So if I can't change your mind, I'll understand. But *I have to try, Em*."

"I don't want to hurt you, Jase," she whispered, meaning it with all her heart. There'd been too much pain between them already.

"And I don't want to be the kind of man who lets the best thing that ever happened to him go, because he wasn't willing to take a risk."

She didn't know if she had it in her. One more risk. Putting her heart on the line for the one man with the power to break it.

"What do you want?"

"A chance, Em." He swallowed. "Just a chance to show you I'm the kind of man you deserve."

Just a chance. It sounded like such a small thing.

"And if I say no?"

Jase closed his eyes and shook his head as if bracing himself for the words to come. "Then I'll kiss your cheek at the next wedding. I'll make you laugh and smile while we have our dance. And when it's over, I'll walk you back to your date. But in the interest of full disclosure, I'm going to iron-hand him and threaten his life if he doesn't treat you the way I wish I'd been able to."

A small laugh broke through the tears that had started to fall.

Jase brushed her cheeks with his thumbs, and when she looked into his face so close to hers...her world shook just a little.

Slowly, he put the space back between them.

"In short, I'll respect your decision. Because more than anything I want you to be happy."

God, she could barely remember what it had been like. Except she knew that before all this, she had been.

She'd been happier with Jase than she'd been in her whole life. Right up until—

"Romeo." She was afraid to ask. "What have you been telling Romeo?"

At that, Jase gave her hands a small squeeze and set them back in her lap.

"I told him to go talk to his wife." Jase stood. "That if he kept listening to me, he'd end up alone and miserable with years of regret that he'd never be able to get back."

Using the sleeve of her robe, Emily wiped at her last tear. Standing with Jase, she nodded. "Okay. You've got your chance."

———

When Emily agreed, she didn't really know what a *chance* entailed. As it turned out, it started with Jase giving her a smile to melt her heart and a quick, firm kiss on the cheek, followed by the promise he'd be in touch.

The next afternoon, Emily was pushing through the revolving door to her office building after lunch with Lena, a hopeful flutter in her chest and belly.

"There's that smile we've been missing," exclaimed Julia, the first-floor security guard.

Emily cocked her head and beamed. "And you're all smiles yourself."

"Hard not to be with all the flowers coming through here this last hour. I've even got a vase for my desk."

Emily's steps slowed as she caught sight of the bouquet of oriental lilies and spray roses prominently displayed on the front desk.

"Those are gorgeous," she agreed, wistfully remembering the flowers Jase had brought her on their first date—the arrangement was almost identical.

Riding the elevator up to her floor, she heard a couple of girls from her office rattling on about the load after load of bouquets that had been delivered.

To her floor?

The elevator opened and she gaped. There were flowers *everywhere*. All the same arrangements.

Inside the glass doors, she stopped beside Avi, who could barely contain herself.

"They all came during lunch. Can you believe this? There are flowers for every woman in the office. I already put yours on your desk."

Emily looked closer at the rolling cart still laden with vases. "They have cards?"

"Just with the names, but the message inside is all the same, 'Have a beautiful day.'"

"Do you know who sent them?" Emily asked, already walking toward her office, Avi taking extra steps to keep up.

They couldn't be from Jase.

No way.

"Probably a client." She held up a hand and whispered loudly, "But I'm guessing it isn't Basker Bourbon."

No, probably not. Emily had barely been holding on to them after the Charlie Teller incident. She quickened her pace.

When she reached her office, she closed her door and turned to the bouquet positioned on top of her filing cabinet. It was exactly the same as all the others, except for the note.

Because I know the best way to get you to smile is to make sure all the people you care about have a reason to smile too.

Have a beautiful day.

~J

Emily's phone pinged with a text. *Jase?* she thought, fumbling for the phone in her bag.

No, Lena. Gushing about the flower delivery to her office.

Oh, he'd gotten her. Good.

Smiling like she hadn't in weeks, Emily checked her phone again. No message from Jase. And when she just happened to walk through the lobby again... no Jase there either.

She wasn't disappointed. Pulling out her phone, she thumbed a reply far too simple for the way she was feeling: Thank you for the beautiful day.

What he'd done was perfect.

Almost as perfect as the surprise Emily got four days after that, when Charlie Teller's assistant phoned her office that he'd give her a meeting. The minute she hung up the phone, she texted Jase, asking if he knew anything about it.

The reply...

Because I know how much you love your job, and everyone just needs a chance sometimes. Good luck.

They talked that night, like they'd talked the two nights before. And it was so good, so easy, so right that a part of her just wanted to give in. To beg Jase to come over and hold her the way he used to. But deep down she knew she wasn't ready. She was still apprehensive about whether she was making another mistake.

To Jase's credit, he hadn't asked to see her.

For now, talking and texting were enough.

Chapter 26

"SO WHAT'S THE DEAL WITH YOU AND JASE?" SALLY asked, bouncing gently from foot to foot while Gloria dozed against her shoulder.

Emily opened one cabinet and then another, finally hitting the jackpot on the third. "Pita chips!" she whispered triumphantly, holding up her bounty. She probably should have grabbed some breakfast, but when Sally had called inviting her to come over while Romeo hit the gym, she'd just pulled on a pair of leggings and a hoodie that had seen better days, whipped her hair into a ponytail, and headed over for some baby love.

Sally nodded from the living room. "Told you I had some. But back to Jase. So it's been three weeks now of taking it slow, huh?"

Three weeks. Of talking every night. Of Jase finding one way after another to show her that he knew her. That he cared about her priorities. And that he was willing to wait as long as it took for her to feel confident about where they were going.

Three weeks of being almost there.

Of feeling her toes wrapped around the edge of the diving board, but no matter how badly she wanted to swim, being too afraid to take that last step and *jump*.

"Yeah. But slow has been working for us. How about

you guys?" Romeo had moved back in, and they'd started marriage counseling two weeks ago.

Sally's voice firmed. "Good. But about the slow thing. Aren't you starting to itch just a little to *speed things up*?"

Okay, so Sally wanted answers. Real ones.

No more dodging.

Emily folded herself into the wingback chair and looked up at her friend. "The slow thing is going good. Really good, I think. I mean, we still haven't *actually* seen each other since that night we agreed to give things another chance. But the talking… God, Sally, I missed talking to him."

Her friend bit her lip, blinking fast. She got it.

How could she not after what had happened with the man she loved?

"It's like he knows me better than anyone. Like we could talk forever."

And sometimes they almost did, not saying good-bye until late into the night or even early the next morning. It felt like he was her best friend.

"But…you still haven't seen each other." Sally shifted Gloria to the other shoulder. "Why?"

The question Emily had been asking herself a hundred times a day…and answering the same each time.

"Because I'm afraid. What we're doing now? It's safe." Like there was still a way out if she wanted it. "But if I see him…if I let him put his arms around me and hold me the way I've been aching for, I'm afraid there'll be no turning back. Sally, when I'm with him, I forget about protecting myself. I lose track of all the reasons to keep a few solid defenses in place."

"You love him."

Emily had been avoiding saying it, trying not to even think it. But just hearing the words was enough to make her heart thump in that slow, heavy, over-full way.

"I love him," she answered helplessly.

Walking over to the counter where Gloria's little SnugRide was parked, Sally carefully tucked her in it. Glancing over her shoulder, she asked, "So Jase hasn't pushed at all to actually get together?"

"No. He said he would give me space, so he hasn't pushed at all."

Tucking a blanket over Gloria, Sally said something in that quiet, singsong voice reserved for private conversations with her daughter. Only it sounded a lot like "Well, maybe someone should."

The door buzzer sounded and Emily frowned. "Sally?"

Sally spun around, hands clutched under her chin, a half-guilty, half-delighted look on her face. "Romeo made me do it!"

Then dashing to the intercom she pressed the access button. "He just can't stand seeing Jase like this. The guy is lost without you."

Emily was out of her chair in a blink, standing in the middle of Sally's living room, looking from the door to her friend and back again as panic spread through her like wildfire. "Wait, why do you have your jacket? You aren't *leaving*?"

Picking up the portable car carrier, Sally gave her the doe eyes Emily would never trust again. "Lena and I agreed it was probably best."

"Sally!"

Sally turned back at the door and frowned a little.

"You have some pita-chip crumbs down your hoodie. And"—she dabbed at her lips—"maybe add a little makeup or something?"

Emily's eyes bugged. "You didn't think to mention that before Jase was on his way up?"

"I didn't want to tip you off," Sally said with an apologetic shrug. A knock sounded at the door, and she quickly shook her head. "Never mind. You look fine."

Sally swung open the door and there he was. Jase, filling the frame with that big, strong body overriding the earth's gravitational force—because with that one glimpse, Emily already felt the pull.

"Hey there, big eyes," he crooned, crouching in front of the carrier to stroke a knuckle over Gloria's plump little cheek. "Your favorite babysitter is here, princess. And I wore the T-shirt you like to hurk on."

He hadn't seen Emily yet. Didn't know she was there.

Looking up at Sally, he grinned. "What's with the car seat? You girls just getting back?"

"So…it turns out," Sally said meekly, "I don't need a babysitter this morning after all."

And that's when it happened. He stood, a confused look on his face as his gaze shifted from Sally, tracking across the living room until—*bam!*

Eye contact.

"Emily…" he started, but then whatever he'd thought to say was gone, and he just stared like he couldn't look away.

"You were supposed to babysit?" she asked, only half registering that Sally had just let herself out. Why did she suddenly feel so uncertain about what to say to the man she'd barely been able to force herself to hang up the phone with at three that morning?

"Romeo called an hour ago and asked if I was free."

That made sense. "About when Sally was calling me to hang out."

Maybe that onset of shyness was because the only words that seemed to come to mind were the ones she wasn't quite ready to voice. Words like "I miss you" and "I need you" and "God, I love you, but I'm terrified and all I want is for you to hold me and tell me this is going to be okay."

His shoulders hunched forward as he shoved his hands deep into his jeans pockets, pushing them low on his hips. "So we've been set up. You mind?"

In those first seconds after Sally sprang it on her, she'd thought she did. But then she'd *seen* him, and just knowing he was that close… It was like all those little broken pieces inside her were falling back into place. Like this soul-deep bruise inside her was finally fading.

"I don't mind if you don't."

"Me?" he asked, taking a step toward her, an incorrigible smile stretched across his face. "Hell, no. I've been going out of my mind not seeing you, but I was afraid if I did, I wouldn't be able to stop myself from doing something stupid like…" His eyes dipped to her mouth and lingered just long enough for her to almost be able to feel what he was thinking. "It doesn't matter. Check me out." Pulling his hands from his pockets, he pantomimed ripping his T-shirt open, Superman-style. "Man of steely restraint, here."

Yeah. She saw.

"Because you care more about me being sure than you do about getting my mouth under yours?" she asked, giving in to that pull she couldn't resist and taking the first step toward him.

Jase's smile retreated, his face turning serious as he watched her take another step. "I do."

"Because you're willing to risk laying yourself bare, giving me everything you have"—another step and she was almost there—"on the chance we might work out?"

"For as long as it takes, Em. You're worth it, and, sweetheart, *I know* I can make you happy."

And then she was finally in front of him, close enough that she had to tip her head back to see those storm-tossed blues staring back at her.

"You're worth the risk, Jase." Pressing her hand over the center of his chest, she uncurled her toes from the diving board and *jumped*. "Because I love you too."

One beat. Two beats. Three beats of his heart beneath her palm and then Jase's breath punched out on a curse as he reached for her, pulling her into that perfect fit, so good and right and strong it brought tears to her eyes. His arms were wrapped around her tight, his mouth next to her ear as he whispered her name again and again.

And then he was holding her face in his big hands, searching it like he couldn't believe she was real.

"Jesus, tell me you really want this, Em. That you're sure."

"Kiss me, Jase. Please."

A low growl rumbled from his chest, and his mouth met hers in a hard press that neither of them was in any hurry to relinquish.

Because it was right.

He kissed her again and again, each tasting like a promise or claim, until she couldn't tell where one ended and the next began. Until her hands were in his hair, her lips bruised as she pleaded for more. For him to hold her tighter, kiss her harder.

Until they were pulling at each other's clothes, and then swearing and laughing as they pulled them back on. Because they were still in Sally and Romeo's apartment. And friends didn't have hot, plaster-cracking, finding-their-forever sex at friends' apartments. It just wasn't cool.

But it didn't matter, because then they were on their way back to Jase's place.

He had one arm around her shoulder and was holding her hand while they walked and talked and laughed and stopped to kiss…and finally ran the last two blocks…

Because forever started now.

Epilogue

May

ON THE UPSIDE, MAX HAD SCORED RINGSIDE SEATS FOR the latest in a string of buddies lining up to get their bachelor-cards punched…and he'd done it *without* having to sweat out the actual best man responsibilities. Nice. Even better, after today's nuptials, he only had one more wedding to suit up for this summer.

Hells to the yeah, man.

'Course before he could check out, he had to make it through both big days without his grooms losing their shit completely. And glancing across to the man seated in the center of the small hotel conference room where the guys were set up, the theme song to *Rocky* playing in the background, that was looking like a tall order for groom number one.

Jase Foster, his formerly cool and collected, badass bachelor comrade, was wound as tightly as any groom Max had ever had the misfortune of managing. Hell, he'd been off the chain even before the limo business. And so much for Brody's assertion that giving in to Jase's "I-can-still-make-it-on-time-if-I-run" plan would help the guy burn off some steam.

What's the harm, right?

"You think she's going to notice?" Jase gasped, still

catching his breath after his sprint from the scene of the flat on North LaSalle Street to the hotel.

From where Max was standing, out of the way by the door, the answer was a resounding *"Hell yeah*, she is going to notice."

The swollen split lip was unquestionably the main attraction, but there'd be no missing the mostly severed jacket sleeve, the pronounced limp, or the seriously bad case of the sweats. Damn, man.

Fortunately, the duty of BSing Jase into thinking otherwise rested on other shoulders. So Max kicked back and let the best man talk his kid down from the ledge.

Crouched in front of Jase's chair, Joe Foster let out a low whistle and shook his head. "Oh yeah, Jase. She's going to notice. There's no hiding all this. It's bad. Ugly."

Max coughed into his hand, while from the other side of the room, Sean cut him a delighted look, the corner of his mouth starting to twitch.

Fuckin' Sean.

"I still don't know what you were doing getting right up behind the driver while he was trying to change the flat, but that elbow"—another whistle—"and then with the running. And Christ, Jase, sliding over the hood of a moving cab only works in the movies. What were you thinking?"

So it looked like Jase wasn't the only one with a case of the nerves.

Amateurs.

Clearly, Sean was happy to settle in and watch the shit show in action, but since Jase looked about one more wedding-day mishap from his own WE tv

Groomzilla special, Max pushed off the wall and walked over. Clapping Joe on the shoulder, he got in on the huddle.

"Forget the split lip," he said, using his cop voice to make sure Jase was listening. "You got here *on time*."

Jase sat back in his chair, relaxing the slightest degree. "I couldn't be late, man."

"I know." Because the dipshit had shared all the truths about the delays of grooms past, which meant the guy was coming undone over making sure he was on time. Because no way was he going to let Emily worry one single minute about whether he'd been getting cold feet or having second thoughts.

Sweet, Max guessed.

Emily was a good girl, so the less she had to worry about, the better. But Max was willing to bet his left nut there wasn't a person left in this city who didn't know how utterly, pathetically in love Jase was or how badly he wanted to make Emily his wife. *Like, yesterday.*

"So you're here, and when Emily sees you, she's going to know you did this for her."

Sean chimed in, "It'll be like an extra wedding gift. Dude, she'll love it."

Jesus, Jase was worse off than Max had thought, because he actually looked like he might be buying this.

"Buddy, you hit your head going over that cab?"

It hadn't looked like that from inside the limo when they'd passed him with a quarter block to go and some Yellow Cab decided to take a right after Jase had already committed.

Leaning in, Max palmed Jase's head for a better look. The door opened behind them and Max glanced back to see Brody backing into the room, his arms out in front of him like he was trying to ward off an assailant.

"*Now, Brody.*"

Or a determined bride.

"Hey, Emily," Max greeted her, satisfied that Jase's brainpan was still intact.

Sean was out of his seat in a flash, adjusting his tie and flashing that polished smile. "You look unbelievable."

She did. She had on one of those strapless dresses that was fitted up top and then flowed down to the floor, and her hair was pinned up in a bunch of soft-looking coils with some kind of pearly clip thing holding it in place.

She really was a knockout.

"You got hit by a car?" she charged, ignoring Sean's compulsive manners completely.

Arm out to the side, one finger held up in warning, she strode past the other groomsmen.

"*I told you*, don't freak out about the timing thing, Jase. I wasn't worried about anything other than you getting here in one piece."

With that last bit, she stared down each of them in turn. She *had* told the groomsmen not to let him out of their sight.

Damn, Jase had always said a scary side lurked beneath all that soft and pretty, but Max just thought the guy was being a pussy. Lesson learned.

Turning back to her future husband, everything about Emily gentled. "Are you hurt?"

Jase was pushing out of his chair, closing the distance between them. "Em, I'm fine. Cosmetic stuff. Molly's getting a stapler for my sleeve."

She was looking up into Jase's eyes, giving him that
smile that said how much she loved the guy—and for an
instant Max remembered what it had been like to have a
woman looking at him that way. Like somehow he was
her next breath.

Turned out he hadn't been. Another lesson learned,
and no question, that one ranked top ten in a lifetime
of them.

"Clear out, will ya, guys?" Jase said, his eyes
still locked with Emily's. "I need a minute with my
almost-wife."

She wrapped her arms around his neck and something in her smile shifted, setting off a quiet alarm in
Max's head.

Uh-oh. "You sure you want us to do that?" he asked,
scanning the room around them. Taking particular note
of the retractable wall dividers. Those things didn't
look very stable. Or soundproof. "We're scheduled to
start in—"

"Make it ten, guys," Emily overruled. "I'm a little
shaken up."

Right. Except that she didn't look shaken up at all.
"You heard 'em. Everybody out."

Joe stopped at the door. "Maybe I should stay? See if
there's anything I can do to help out."

"You know, I think Jase has got this one," Max
answered, poker face in place. Ushering the elder Foster
out, he suggested Joe go check on his own bride-to-be.
See if Clara was picking up any ideas for the ceremony
they'd be having in two months' time.

Forty-five minutes later, Jase was unequivocally the
happiest man Max had ever seen. The ceremony had

gone off without a hitch. Emily had been grinning ear to ear, a dreamy look in her eyes as she walked down the aisle on her father's arm. That pretty clip that had been so neatly tucked into her hair was sitting off-kilter, and her dress was sporting a black smudge on the rear that looked a lot like the one Jase had on his hand from the limo's lug nut.

There'd been tears in their eyes as they spoke their vows, and even he'd had to fight that misty feeling when the rings were finally exchanged and Jase dipped his wife back into a kiss that nearly blew the roof off the place.

Marriage wasn't for him. Max knew that.

But hell, days like this one were almost enough to make a guy like him wonder *what if*.

Acknowledgments

A huge thanks to the enablers facilitating my continued belief that writing is a team sport.

First and foremost, to my fairy god-agent, Nicole Resciniti, the woman behind my dreams coming true. Also to Cat Clyne, for her patience, insight, and guidance in helping me to get this book where it needed to go, and to Deb Werksman, along with the rest of the amazing team at Sourcebooks, for being as enthusiastic about this series as I was.

To Liz Lewis, for taking the time to share some of her PR know-how with me—and also for being one of the sweetest, funniest, goofiest girls in the Windy City. Wish we lived closer!

To my sanity savers, Lexi Ryan and Megan Mulry, for the chatty brainstorming...and even more for the chatty non-brainstorming. These girls just get it. They get me, and I'd be lost without them.

To my husband, kids, family, and friends, for putting up with the deep-in-the-zone Mira even I can barely tolerate!

And especially to my readers, for making it all worthwhile!

I love you guys!

About the Author

USA Today bestselling author Mira Lyn Kelly grew up in the Chicago area and earned her degree in fine arts from Loyola University. She met the love of her life while studying abroad in Rome, Italy, only to discover he'd been living right around the corner from her back home. Having spent her twenties working and playing in the Windy City, she's now settled with her husband in central Minnesota, where their four beautiful children and one naughty dog provide an excess of action and entertainment. When she isn't reading, writing, or running to keep up with the kids, she loves watching movies, blabbing with the girls, and cooking with her husband and friends.

Visit Mira at www.miralynkelly.com.

Test Drive

Body Shop Bad Boys

by Marie Harte

New York Times and *USA Today* bestseller

Get to Know the Body Shop Bad Boys

Johnny, Foley, Sam, and Lou are the rough-and-tumble mechanics of Webster's Garage. These reformed bad boys are used to living fast, but it's the women in their lives who take them from zero to sixty in a heartbeat.

Johnny Devlin

Johnny's a charmer with a checkered past. He's had his eye on scorching-hot bartender Lara Valley for ages, but she's rejected him more than once. That doesn't mean he won't come to her aid when some dirtbag mauls her. When she asks him on a date as a no-strings-attached thank-you, he can't say no. And then he's saying nothing but *hell yes.*

Praise for Marie Harte's McCauley Brothers series:

"Packed with sass, sensuality, and heartwarming emotion…an absolute delight!"
—*Romance Junkies* for *What to Do with a Bad Boy*

For more Marie Harte, visit:

www.sourcebooks.com

Roadside Assistance

Body Shop Bad Boys

by Marie Harte

New York Times and *USA Today* bestseller

—◦—

Underneath the Axle Grease and Tats He's a Gentleman

Foley Sanders figured he'd always be content with a life of cars and casual hookups. Until a run-in with Cyn, a statuesque firecracker with a hate-on for men, leaves him bewitched and intrigued—much to her annoyance.

Maybe Cynthia Nichols was a *little* hard on Foley, that muscular, tattooed, superhot mechanic next door. But she's tired of feeling defensive about her size and has sworn off men. She's got a new job, new life, perfect plan. Foley has trouble written all over him—no way is she going to fall for his charms.

Foley might look like a bad idea, but underneath, he's all gentleman. Too bad Cyn's not buying it. What's a bad boy to do when the goddess of his dreams won't give him the time of day?

—◦—

Praise for *Test Drive*:

"High-octane chemistry keeps the pages turning and your engine revving!" —Gina L. Maxwell, *New York Times* and *USA Today* bestselling author of the Fighting for Love series

For more Marie Harte, visit:

www.sourcebooks.com

Trouble Walks In

The McGuire Brothers

by Sara Humphreys

New York Times and *USA Today* bestselling author

~~~

Big city K-9 cop has a problem

Ronan McGuire loves women, loves his dog, loves his job—but when old flame Maddy Morgan moves into his jurisdiction, he can't think about anything else. Ronan knows she's way out of his league, but he's determined to help Maddy live life to the fullest.

Hometown girl could solve it—if he'd let her

With tragedy in her past, Maddy has immersed herself in work and swiftly made a name for herself in the hot New York City real estate market. She's looking for safety, not love, but Ronan McGuire is as persistent as he is sexy, and his crooked smile is hard to resist. But all other concerns are wiped away when Maddy goes missing and Ronan and his bloodhound K-9 partner are tasked with finding her and bringing her home.

~~~

Praise for *Brave the Heat*:

"Boasts suspense that burns as hot as the love scenes."
—*Publishers Weekly*

For more Sara Humphreys, visit:

www.sourcebooks.com

Every Bride Has Her Day

Magnolia Brides

by Lynnette Austin

———

Cricket O'Malley can't wait to plant roots back home in Georgia, where she's returned to restore an abandoned flower shop to its former glory. The only blemish? Her neighbor's house is even more neglected than her old flower shop, and its occupant seems as surly as he is darkly handsome.

Devastated body and soul after a tough case went south, New York City detective Sam DeLuca thought he'd have no trouble finding solitude in the quiet Georgia town of Misty Bottoms, but his bubbly neighbor seems determined to shine happiness into Sam's life. Sam is equally determined to close himself off, but his heart says otherwise…

———